I0521220

Vegas Fever

by Bill Collins

Cherise Kelley, Editor

Karlie Lucas, Developmental Editor

ISBN: 0997087218

Fiction

Rated: ML/V

(Occasional Mild language and violence)

Table of Contents

Dedication

I dedicate this book to my wife, Sue, who accompanies me on my Vegas craps shooting adventures. And who put up with me while I struggled to write and polish Vegas Fever.

You're one special lady, Sue.

Introduction

Strangers often ask if my brother, Joe, and I are twins. We share the same tall muscular body type, facial looks, and sandy-colored hair.

Join us on our week-long jam-packed craps-shooting vacation as a newbie craps player and Vegas virgin trying to win in Las Vegas. I'm a just-turned-twenty-one self-taught precision shooter who tries to use my dice-setting skills and cunning to gain an edge over casinos. It's a wild ride.

One thought keeps running through my mind as I write this: *What would you be willing to do to accomplish your dream?* Find out what I did to try to realize mine. It might amaze you.

You get to tag right along at arm's length through all our adventures, misadventures, dangers, excitement, romances and the emotional highs and the lows—so it's like getting to take a free week-long Vegas craps adventure vacation on me.

Ray

Eighty-five percent of all the fun in a casino happens at the craps tables, where most of the non-stop action, excitement, and wild and woolly gambling is found. You'll feel like you're right in the heart of all that action. It's the next best thing to going to a casino. A lot more interesting things happen in the Vegas Fever's craps action in a week than you'll see in a month of Saturday nights at a live casino table. Oh, did I mention that a lot more than just craps playing happens, too?

The Bonus Reading Material section contains detailed info to keep casual readers from having to research how what's known as "dice setting" and My Five-Level Parlay-like Progression Place Bets work— just to reach the heart of our adventures. In its own way this info is an important part of the story. It might even teach you how to do what I did with a pair of dice. It also tell what I've learned about craps since this Vegas adventure.

Craps has many betting rules which make the game difficult for non-players to understand when first encountered. To overcome this, I tried to limit the craps rules discussions to only what effects the story.

Anyone with questions or comments about Ray's adventures may contact me at: pokerbillcollins at gmail.com. I'll try to answer your questions.

Prologue — Joe's Discovery

It was a fall morning and the air was crisp when Joe went out to the seldom-used outer barn on his family's farm near Council Bluffs, Iowa. As soon as he entered and flipped the light switch, he noticed a big brown tarp covering something.

Curious, Joe walked over and lifted one edge of the tarp. He saw stacked-up sheets of thick plywood, two by fours, a roll of simulated leather, and some material rolled up that had inch-square rubber diamonds sticking up all over it. Next he found a wide roll of heavy green felt. Unrolling it, he discovered it had a full craps table betting layout silk-screened on it.

What the f... Ray? You're up to one of your hair-brained ideas again. You never cease to amaze me, Bro.

Joe replaced the tarp and shook his head. *Bet Dad doesn't have a clue.*

Chapter One — Getting Joe to Help

Early the next morning I had Joe tag along while I went looking for Dad. We found him under the tractor, repairing it. I asked him, "Can I use the outer barn? I wanna build something."

Dad kept working on the tractor and didn't answer.

Nineteen at the time, I again asked, "Dad, can I build something in the outer barn?"

Dad grumbled, "Ray, don't bother me when I'm working."

"Dad, please. If you'll answer my question—I'll get out of your hair."

If I can just slip this one past him, I'm off to the races.

"Alright. Keep it in one of the unused stalls. Now get outta here."

******

Growing up, I'd secretly wished I could be more like Joe—I looked up to him and maybe even idolized him. Joe is smarter and a couple of years older than me. There's always been some sibling rivalry between us. As far back as when I was seven, despite being younger, I saved his ass a couple of times in fights with older kids. I'd always been able to whip butt when I had to. Dad said I had the fight in me, and he taught me how to defend myself. Joe was peaceful and bookish.

As soon as we got out of Dad's hearing range, I stopped. "Can you keep a secret?" I shifted my weight back and forth and dug at the dirt with my toe.

"I've got your back. What is it?"

I scuffed some more dirt with my boot, dug my hands into my front pants pockets, then got serious. I took in a deep breath and finally made strong eye contact, getting my brother's attention. I removed the ball cap and rubbed the back of my neck. "Promise you won't laugh? It's probably going to sound crazy."

"Do I look like I'd laugh, Ray?"

"I dream about becoming a constant winner at craps by using a skill called 'dice setting' I learned about on the net. I've got to see if it works and whether I can do it."

Joe rolled his eyes. "Is this going to be like last year when you decided out of the blue to braid twenty nylon-paracord bullwhips and learn how to crack two whips at the same time?"

"Well, I did it, didn't I? What was wrong with that?"

"Or like when you were sixteen and decided to learn to ride a motorcycle? We couldn't get you off it to even come eat."

Unlike Joe, I'd always been a pit bull. When I got hold of an idea, I never let go. Not until I mastered it.

Joe was different. He was happy to go along and get by however he could. "Don't believe everything you read, Bro. There's all kinds of crap on the net."

Looking around for a second, I blew all the air from my lungs. "I've got to build a craps table to practice on. That's all there is to it."

Joe wore a big grin. "Is that what you got Dad's permission to build in the outer barn?"

I nodded. "Only, he doesn't know it—yet." *And I'm not going to tell him.*

"Ray, Dad's going to be pissed when he finds out what you're doing."

My voice rose almost to a squeak. "Joe, you've got to help me." I always spoke twice as fast as Joe. My mouth couldn't keep up with my thoughts.

"What do you want from me?"

I cracked my knuckles. "I need to know the table length and the heights of the surface and chip rail on Hollywood Casino's tables. It's the only way I'll know for sure how tall and how long to make mine. Everyone on the net says something different about the table length."

Joe straightened his glasses. "And you want me to get those measurements for you?"

"Yup. I'm nineteen, too young to get into a casino, or I'd do it myself. You're the only one I can turn to. I'll owe you. Big time."

I shoved my long fingers deep into my hip pockets and rocked back on my heels. I looked at Joe with my best dog-begging impersonation.

Joe shook his head from side to side. "Ray... Ray... Ray."

"It wouldn't take you any time at all to get that info—a couple of quick measurements when nobody's looking. I'll even buy you a laser tape measure, so you can point and press a button to get your reading. Nobody'll have a clue what you're doing."

He ignored me.

Maybe he thinks I haven't begged enough...

"You going to cheat at craps?"

Don't go there, Joe. "No, nope, not at all. Get me the info... I'll clue you in." I thought for a moment. "Look, we both know I'd help you if the situation was reversed, right?" We stared at each other. Neither of us flinched. "Dad's in danger of losing the farm. Mom let it slip last week. I think this might help."

Man, you're a tough nut to crack.

"You can do it, Joe, and be totally undetected. Besides, it's not like it's illegal to measure their table. At worst, they might ask you to leave, but I doubt it." I shot my brother a pleading look, raised my eyebrows, and turned my palms up.

Well, this isn't working.

I put both hands together in a prayer position. "Please, Joe. Pretty please? You can't begin to imagine how important this is to me. Don't you even care?"

I hate to have to beg. It feels so undignified.

"Why should I care? Jeez. Ray, you're not going to let me get out of this, are you?"

Nope.

"Hey, isn't that what bros are for?"

"Ray. You really know how to push a guy's buttons."

Darned right, I do. Got you figured.

Chapter Two — Building the Table

I'd made sure Dad knew no details about my project. He'd given his approval without giving it any thought. I had timed my request to catch him at his busiest, when he was least likely to want to chitchat about it.

About a week later, Dad came wandering into that out-of-the-way barn, searching for a misplaced tool. He got the shock of his life when he discovered us listening to rock n' roll music while we worked on building an instantly-recognizable mostly-built full-size craps table.

Dad exploded, cussing and calling me every foul name he knew, and a few he might have invented. "You betrayed my trust! You tricked me into giving my approval! You made sure you didn't let me know what you were up to."

I rolled with his verbal punches.

"D-D-Dad, I've read about something called 'precision dice setting' and 'dice influencing' on some internet forums." I slumped and kept my head down. "I'm curious about it. What's the harm in getting a little educated?"

Dad didn't move, or respond.

"I promise to never gamble on my table." I raised my eyebrows and straightened up. "I'm only going to practice on it. I'm not going to do anything bad."

Dad's face grew bright red, and his fists clenched. He locked eyes with me and got right in my face. "Ray, I raised you to not become a shifty character. You've let me down—I want you to know I think so. How you went about all this flat-out disappoints me." He wagged his finger at the craps table and spat in its direction, "What in Hell are you aiming to do with that damn thing after you've built it? What's it for?"

I took a submissive stance. "Dad, I'm sorry. I never thought you'd take it this way."

I was hoping Joe would jump in and help me. He'd been on the receiving end of Dad's wrath before. Now Joe probably wished he wasn't even here, probably feared being judged guilty by association.

I shifted my weight to my back foot, trying to avoid Dad's angry gaze but knowing I couldn't hide. "I-I-I-I..." Then I gathered my thoughts and faced Dad, taking in a deep breath. "I'm going online to order some poker chips and some real casino-quality dice. I aim to find out if there's anything to what I've read online about this 'dice setting'."

I didn't back down. "Dad, this idea fascinates me. I think about it all the time. I've got to see this through and see where it takes me."

Come on, Dad. Cut me some slack, will ya?

"Dammit Son, you're way too young to even step inside a casino. Why become involved with shooting craps? Isn't trying to control the dice illegal?"

"No, Dad. It's not. As long as both your dice bounce off the end wall, it's legal. That's all they require. The only other restriction is you can't try to slide them on the table-top, instead of tossing them."

Dad closed his eyes, dropped his head, and threw both hands up in the air. He shook his head, then turned and left.

Dang, this isn't turning out right.

******

Dad stewed for more than a week. He shot us daggers at mealtimes. We remained quiet in his presence, not wanting to aggravate things. We managed to stay out of his cross hairs—fearing he might get mad again.

Dad remained a man of his word like I knew he would. He'd given my project his approval, so he didn't try to nix it—even though he now realized I'd gained his approval by crookery.

"I'm worried about what will happen," Joe said. "I'm afraid you've bitten off more than you can chew."

I didn't care. 'Lie low and go forward' was the plan.

******

Joe worked on our small Iowa corn farm and enjoyed farming as much as Dad did. One day, if it survived, the farm would be passed down to Joe and me to work as our own. Dad was a first generation farmer who had struggled his entire adult life trying to get the farm to where it could support our family after he retired.

As he was approaching seventy, it was questionable if Dad would ever be able to afford to retire, or worse, if he'd even be able to hold on to the farm. He still had about another ten years left on the mortgage, and Mom had let it slip that Dad had fallen behind on making the payments.

I helped farm too, but didn't love farming. I also worked a part-time job cleaning up used cars for resale at the local Toyota dealer.

After I suckered Joe into getting the needed measurements by going on a spy mission for me inside the local Hollywood Casino, we built the craps table rectangular with rounded corners—like those in casinos. Both of us worked on the table off and on for more than a week. I felt confident Joe had gotten me all the information I needed to make the table accurate.

Utilizing our circular saw, Joe produced parallel kerf cuts spaced half an inch apart and two-thirds through the outside surface of the plywood in each outside third of the vertical end walls to make them bendable in the corners. Those corners bent to resemble a roll-top-desk's cover stood on its edge. Cutting them only part-way through left a smooth quarter-inch solid inside surface that wrapped around all four corners. The middle third of each vertical end wall remained straight and uncut.

The table looked mighty fine when done, sporting vertical end walls we lined with glued-down molded material that had hundreds of one-inch pointed rubber diamonds covering it—like they had on craps tables in casinos. The rubber diamonds' intended purpose was to disperse dice randomly after striking that end wall—which supposedly made what I tried to do with the dice impossible.

Joe knew I hadn't gone to the hardware store to acquire such a specialized item. "Where did you get that rubber diamond material, Ray?"

"Same place I plan to get the dice, Joe—mail order from Gamblers General Store [*sic*] in Las Vegas. Their web page offers all kinds of goodies gamblers can't find anywhere else."

We used only top-grade three-quarter-inch plywood, putting sawhorses underneath to bring the table to its proper height. I covered it with a heavy dark-green felt. It was silk-screened with a full craps-table layout, "Don't Come Bar" and "Hardway Bets" included—another purchase from Gamblers General Store.

"Joe, help me stretch and staple down the padded simulated-leather railings. I'll be able to rest my elbow on it while I shoot."

Fifteen minutes later we had the task done.

I took a couple measurements. "Let's make a couple of chip rails in front of the elbow rests. Be sure to space them to allow me room to rack up two rows of chips, one in front of the other. I want each row to hold up to fifty poker chips when they're stacked on their edges."

Joe plugged in the hot-glue gun and got the dowel rods to make the chip rails. Five minutes with the hot glue gun completed that task.

Joe's really getting into this project.

I slapped him on the back. "The chip rails are necessary. I'll bet like in a real casino, then roll the dice. I want making progression bets to be completely automatic."

We built the table in front of the stall, where we had more space. The day arrived when we had to fit the now-finished craps table inside the empty stall. We needed to get it out of the way and give it a permanent home.

It had gotten cooler outside and the days were getting shorter. The old barn had taken on a smell of fresh sawdust from all the sawing we'd been doing for the table.

I chomped on a piece of tall prairie grass I'd stuck in my mouth. Joe hated the habit, but it somehow fit me. "We'll have to set up the sawhorses inside the stall first, then turn the table bed sideways to get it through the stall door."

Joe measured the stall. "It's going to fill it up from front to back." He pointed at the stall to emphasize. He must have wanted me to pay more attention to him than the prairie grass I was chomping on.

Yeah, I was busy daydreaming about when the table was done.

I tossed the shoot of grass aside and grabbed a sawhorse. Joe grabbed the other one. We set both in place inside the stall. We wrestled the forty-pound table top through the door on its edge. Once it was on the sawhorses, we slid it into position against the wall. We had room to walk along the other side to retrieve the dice after they'd been tossed.

I put a carpenter's level on the playing surface, then added a couple of shims under different sawhorse legs to make it level. I discovered one thing we hadn't considered after the table got its new home. We'd have to crawl under the table to get out the door.

"Uh, I'll have to shoot through the open door from outside the stall." I rubbed my head. "But, the table is completely blocking the door."

"Yup. There's no way to get through the door to retrieve the dice."

I smacked my forehead. "Shit. We goofed big time."

"We sure did."

I put a tape measure to a plank by the door. "Joe, let's ask Dad if he'll let us take out a couple of planks."

"We could save them, so we could put them back later."

We both stood there, arms folded. Joe looked dejected. I was pissed. We brainstormed. Joe pointed out the obvious. "Unless you want to get down on your knees and crawl every time you need your dice back, there's no other choice."

I shook my head. "Even if I toss ten different pairs of dice before going to retrieve them, that's more crawling than I want to do."

"Maybe we could make a long rake-like stick to rake them back with?"

I shifted my weight, putting both hands on my hips. "That wouldn't be convenient...too long. It'd work from the middle of the table, but I'm shooting from one end to the other. I'd rather go with making a new opening."

Neither of us savored the prospect of going to Dad and telling him we now needed to modify the front of the barn stall so we could use the table he'd been conned into giving us permission to build.

Joe shook his head. "Might as well get it over with. Putting it off isn't going to make it any easier. Say," he asked, "which one of us gets the blame for this screw up? Didn't you think of this before you decided to put the table in here?"

I sucked in a breath in disbelief. "Why didn't you point it out earlier?"

"I didn't know it would happen. You should have covered your bases better, Bro."

"Joe, it doesn't matter whose fault it is. It is what it is. No point in assigning blame. We'd both probably take a double helping."

******

We waved our arms over our heads from the edge of the field to get Dad's attention, then ran to the tractor when he stopped.

"Joe and I need a favor," I yelled up to Dad.

He shut the engine off and climbed down. "What's the problem, boys?" He looked first at Joe, then me. He wiped sweat from his brow with the handkerchief he took from his bib overalls. He was red-faced.

I started off cautiously. "W-We got the craps table moved into the stall, but it's so big it blocks the door. We can't get in to retrieve the dice."

Dad narrowed his eyes. "What you want from me?" His lip twitched.

Is that a smile? He's enjoying this.

14

"May we take a couple of the planks out next to the door? We'll reinstall 'em when I quit using the table. M-May we do that, Dad?"

Joe tried to help. "We didn't want to do it without asking."

Dad looked me up and down, avoiding eye contact.

He's stalling. Jeez, he enjoys seeing us stew?

Then Dad surprised us by spitting on the ground and remounting the tractor without answering our question. We stood there and watched him start working again.

I spat, too. "O-O-Old man's still pissed."

Joe said, "Why not put a stool inside the stall? I can stay in the stall and pass the dice back."

"When you're not around, I'll crawl under the table after each dozen tosses."

Will it always be this difficult dealing with Dad?

Chapter Three — Practice Makes Perfect

Joe came out to watch me practice the night I started tossing dice. A loud boom shook the barn and then a bright flash of lightening spread its fingers across the sky. Rain started pouring by the bucket-full.

"How's this dice setting supposed to work?" Joe asked.

"I'll use what's called the V3 dice set—threes always on top of both dice and a six and two on the side facing me. I want to get so good at arranging them into the V3 set that someday soon I'll do it one-handed in less than three seconds. I'll try to modify what's called the ice-tong grip so that the dice rotate more."

Satisfied with the dice, I began my practice session on what's probably still the only privately-owned craps table in this part of the state. I positioned my bets on the layout, making my progression place bets on six and eight. "I want to get my betting down so pat that I can parlay all five levels of my progression bets without even thinking."

Joe watched intently. "Are you any good? Think you'll be able to win?"

"I'm a total newbie, but I've got to start somewhere. I'm trying to get my mind blank on each toss. I never want to think of bets as real money. They say 'Scared money never wins', 'Don't sweat the money', and 'Do your job; the money will take care of itself'."

The thunder crashed again. A bright flash filled the night sky outside. I'd been afraid of thunderstorms as long as I could remember. Icicles worked their way up my spine.

But I was on a mission. Not even the fear of thunderstorms stopped me. I squared up to the table, readied the dice, and let them sail toward the other end.

"I need to get my running average for the last 500 tosses up to about ten numbers rolled between each losing seven to win consistently. That's a tall order."

Joe was now sitting on the stool inside the stall, splitting his attention between the conversation and the growing storm outside. He logged the results of each toss into my newly acquired Bone Tracker database that figures all my stats.

I wish I could go play right now. This waiting to turn twenty-one's going to be a drag.

"Casinos love dice-setter wannabees. They make a fortune off their learning attempts. Most never make it. They go broke first."

"Is that right?" Joe covered a yawn, looking outside at the storm raging there. Storms always made him sleepy. Unlike me, storms never bothered him.

Maybe all my talk was boring him, too?

I had a tape recording of a casino's craps-table-gambling noises playing in the background: an ever-changing symphony of bells dinging; coins dropping into metal trays; and people cheering, laughing, and betting filled the air.

I tried to think of everything. Not miss a trick.

I tossed an eight, then rolled sideways to rest one elbow on the railing. I played with the pair of dice in my hand.

"The guys on the net say to limit practice sessions to about fifty tosses each and then take a short break...and to log the exact result of each die."

I tossed a hard eight.

"I'm supposed to make each toss flawless—rather than to just try to log a lot of tosses—because I'm training my forearm's muscle memory. Fatigue introduces bad habits, so I'll avoid it." I turned, squared to the table again, and made another toss.

Joe kept his eye on the storm outside. It worsened every minute. He logged the six-two eight.

"Quality during practice would be more meaningful than quantity."

I put out my bet. "I want to slip into a relaxed comfort zone where I'm not thinking. I'm trying to experience no pressure and have no feelings or emotions."

"Totally spaced out, huh?"

"When I'm in my zone, muscle memory is supposed to do all the heavy lifting—a perfect toss every time. I only focus on the dice's desired landing spot."

"So the mental aspect is critical, too?"

I tossed a nine. "Yeah, Joe. Being in the zone should make my practice pay off. I'll try to eliminate all my toss's variables I can. Muscle memory should make my forearm a robotic dice-tossing machine."

"What's with that tape recording with the gambling sounds?"

"A buddy on the net uses it to help him tune out distracting gambling sounds when shooting. He sent me a copy. Kinda neat, isn't it?"

A bright flash lit everything up, followed by a loud boom. Everything went totally dark. The electric transformer atop the light pole next to the main barn burst into flame. Lightning had struck it. Joe scrambled to get the flashlight we kept handy. Upon finding it, he turned it on. I finished the practice session in near-total darkness. The flashlight Joe held barely lit the table's surface.

Watching me practice and seeing the results, Joe said, "You're doing all your homework right, Ray. I've conjured up an image of your arm being a dice-tossing robot."

It made me chuckle. Joe was always good for a laugh.

Just call me 'Robot-Ray'.

Chapter Four — Ray Drops The Bomb

I would now turn twenty-one soon and had tossed the dice more than 30,000 times in practice, logging the results. I'd been honing my skills a year and a half with no way to verify them. I'd soon be able to go to a casino to actually test my craps-shooting skills. Sitting on this ability was pure torture.

"Hey Ray, let's go into town, let off some steam, and have some fun."

I rubbed the back of my neck, "Leave me alone, Joe."

"Come on, Ray. It'll be good for you."

I spun the class ring around my finger, then frowned. "Nah, Not in the mood. Go away."

"You're not much fun, Ray. Let's go to a movie."

I rocked back and forth in place. "Look, shit-head, let me be. Got it?"

I'd rather stay home and mope.

My behavior seemed to get on Joe's nerves. He would have probably liked to kick my ass more than once.

Roll on, twenty-first birthday. Maybe I can stop being such a prick.

I volunteered every Saturday morning at the local no-kill animal shelter. I always liked petting the cats and dogs there, because they didn't ever seem to get enough petting. Lately I'd been volunteering even more, going in more often, trying to fill up the day. I hadn't even been dating anyone lately. I only wanted to stay hunkered over the craps table and get better.

This dice-setting obsession is eating me alive, and all I can do is spin my wheels.

Joe hadn't been interested in women for more than fifteen months, either. He dumped his sweetheart less than a week before their wedding, when he caught her cheating with one of his friends. He wasn't anxious to get hurt again, so he lived like a hermit. The hurt had eased, but bets were on the pass line that the memory lingered. He hated losing his friend too. He'd known him since grade school.

*****

Three days before my twenty-first birthday arrived, I dropped the bomb—during Sunday dinner, right in the middle of Mom serving fried chicken and mashed potatoes.

"I'm going to Vegas for a week to test my skills," I announced with a smile, a head nod, and not a sign of stuttering. "I'll take the dice-setting seminar I signed up for when I arrive, then shoot craps for real money. Saved up half a year's pay." I flashed a huge confident Ray-grin.

"Who said you could go?" Dad's face reddened, his jaw drew tight, and his eyes narrowed. He shot questions like they were bullets out of a machine gun: "Where'd this idea come from? What's this about a dice-tossing class? Whose idea was all this, anyway? Who gave you the right to go?"

Joe took a quick glance at Dad and then at me. The situation had gotten out of hand. Mom continued to dish out the mashed potatoes.

"I-I'm turning twenty-one. I've got a year and a half of practice invested... There's this weekend dice-setting class in Vegas I need to take."

Joe listened with interest.

I forged ahead. "C-Cost $750, and I paid weeks ago. I've earned the chance to test my skills." I met Dad's surprised stare head on. "Look Dad, this is happening, one way or another."

Mom put down the mashed potatoes, realizing what was going on. "Ray, why so secretive in how you did this?"

I slid the chair back and shifted my weight forward.

Mom's eyes teared up. "You dumped this on us all at once. Why are you doing this? I don't want you gambling."

"Sorry, Mom. Hurting you is the last thing I want."

Mom and I turned toward each other. Neither spoke. The air hung thick with tension.

Rising from the table, I gripped it with both hands. "I'm going— that's final. I've got to have the chance to succeed."

I felt my face redden. Sitting back down, my body relaxed.

It's finally all out in the open.

How I had handled all this made Joe scowl—me not thinking about everyone's feelings. I had a force deep inside driving me that was beyond my ability to control.

I don't like myself, anymore.

For once, Dad didn't have anything to say: he and Mom looked dumbstruck, almost like I had declared I had disowned them. Both turned ashen as their chests heaved with heavy breathing.

Mom closed her eyes and clinched her fists. "You'll end up like your Great Uncle Mike. Gambling cost him everything. You know he became a drunk and committed suicide."

"Mom, that won't happen to me. If I lose my bankroll, I'll quit and walk away. Forever. Promise."

Joe couldn't stay silent any longer. He surprised me when he jumped in on my side. "Mom and Dad, you're blowing this out of proportion. Ray's a man now. He's going to do what he's got to do. Have a little faith he's smart enough to handle whatever life throws him. Give him the chance to be happy."

Setting my jaw firmly, I looked Joe straight in the eye. "Joe, you're going, too." I nodded then winked. "Need you for moral support and as my wingman. Besides, we'll have a blast—the adventure of a lifetime."

I need to repay Joe for all the times I whimpered as a child to get Mom to make him let me tag along when he got to go somewhere special. I know he didn't appreciate having his little bro go along, especially when he was with his older friends. I couldn't help it. I didn't want to be left behind. Besides, Mom was an easy mark.

Mom, chewing her fingernail, looked over at Dad and nodded as she choked back a tear. She'd always been a strong woman who kept her emotions hidden, but now she revealed a side of her Joe and I had never seen before. Love, worry, concern and fear—all rolled up together. I gave her a loving hug and a kiss then wiped away her tears.

Her boys are grown up.

She returned my hug, squeezing me around the waist.

I smiled. "Everything'll be okay, Mom. Promise."

Dad laid his glasses on the table, then wiped a forearm sleeve across his eyes. He shook his head slowly, then turned to Joe. His voice sounded low and controlled. "We've got the corn planted. I'll manage without you, Joe. Go with Ray. His mind's made up."

He rested both elbows on the edge of the table, cradling his forehead in his hands. Dad didn't move and his face remained hidden. He sat for a minute longer, his forehead still buried. He lowered his arms and looked over at me. Peace flushed his paler-than-normal face. "Ray, go learn your lesson. It'll make you more of a man—no matter the outcome."

"Sorry, Dad." I bowed my head. "You dream of me being a farmer. But farming's not in my heart like with you and Joe. I've got to see if dice setting's my calling. Can't deny it."

Dad got up and hugged me. His eyes were moist, but he wouldn't allow any tears to flow. He turned toward Joe. His lower lip quivered and his voice choked-up. "Joe, keep Ray safe."

"I will."

Mom smiled at me. "Call home frequently. Don't worry us unnecessarily."

I hurried to her side to embrace her. "We will, Mom. Scout's honor."

Likely, what I have planned will prove foolhardy, but the world is calling me. I can deny it no longer, and I only have to reach out my fingertips... No matter how bad the outcome, I'll take the rap. Maybe Joe's right—have I bitten off more than I can chew?

Oh, well, at least Joe'll be there to help keep me safe. Maybe we'll stay out of jams and not embarrass ourselves too much, or too often. God willing, we'll come out the other end of our adventure alive, still kicking—our scalps intact.

I had more tenacity than Joe, but would tenacity alone carry the day? It might get me chewed up and spit out.

Despite Joe being a couple years older than me, he wasn't wise in the ways of the world, having lived all his life in a rural setting. To be honest, I thought this adventure we'd be taking on might scare the hell out of him. We'd both stand out in any Las Vegas crowd, being recognizable as a couple of hay seeds from the Midwest.

Call us The Lone Ranger and Tonto, or Lewis and Clark, because we'll have a lot of exploring to do in Vegas. What'll we encounter in Sin City that we haven't planned on or prepared for?

I continued to try to psyche myself up.

Oh, well. Nothing to do but go do it. I'm ready. Bring it on.

Chapter Five — Friday, Vegas Bound

Weeks before our departure, I checked prices and booked rooms online, receiving decent rates and even a couple of free nights included midweek. Before we went to Las Vegas, the farthest we'd ever been from home was nearby Omaha.

Everyone back home celebrated my twenty-first birthday on Wednesday. We threw an enormous party.

At breakfast Thursday, I helped myself to a big plateful of scrambled eggs. "Everybody we knew showed up; must've been 150 here."

Joe buttered his biscuit. "I'm glad we booked Dino Rhino for the music. They were awesome."

"Did we really go through three kegs of beer?"

"Yup. What time did the party end, anyway? I never even checked."

"The last guests left after three a.m." I poured coffee. "I was so ready for bed by then."

"We told everyone we were going to Vegas. But does anyone know why?"

I lowered myself into a chair at the kitchen table. "Joe, unless you've told someone, not one of our friends even knows we have a craps table in the barn. I've kept it a secret."

"I never told anyone."

******

Our plane took off from Omaha International Airport for Las Vegas' McCarran Airport at 7:10 a.m. on Friday.

Before entering security, we exchanged hugs and kisses. Dad wiped away a tear. I pretended I hadn't noticed.

Mom forced a nervous smile. "You keep safe now." Her voice trembled.

Dad said, "Boys, be careful of pickpockets in the big city. I got my pocket picked once right here in Omaha."

"Really?" I had never heard about it before.

"Yes, when you were youngsters. Pickpockets work in crowds, where an accomplice yells out 'There's a pickpocket in the crowd!' when a target's spotted. This makes the target check his valuables to see if he's been hit. Now the pickpocket knows where those valuables are and lifts them at his leisure."

"Pretty slick," I said.

"If you ever get bumped into or hear someone yell something about a pickpocket, the last thing you want to do is check your wallet."

I nodded my understanding.

Dad concluded, "If you do, keep your hand covering wallet until you're safely out of the crowd and there's nobody near you. Your wallet will be harder to pick if you carry it in your front pants pocket, too."

"Sounds like a country boy can't be too careful in the big city," Joe said.

Dad bit his lower lip and nodded. "You guys take care of each other, okay?"

"We will," I assured him, shaking hands firmly, followed by a quick wink. "We'll be fine, Dad."

Joe and I gave out final hugs, then went through the security check-in area.

******

I stiffened up at takeoff. I had no idea it would be such a steep climb. Most people probably would have called our Las Vegas flight pretty uneventful, but to us every shudder of turbulence was a new sensation, scary and exciting—because we'd never flown before.

In the far distance, another airliner passed us headed in the opposite direction. The clouds below were puffy. The tiny squares in differing shades of green proved to be farms. Cities looked even stranger from up so high. The Rocky Mountains provided an amazing view.

We passed time discussing our plans for our week-long trip. I had purchased tickets for three shows: the topless *Folies Bregere* at the Tropicana on Sunday night, *Riverdance* a couple days later at the Mirage, and *Santana* on Thursday night at the Hard Rock.

Joe entertained himself by playing chess against a computer opponent on his phone, one of his favorite hobbies. He also read a lot—up to three different library books at the same time. He read a while in one, bookmarked it, and set it aside. He picked up the second and started it. Then he did the same with the third. After that, whichever held his interest the most got the majority of his reading time. He never had trouble keeping track of what went on in all three, and that ability drove me crazy.

As a kid, Joe had once listened to an audio book through earbuds. Without thinking, he picked up a library book and opened it. A good forty-five minutes passed before it dawned on him he'd been reading the library book while listening to the audio of another book at the same time. He had been able to keep both of them separated in his mind, without missing any details from either.

Growing up, I had always enjoyed running and horseback riding.

When Joe finished his chess game, he turned his phone off and closed his eyes, likely listening to the drone of the jet engines.

Everybody seated around us appeared excited to be vacationing in Vegas, too. We listened to their plans and shared ours, which caught the interest of the older married couple across the aisle. Their names were Carl and Nancy. Both were retired and from Omaha.

Carl raised his eyebrows. "Good luck. You're brave to take on such a difficult challenge."

Twenty to thirty minutes before landing, we viewed what might have been the Grand Canyon, then Carl urged me, "Tell me more about this 'place-bet progression' you'll use in Vegas."

"I'll bet on my ability to toss sixes and eights twice as often as a random roller, while also tossing half as many losing sevens as normal. Heavy Haltam, an expert precision shooter from Texas, helped me over the net. He came up with my parlay-type progression bet for me."

Joe listened in while working a crossword puzzle in the newspaper he'd found in the pouch on the back of the seat ahead of him.

"My progression place-bets win big when I toss any combination of sixes and/or eights five times, before I toss a losing seven. But, I lose small when I fail." I cocked my head sideways to see Carl and Nancy better. "Those progression bets are powerful. I can suffer two or three quick seven-out losses, then win my progression bet once and still win more than double what I lost. I'm not under much pressure to perform." I pushed the fingertips of both hands against each other.

Joe smiled at Carl. "He seems to win his progression bet all the time in practice. Usually more than once."

I took a PayDay candy bar from my shirt pocket, unwrapped it, and took a bite.

"Hey, Ray, mind sharing?" Joe had already eaten his candy bar.

"Here ya go, Joe." I broke the candy bar in two and gave him half.

"Thanks, Bro."

"It's a good thing you come from a line of tall skinny people, Joe. You're a nonstop eater. Most people who eat like you weigh a ton."

I was right. His mind always focused on what to eat next, anytime he had time on his hands. It was an addiction with him. Either he remained in control and ate right, or he was totally out of control and scrounging for some junk to eat. No middle ground existed.

"Yeah, I guess my genes are saving me from myself." He took another bite.

What I'd told Carl was how I believed things would go in Vegas. Then again, I hadn't yet stepped inside a casino, and we were both what locals in Vegas call *Vegas virgins*—first-time visitors. I had already envisioned all this in my mind, though. To me, visualizing it meant half the battle had already been won.

"I expect to win a couple progressions per session, then move on to another casino in a quick hit-and-run fashion—to avoid management noticing my wins too much."

I took out a pair of practice dice and gave them to Carl. "A souvenir. Keep 'em. I have three more pairs in the carry-on."

"Thanks. Be sure to win one of your progression bets for me."

A bit puzzled, Nancy asked, "This may be a stupid question, but what is a 'place bet'?"

Joe continued to work his puzzle, half-way listening.

"On a simple place bet, I'm betting the casino my number will roll before a losing seven does. With place bets on both six and eight, I win seven dollars for each six dollars bet every time either six or eight rolls before a seven appears. If seven rolls first, all the place bets are lost."

The "fasten seat-belts" light came on and the pilot announced weather conditions in Las Vegas, saying we would soon be landing. While our plane settled into its landing pattern, slowed, and started to bank, Lake Mead and Hoover Dam appeared below.

Landing both scared and excited me. The plane bounced once on touchdown. Several famous hotels came rushing into view while our plane slowed. Next, I experienced a jolt when the air brakes slowed us down.

I recognized the pyramid shape of Luxor and could read Mandalay Bay's name atop their hotel. Excalibur and Tropicana next rolled into view. They were all there, waiting for us. They were far enough away from the runway that they each appeared to be foot-tall miniatures. Even though those hotels looked more like movie-set miniatures from our plane's tiny window: they'd assume their full grandeur when we got closer to them. This naughty jewel in the desert called out to us, "Come, it's time for fun."

Joe pressed his nose to the window. "Wow! Disney World for adults."

******

The stale smell of the airport greeted us when we disembarked down the long lit corridor. We followed overhead signage and boarded a rail tram to take us to the main terminal. There, we used a moving walkway to work our way toward the baggage area. Nothing seemed impossible.

In the main terminal, we took in rows of slot machines with travelers playing them and many huge screens advertising super-star acts appearing at Strip hotels. We passed dining spots, souvenir shops, bookstores, and car rental booths. This week promised to offer sensory overload.

After what seemed like a twenty-minute wait in the baggage area, a light at the end of our baggage carousel started flashing, a buzzer sounded, and our carousel sprung to life. Soon bags of all sizes and shapes popped out of the carousel's mouth.

Joe checked each when they came by, trying to spot our bags, but so many of them resembled ours that he had to pull them off to check name tags and then put them back on when he learned they were someone else's. Finally, when the last bags emerged, Joe and I finished gathering our belongings.

On our way out, we encountered about a dozen tightly-grouped people holding signs with different people's names on them, waiting to whisk them off for limo rides to their various destinations. Our names wouldn't be among those listed.

We wheeled our bags outside the main terminal doors and got in line to get a taxi. After waiting our turn, our bags got loaded in the taxi's trunk. We were off for what should have been a five-minute taxi ride. Due to heavy traffic, it took us a bit longer to arrive at the Tropicana.

******

Signs advertising the TV Show "Let's Make A Deal" caught our eye when we checked into the hotel. They stated the show would be filmed in one of Tropicana's many theaters.

"How do we get on 'Let's Make A Deal'? I asked the check-in clerk.

"You have to already have tickets that were mailed out months ago."

Oh, well. Guess they'll survive without us. Joe and I are probably too quiet to have gotten selected.

We gawked at the bright lavishly-ornate golden-colored casino area that glittered not more than fifty feet in front of Trop's check-in desk. They didn't want us to miss it.

Talk about marketing, the management gave us no choice about discovering Trop's casino. We had to cross through the main casino floor to get to the long hallways at the rear, which lead to the towers housing our rooms. Not all new guests even made it across the casino area without succumbing to temptation and parking their bags beside a bank of slots to try their luck.

All the gambling going on right in front of us quickened my pulse. The noises from slot-machines and the happy and boisterous shouts from black-jack and craps-tables mixed with loops of what would barely pass for music to create a breathtaking sound-mat.

Coins dropped into a hopper nearby. The sound of people losing money couldn't be heard. The losers remained silent, wishing their luck to change.

I leaped up in the air, clicking my heels together. "Did we die and go to Heaven, Joe?"

******

The journey to our room took us a full ten minutes. Not only did we have to cross the huge casino area, but we also had to go down never-ending corridors and cross an outdoor park-like tropical area.

Up in one of a neighboring pair of towers—each housing hundreds of rooms—we had a two-room suite featuring a strong tropical theme, with massive pieces of light-colored furniture accented with split-bamboo trim.

"Both these beds are gigantic." Joe flopped on the nearest bed after we entered and sank so deep he had trouble getting back up.

I stuck my head inside the bathroom. "Check this out. Our bathroom's bigger than either of our bedrooms back home—marble floor, too."

Light warm-creamy colors covered everything. Beautiful wall-sized framed photos of tropical sunsets graced the walls.

"Look," I pointed across the room, "a fridge." I went and opened its door. "Hey, it's stocked with mini-bottles of liquor and has a small microwave on top."

"Staying here promises to be fun." Joe rubbed his hands together in anticipation.

"Joe, don't take anything out of the fridge. I bet they charge big prices for each little bottle of liquor you drink."

Excitement gripped us. We were anxious for our adventure to begin. We unpacked our bags at lightning speed, shoving our clothes into drawers and closets. I broke out the dice, threw a few practice tosses onto what I'd decided was my bed, and liked the results.

Back home, I had divvied up my $3,000 gambling bankroll by putting four hundred-dollar bills into each of seven envelopes. Each was labeled with a different day of the week on the front, to guarantee the bankroll lasted all week. One extra envelope marked "Second Friday" held two-hundred dollars for our final, partial day in Vegas.

"I will be an intelligent, responsible gambler," I promised myself.

I took the money out of the envelope marked Friday and put those bills in my wallet. I then locked all of the remaining envelopes inside our room's wall safe and chose the new combination. I put my wallet in my front pants pocket.

"They say Vegas is a pick-pocket's paradise."

"Remember what Dad told ya."

******

"Let's go look around," Joe suggested, champing at the bit to begin exploring Vegas and learn all its secrets. I was in the hallway before he got his words out. We skipped our way down to the elevator like a couple of kids with enough pent-up energy to explode. We found ourselves alone when we reached the ground floor. We couldn't resist punching all the elevator's buttons before we exited.

The casino's decor still overwhelmed me; so did the vast number of slots and table games that produced constant gambling sounds—dings, coins dropping, reels spinning, and people hollering and shouting—

that lured us to check them out. Neither of us resisted the temptation to play a few of those flashing noisy slot machines beckoning us. We played the cheapest ones we found, but won nothing. Chalking it up to the cost of entertainment, Ray and I both controlled our losses.

During our initial foray, we were most amazed by the live entertainment on a raised stage protruding into the casino's gaming floor. We noticed the male/female acrobatic act who employed silk scarves and interlocking arm grips to grasp onto each other while they sailed above the casino floor on a long swinging velvet-covered rope.

They accomplished amazing and dramatic acrobatic moves we'd never seen before. The guy released his grip on the girl's waist, making you believe he'd dropped her before catching her upside down by her ankle.

She slithered back up her own legs using her arms, up his legs, then worked her way into a one-handed handstand on his head. His anchoring arm remained intertwined around the silk scarf, attached to the swinging rope.

From her one-handed handstand, the woman pushed off strongly and turned a midair flip during her dive toward the floor, to reach out and grasp her partner's ankles and swing below him. She released her grip with one hand and waved to the slack-jawed gawkers below, who gasped, emitting a loud "Oooh!" together, then offered their applause.

The acrobats got swinging back and forth, in unison, like he'd become her trapeze. To gasps from shocked onlookers, she shot upward far enough to grasp his wrists.

Then he started spinning his rope fast, moving them both around in circles while holding his rope at arm's length away from his body.

She moved her free arm to his thigh and pushed herself straight out perpendicular to his vertical body so they could spin together.

The muscular and attractive acrobats completed their act, not breathing hard but glistening with perspiration. They took their bows and left the stage to thunderous applause and cheers from those who had been frozen in their tracks, heads straining skyward to follow the couple's graceful maneuvers.

A rock band swung into action on the casino stage.

Nonstop live entertainment. Cool.

When their act ended, we felt an urgent need to get exploring again.

******

I eyed the roller coaster atop neighboring New York-New York's casino. "Joe, we're riding that sucker before we go home."

He agreed while we both looked up, shading our eyes with our hands. The coaster went up and down and twisted along its metal tracks. Muffled screams floated down from high atop the building that sported the skyline of New York City.

Someone's having fun.

We noticed a big golden lion statue across the intersection at the humongous emerald green MGM Grand Hotel. On up The Strip, we saw The Monte Carlo—tall and impressive in its outer covering of all white. The Strip swarmed with shoulder-to-shoulder tourists squeezing past each other in both directions.

We stopped to grab eighteen-inch-long hot dogs—the world's largest? We got them at an on-the-street cubby-hole-sized eatery right next to a souvenir shop. We were dumb enough to get one each. We'd needed to quench our growing hunger, but neither of us could eat even half our hot dog. While we ate we people-watched and enjoyed the light breeze.

One of the casinos had a billboard-sized LED screen outside for all to see, advertising Paul Anka's upcoming show. Most Hotels had some kind of a skin review, featuring either scantily-attired showgirls or Chippendale-type guys for the gals to see.

"Man, Joe, each casino looks so close, but they're so gigantic we walked forever before getting to the next one. They seemed to be up to half a mile apart." Each appeared bigger and fancier than the one before.

Two members of the Las Vegas Mounted Police Patrol came moseying single file down our side of the street. The one in front kept an eye on everything around him while his horse nodded to tourists as it passed. The other was a mounted policewoman who moved along at a slightly slower, more relaxed pace. I enjoyed seeing their beautiful horses and waived briefly, but wasn't noticed.

We stopped and studied the neon that made up the five-story-tall by half-a-city-block-long marque sign in front of Riviera Hotel and Casino. It appeared to be more than thrice the size of our main barn and covered by lit and flashing neon. It reeked glitz, in the most flamboyant way. Tons of small souvenir shops and eateries populated the area.

We did our best to avoid the dark-skinned foreign-looking men shoving fliers for prostitution-outcall services into our faces. They held out their literature at arm's length, flicking it fast with the fingers of their free hand to create constant noise to get your attention. "No" wasn't in their vocabulary. When we first encountered them, I took their literature out of curiosity to find out what it was and was surprised by its nature. I asked the guy, "Why are you handing me this?" He replied, "No Ingles." Their behavior became annoying. I quickly discarded the flier.

Sin City, indeed.

Banks of a half dozen of what I'd normally call newspaper vending machines were at curbside. Except they all said "Free" on them and the literature they contained weren't newspapers, but tabloids with photos of women on the front pages, promising guys a good time.

Rolling billboards for a variety of outcall services also traveled up and down The Strip on long low-slung flatbed trucks. Those mobile billboards displayed revealing photos of stunning, sensual women and a phone number to call for one of them, or someone similar, to visit your hotel room.

Not for us, but tonight would be an excellent time for me to lose my dice-setting cherry.

Chapter Six — Friday Night

"Why are we here?" Joe asked me, probably wondering why anyone would leave Vegas to go gamble somewhere else. We had arrived by taxi at Green Valley Ranch Casino in Henderson—one of Vegas' suburbs.

"Everyone taking the dice-setter course is gathering here for a meet and greet and a possible craps-shooting session at seven p.m. They picked the place—I didn't."

"There must be something extra special about this place for them to want to bring us all out here. Guess we'll find out if that's true."

I looked around. "Yup. Didn't want to miss it."

Joe checked his watch. "We're a bit early, Ray."

I headed to where I'd been told the group would join up—at the edge of the craps pits.

Joe followed right behind. "There aren't any groups around here. Are you sure this is where we're supposed to be?"

"Let's check out the action."

We were in the heart of the bustling casino, with the floor laid out like a maze. Overhead spotlights lit each gaming table, with everything around it falling off into darkness. A few craps players were in action there. Joe and I stood behind a player with a backward baseball cap as he tossed the dice.

We watched the players shoot. There were six tables in the craps pit area, grouped in two rows of three tables each. They sat end to end lengthwise, with about five feet between each table in all directions. With floor space so valuable, they packed 'em in tight, to accommodate the greatest number of players. All their tables featured a tasteful light-tan covering with "Green Valley Ranch Casino" emblazoned atop their betting layout.

"Hey, Joe, look at that." I pointed to what had caught my eye, exciting me. Without thinking, I dragged Joe by the elbow to the back of the craps pit area. A bubbling waterfall cascaded down a freestanding glass wall. The water glowed from the bulbs submerged in its depths.

I stared up at it with my mouth gaped open. My eyes grew large and a giant smile came across my face. I was hypnotized and stood motionless for a long time.

Finally, I said to Joe. "This waterfall is the most relaxing thing I've ever seen. It's mesmerizing. I need to buy one so I can feel this relaxed at home."

Not only was it visually relaxing, it also made the tranquil sounds of water splashing into a little babbling brook at floor level. The sensations of sight and sound intertwined to weave their magic. The waterfall zapped the tension right out of my body. I don't know how long we stood there as the water continued to cascade down the sheet of glass, with little air bubbles rising through the water.

When we eventually slipped out of our transfixed state, we looked around again. We joined up with the other precision-shooter wannabes, who had gathered outside the craps pit area, not twenty-five feet away. Everyone was dressed like casual tourists. All were men, ranging from my age to over sixty. At one of the instructor's encouragement, everyone introduced themselves, telling where they were from, how they'd become interested in dice setting, and what numbers their tosses favored. I remember thinking that if they were like us, they were anxious to get straight into some team play.

I introduced myself.

When Joe's turn came, he said, "I'm Joe, Ray's older brother. I'm here to lend him moral support."

Everyone welcomed him to tag along for the rest of the evening.

Joe got one of the instructor's attention. "Can I attend Ray's seminars with him? I don't intend to participate. If not, I'm good with casino hopping till he's done."

"Someone'll get you an answer to that question before we leave."

Everyone split into two groups, with each group of five going to separate craps tables. Tonight's gathering gave everyone a chance to bet on each other before our seminars got underway on Saturday.

Standing at a real craps table ready to play excited me. Joe stood out of the way behind me, but close enough to talk.

The dealer looked at me. "I'll need to see your driver's license, please."

"Why?"

"We need to make sure you're of legal age to play."

I passed him the driver's license. "Turned twenty-one a couple days ago."

Driver's license checked, the dealer passed it back. "Congratulations, and good luck."

I took out today's four one-hundred-dollar bills, dropped them on the table, and received four-hundred-dollars' worth of chips. A player two table positions before me tossed a losing seven. I surveyed the surroundings and assessed the action. I had learned a lot about craps while waiting to come to Vegas.

Nudging Joe, I pointed out the stickman, who stood at the middle of the table, opposite the dealers and the box man, who received player cash, counted it, then dropped it through a slot into the table's lock box. The stickman used his bamboo stick to return the dice to the next shooter.

"The guys online say that after seeing what your dice set is, a good stickman always passes the dice back with your chosen numbers already on top," I whispered. "You're supposed to tip the crew the first time the stickman returns your dice with your numbers turned up for you. The pit crew can make it easier for you to win, or harder, if they take the notion. It's better to have them on your team, instead of working against you."

I played with a few of the chips, shifting them from hand to hand. I'd waited a very long time for this moment. Now it stared me in the face and needed to be savored and enjoyed.

I could smell the cologne on the guy next to me. It had a light, clean fragrance of oriental spices. I also got a whiff of the talcum powder he probably carried in his pocket to keep the dice from getting sticky. The guy wore gold jewelry and a diamond ring the size of a quarter on each hand. I'd never seen a man wear that many signs of wealth before. The thought of him being rich enough to buy anything his heart desired ran through my mind.

My turn to shoot arrived. Firing a glance over my shoulder, I gave Joe a thumbs up and smiled. I took a deep breath, then set seventy-two dollars in chips on the table. I turned and squared to the table, telling the dealer, "thirty-six dollar place bets on both six and eight. All place bets work on all my come-out rolls."

The dealer nodded, then made the bets for me. In practice I always had my bets working on my come-out roll to make it easier for me to win the big progression bet payoff. This move often got me one step closer on the first toss. I rarely opened by tossing a seven, so I didn't worry about that.

I'd experienced a huge leap in results when I modified my grip to put more spin on the dice. That kept them rotating around my desired axis through the very top-front corners of the dice, where I ice-tong gripped them as lightly as possible with the end of my first finger and thumb. All the practice had paid off. Those rubber diamonds at the end of the table no longer seemed to affect my toss's outcome—almost like they weren't there. The dice came rolling straight back down the table together after hitting the very bottom part of the end wall—maybe that dampened the diamonds' supposedly randomizing effect? Those protruding rubber diamonds now didn't do much to spoil my efforts.

I selected a pair from five matching dice the stickman slid in front of me with the tip of his bamboo stick. The remaining dice were pulled back and deposited in a tiny shallow dish.

My hands automatically set the dice in a V3 pattern as I put them down on the table surface, touching and lining up on the pass line. With a three-foot-long straight-upward snap of my stiffened wrist and forearm, I launched them while they still rested right on the table surface. In flight, the dice stayed less than two inches apart and rotated together at the same rate, seeking their targeted landing zone at the distant end of the table.

"Point is eight, easy eight," our stickman announced.

I upped the place bets on six and eight by having half my winnings added to each. The next roll produced a five, then a hard ten, which can happen when one die goes off its desired rotational axis. A hard eight won my bet.

I used those winnings again to increase both the bets to my third progression level, saying, "all my place bets work on all my come-out rolls."

One of our dice-setter wannabees pointed. "Look how those dice travel together. He's nailing sixes and eights, too." The action on six and eight picked up. The chatter rose in volume. As a player wins, excitement grows.

"Three-three six. Hard-way six. Point is six. Get your bets down, hard ways, yo, field bets, get 'em down," our stickman sing-songed, smacking the table surface with the tip of his stick for effect.

I split the winnings to increase both bets again to the fourth level of the progression bet. I threw a five then a four, then paused and sneaked a peek over at my favorite lighted waterfall for a couple of seconds. I launched the dice again from the tabletop.

"Six. Winner six. Pay the line, take the don't," our stickman said.

I relaxed my body with a deep sigh. If I threw one more six or eight before the devil-seven rolled, I'd net $699 on this progression bet.

After my next throw our dealer barked, "Easy eight. Point is eight."

My eyes lit up. I looked over at Joe, flashing him a relaxed grin.

He smiled back. I had won my progression bet.

But the dice were passed back to me without my big progression bet getting paid off.

I frowned. Instead of picking up the dice and shooting again, I stopped and asked the dealer, "Why didn't you pay me? I should have won about $700."

"You didn't say your place bets were working on that come-out roll," the stickman replied dryly. He didn't want to discuss it. He went on about his duties, not even looking toward me.

"Maybe I forgot to say it this time—I thought I did. I know I stated it each time before. I said my place bets work on ALL my come-out rolls," I protested in a panic-filled voice.

Nah, they wouldn't cheat me out of my first ever big win, would they?

"You heard me say my place bets always work on ALL my come-out rolls, didn't you?"

My dealer didn't even look up at me. "Yes, I heard you say that."

"He said it," the dealer at the far end of our table volunteered.

"Pay the man," ruled the pit boss I hadn't even noticed standing nearby. "He clearly established his betting pattern."

Decision rendered, dispute settled. $699 in chips flowed my way. Actually, the dealer had me toss him a one-dollar chip, then gave me seven black $100 chips. Players flashed me the thumbs up. Joe patted me on the back. Others celebrated with applause, whistles and high-fives.

Everybody celebrates when a large win occurs. Everyone likes winning and winners. Only Joe and I knew this was my first time shooting the dice with real money at stake. I had a feeling that if the others knew I'd won big while losing my cherry, they'd have celebrated much louder and longer.

Joe pumped my hand. "Welcome to becoming a real craps player."

I tossed a green twenty-five dollar chip to the dealer as a tip. "For the boys."

The dealer tapped the edge of the chip against the Plexiglas tip box, then dropped it in.

I'd already established eight as my point to make with the last roll. Since I'd won my bet and not tossed a losing seven yet, I got to continue shooting. I tossed another six and an easy eight, then devil seven showed its ugly face to end my turn.

Wow! Welcome to Vegas. What a sensational way to begin our trip.

I spotted some orange chips in the center of the house's chip rack and asked the dealer what they were.

"They're called 'pumpkins'. They're $500 chips.

Then Joe asked, "Why are the pumpkins kept in the middle of the other chips?"

The dealer chuckled. "That's on a need-to-know basis."

"Really? You can't tell me?"

"Nah. Just kidding. We stash the pumpkins in the center of our chip supply on both sides of the thousand-dollar chips to ensure they're most difficult for anyone to swipe. The smaller chips on both sides help protect them."

Joe thought about it. "Thanks."

He tapped me on the shoulder. "Tip the man, Ray. He answered our questions."

I tossed him a couple of five-dollar chips.

Our dice-setter classmates shot around the table again, without me getting another win.

When our game broke up, I chased down a heavyset guy leaving our table.

"Are you Heavy?" I asked, referring to his craps nickname.

"Sure am. By the way you shoot and bet, I'm guessing you must be Ray from Iowa." He shook my hand.

"That's me. I won the progression bet you thought up for me."

"Yes, I saw you win it. Congratulations." Heavy tipped his hat. "Nice toss you've got there. I won some money betting on you, too."

I smiled from ear to ear. I had put a face to the name I knew so well from those dice-setting forums, the name of the man who had advised me many times over the past eighteen months. I'd told Joe earlier I knew I'd recognize Heavy by his size, shooting style, betting patterns on all four outside numbers, and the Texas-cowboy getup he'd be wearing. Heavy had arrived late, missing our group's meet and greet.

Heavy shook my hand again. "I look forward to shooting with you some more."

He tipped his hat and moved to another table to find a new game. Ours had closed up shop when everyone walked away at the same time—like someone, for some unknown reason, had pulled the plug.

Our group's head honcho—I hadn't learned his name yet—pulled Joe aside. "If you're willing to drop $200, you may attend all seminar sessions as a nonparticipating observer."

I gave the honcho two of my black chips, satisfying that requirement. Joe thanked me.

These professional gamblers could sniff out a dollar bill hidden under a rock.

******

I called home on the way back to the Trop via taxi and brought our parents up to speed about the goings-on of our first day. Mom and Dad's whoops and yells came over the speakerphone about my right-out-of-the-gun big win.

Mom's voice sounded full of excitement. "Yeah, that's some win. We're rooting for you, Son."

"Good luck the rest of the week. Keep on winning," Dad said.

I imagined they'd been anxiously awaiting that call, too. I was glad it helped put their minds at ease.

While we settled in for some sleep, Joe told me, "If the rest of the week proves to be anything similar to today, we're in for one hell of a good time."

"New doors might be opening for me." A new fear washed over me. "I hope they don't ever slam shut in my face."

I took in a long breath, managing to regain my composure. I looked Joe's way with my heart in my throat.

"I'm so close to succeeding, I can taste it, Joe. I don't know if I can handle it, if it all falls through now."

I took in another deep breath and buried my face in the pillow.

"Ray, you did your homework. Everything's going to turn out fine."

When I looked up again, Joe shot me a warm smile and nodded.

"Think so?" I asked, seeking reassurance.

"Absolutely, now get some sleep. We've got to get started early tomorrow."

I rolled over in bed, pulled up the covers, and turned the lights out.

******

The sound of me pulling on jeans woke Joe at 3:30 a.m.

Joe rubbed his eyes. "What's up?"

"Can't sleep. Goin' downstairs to play some slots." I checked to make sure my billfold had enough money in it. Yep, I had my $500 in winnings.

"Is that wise? You need to be your sharpest tomorrow."

I put on my shoes. "I'll be fine, Joe."

"You've got a case of Vegas fever. I read that's where people get so excited they can't stop gambling long enough to get some sleep."

My mind remained unchanged. I'd become too wound up to sleep.

Joe dressed. I could tell he was set on making sure nothing bad happened to his little bro.

******

We bought a bucket of coins at the cashier's window and played slots for more than an hour. Cha-ching! Jackpot symbols lined up on all three wheels on the single pay line. Joe looked up at the payoff chart at the top of the five-cent Double Diamonds Deluxe slot he was playing.

"Ray, I hit an eighty dollar jackpot."

No coins fell into the machine's coin tray. Only a light flashed on top of the machine.

"What do I have to do to get paid?" Joe asked.

"Sit tight and wait. A slot attendant will come and hand-pay your winnings in folding money," said a lady of about forty, who sat next to Joe with two other women of similar age.

We all got to talking as we waited.

"Another friend came with us to Vegas, too, but she got gambling fever real bad during our first couple of days here. She stayed up day and night gambling, lost all her money, then maxed out all her credit cards trying to win it back. Now she just lies on the bed upstairs and cries. It makes us feel really bad and has nearly ruined our trip. She wouldn't stay with us on the cheap slots," the lady confided.

Joe gave me a warning look, flicking his eyebrows menacingly.

The slot attendant soon arrived with Joe's jackpot.

"You should tip her a couple bucks," the lady player said. "They expect a tip when they come hand-pay you in cash."

Joe collected his money and tipped the attendant.

"Ray, we're going back to bed, now."

Does he expect to drop the hammer and nip my Vegas fever in the bud?

40

I smirked and stuck out my tongue.

"Nah, baby, nah. I'm having too much fun. Go to bed if you want to. I'm staying up."

What could Joe do? I'm too big for him to toss me over his shoulder and carry me off to bed.

"You're going to end up feeling terrible tomorrow, when you'll be needing to feel your best," he argued.

I continued to feed coins into the slot.

"If I do, you can throw it in my face with an 'I told you so'."

"Okay. I know when I'm whipped, but you'll be sorry. It doesn't matter how crappy I feel tomorrow. I'm not the one who'll be trying to do spectacular feats with the dice." Then Joe said under his breath, "Let the little prick learn from his mistakes."

I heard what he said, but let it go.

He stayed up despite being tired. Joe didn't want me to do something crazy without him being there to save me from myself. His intentions were good, but in a way, it felt smothering. I was ready to cut loose and have some fun.

How will Vegas fever affect me tomorrow?

Chapter Seven — Saturday

My dice-setting seminar began at nine in the morning in a small dealer's school near Downtown, a few miles away from the Strip. The school was nestled in a narrow storefront in a strip mall. No glamorous decor existed in this place. It was where potential casino employees learned their trade. Today, our presence kept it from being empty and lifeless. Every type of table imaginable sat there: blackjack, roulette, pai gow poker—all of them well worn. Several had chips scattered about on them.

The instructors guided us to the back, where two craps tables sat crowded beside each other. Nine others had signed up to get their throwing styles analyzed and listen to experts cover everything imaginable concerning precision dice setting. They had all been present at our meet-and-greet the previous night.

I looked around for Heavy, half expecting him to be teaching the seminar, but he wasn't in attendance.

One student, Henry, ran around showing everyone a video he'd taken a month before on his previous trip to Vegas. "Watch, watch... that's my girlfriend, there. We were hiking out in the desert after we got into town. See that huge rock? There she goes, jumping up on top of it. But what she doesn't know is...whamo! Did you see that? Wait, let me replay it. That's a rattlesnake, there. I can't believe I caught the whole thing on video. I posted it on YouTube after we got home."

Henry played the video for each person there. His girlfriend always jumped when that snake bit her. Every person watching the video jumped, too.

"We lucked out getting a cell phone signal and called 911. A helicopter flew us to a nearby hospital, saving her life. She spent the whole week in the hospital and barely recovered enough to get released to fly back home. Our complete vacation was ruined." He then complained, "All I got to do was visit my girlfriend every day in the hospital on our last trip. This trip, we're staying out of the desert."

Henry showed the video and repeated his speech word for word several times in ten minutes. It gave him a few seconds of fame. Oddly, his face showed pleasure at each person's shock when the snake bit his girlfriend and she jumped. Nobody told Henry what a stupid thing they'd done.

I was glad he'd shown me the video. Being a newbie to the desert myself, I otherwise wouldn't even have been thinking about such possibilities. It opened my eyes.

Poor fellow, poor girlfriend. What rotten luck.

The head honcho called everyone together. Tall, thin, and gray-haired, he introduced himself as Terry Matherson, author of numerous top-selling gambling books. The other instructor called himself Doctor Bones.

Terry outlined Saturday's and Sunday's seminar agenda, then gave each student a packet jammed full of handout materials to study.

I stared at the craps tables, shaking my head "These craps tables look four or five feet longer than the one I built. What am I going to do?" I asked Doctor Bones, "How long are they?"

"Sixteen footers," replied the short, heavy-set instructor, looking them over. He planted his hand on his hip. "Most Vegas casinos use fourteen footers. Some use sixteen footers. The San Remo, down next to the Trop, has tables at least eighteen feet long, maybe longer. Ellis Island Casino has a short eight footer that's pretty popular with locals."

Both the craps tables were in use, with students being called up for their turn to warm up and shoot. My turn to warm up came. I made several tosses from the table's end and had trouble adjusting my throw to the table length. I tossed several trash numbers without the normal abundance of sixes or eights. Several of the throws failed to reach the far wall.

Doctor Bones passed the dice back. "You could move nearer the table's center."

"I might try a shorter distance, but I shoot from straight out and would prefer to continue shooting from there, if I may." I said with nervousness in my voice.

Doctor Bones, who owned a dice-coaching business in Vegas, studied my throws. "The ice-tong grip fails for most people shooting from straight out. The ice tong doesn't get enough rotation on the dice to control 'em."

He'd started demonstrating a new grip for me to try when Terry told him, "I've read online about the sensational results Ray tossed during practice. Let me watch him make a couple more tosses, before we go trying to change anything."

Terry watched me make a couple more tosses. "No, I believe he's got something with his grip and throw. I'm liking the way his dice travel through the air and the way they rotate and stay together. He should be able to adjust the landing spot a little farther down the table and be fine."

I was relieved by this appraisal. After a few tosses, more sixes and eights appeared. Zeroing in took me less than ten minutes.

Everyone not being coached circulated. "Glad to meet you, George. I'm Albert. I toss the outside numbers with the V2 dice set."

George flipped open a small notebook and wrote down *Albert V2 outside numbers.* "I use the straight-sixes set and go for a ton of sevens on the come-out rolls, then try to make the point." Albert made his own notes for when they played together and tried to win money on each other's tosses. A few students, including me, listened to the coaching others received, hoping to learn something new.

After all the students had taken advantage of their private time with both coaches, Terry called everyone together, announcing, "We're going to hold a long-roll competition. Everyone gets one turn to shoot. Our winner'll be the one tossing the most numbers before rolling his seven out."

Everyone took their turn, with Terry tracking the score. I tossed eight numbers. A Michigan shooter named Wayne won, throwing seventeen numbers. For winning, he picked the Golden Nugget for his group's Downtown casino team play later that night, saying he'd played there before with winning results.

******

We broke for lunch. Everyone grabbed a bite to eat at a pizzeria in the same strip mall. We then piled into two vans and went to the afternoon's Downtown casino session.

While we rode in the middle seat, I told Joe, "I'm still unsure what results I'll produce on longer tables. I'm going to start with only half my normal opening bets."

Four or five conversations were going on at the same time around us, which made it difficult for Joe to hear, so he scooted closer to tune out the excited chatter.

"I'm going to make safe offsetting warm-up bets until I throw the numbers I want. I'll only bet on myself, too," I said, more to myself than to Joe. "They say online a lot of dice setters slip into a habit of winning on their own turn tossing the dice, but then lose all their winnings by betting on random shooters while waiting for their next turn to shoot."

Joe nodded while we rode onward. I was determined to be a smart, educated gambler. The van ride was bouncy: it threw us into each other every time the van rounded a corner.

"Guys like that are action junkies. I'm never going to be one. I'm never making any crazy bets on my own tosses, either. I'm sticking to my progression bets. I'm going to stay focused, patient, and disciplined, betting on what I'm convinced will bring me money."

Joe punched me playfully in the shoulder. "Way to go, Little Bro. You've got your head on straight and know what to do. Don't let longer tables bother you."

******

We entered the casino through their parking garage. I didn't know which one, because I hadn't been paying attention when we pulled in. I'd been talking to Joe.

A reserved table awaited our group. The other craps tables were full of rowdy players and tourists. The seminar students stepped up to their favorite spots and put their money on the table.

Most students sought spots closer to the center of the table, but there were more people than space at those available prime spots. Terry told them to run what he called a "Chinese fire drill" for those throwing positions, moving to those prime table spots when their turn to shoot arrived.

Joe stood behind me. Terry and Doctor Bones observed from similar positions behind the students. Doctor Bones recorded exact results for each toss on individual index cards for each shooter. After each turn ended, the student stepped away from our table to join Doctor Bones, who then showed him the results he'd tracked for their tosses.

On my turn, I made five-dollar-pass and don't-pass bets that canceled each other out, to see if I'd brought my A-game before risking serious money on my toss. I'd used these offsetting warm-up bets to start practice sessions at home.

I tossed ten numbers before I lost my turn. Only three sixes and eights appeared among those numbers, not enough for me to put my regular bets down.

Other students experienced varying degrees of success with their throws while the dice worked their way around the table, but no one got a long roll going.

On the second turn shooting, I got braver and made opening eighteen-dollar place bets on each the six and eight. "Always working on the come-out roll," I told the dealer. I immediately rolled an opening seven. Since the place bets were working, I lost both of those bets. That put me down thirty-six dollars, but it didn't cost me my turn with the dice, since a seven wins pass line bets on the come-out roll.

Joe winced as the dealer took away my losing place bets. I couldn't remember the last time I'd tossed an opening seven.

Maybe I'm not going to be able to do well on the longer tables? Not a good start.

I replaced the eighteen-dollar bets I'd lost and threw again.

"Eight, easy eight." The dealer placed the white circular six-inch point-marker disk on eight.

Each toss I made now showed lots of my favorite numbers.

My dice always traveled in a chest-high arc for three-fourths the table's length. They hit their landing spot, bounced once into the base of the back wall, then dribbled straight back together. They usually were still on their desired rotational axis when they stopped a foot or so apart. My dice spun fast through the air in perfect unison, sometimes giving the appearance they were glued together.

My modification to the ice tong grip moved the dice's rotational axis points to run straight through the top-front corners of the dice—where I gripped them—instead of through the middle of the dice. This shift in axis points made them loop through the air without wobbling. They moved similarly to the way a basketball would if it had a heavy weight glued to one side of its inner surface then thrown down the length of the court. My dice leaped forward on their first half of each rotation, slowed on their second half, then repeated their wobble-free looping over again, and again. It became a show in itself.

I entered my mental zone and cranked out sixes and eights. I held the dice for more than half an hour, winning the progression bet four times. On the final toss, I blew on my fingers, picked up the dice, and threw a four-three on-axis seven out. The right die had over-rotated by exactly two die faces, making the devil seven appear.

I went to where Doctor Bones stood with my score card. Joe followed in order to hear what he told me, too.

"Ray, you threw forty-two numbers before you sevened out. Of those forty-two numbers, you rolled an amazing twenty-four sixes and eights."

All my sixes and eights were circled on the index card.

He showed me where he wrote on his card; "7-out" circled twice.

"I wrote that down before your final toss. I knew you would throw a seven. I'd have bet a hundred dollars on it." He paused and drew closer. "Before you threw your last toss you did something new. You stopped and blew on your fingertips before you tossed your dice. When you did, you took yourself out of your mental zone. I knew you'd ended your turn."

He poked the index card with a finger for emphasis.

"You were knocking them dead. Up until your last toss, you stayed deep in your zone. You only needed to stay there to continue winning, but you did something different and jerked yourself right out of your zone and made yourself throw a seven."

"You're right. I was thinking to myself, right then: 'I'm going to reach down deep and pull out a string of super tosses to run my progression again. I'm going to try harder and get this done again.' That's when I blew on my fingertips, attempting to double my effort. Lesson learned. Thanks, Coach."

All this happened so quickly after the end of my turn that we didn't even get a chance to celebrate properly. The win felt more like a practice session than a big win. Weird.

I'd also been keeping an eye on what went on at the table.

As soon as my turn ended, a pit boss with a small vice-like metal gizmo in his hand asked the stickman for the dice I had used. He sat the gizmo on the table surface and mounted one of the dice in it so that it balanced on two opposite corners in the gizmo. He then spun the die with a finger and closely studied how it spun. He did the same thing with the other die I'd used. He gave the dice back to the stickman, shrugged, and left without saying a word.

I concluded he must have been checking to make sure I hadn't slipped loaded dice into the game.

Terry raised both hands and gave a shrill whistle. "I'm sorry, gang, but we've run out of time. We need to get back to the school."

Terry motioned to me. "I want you and Joe to ride back with me. I want to talk to you." On our way to the van, he asked me, "How much did you win?"

"I cashed in for $1,032, clearing $832 over my buy-in." I didn't add that my buy-in had come out of last night's winnings. That seemed like it would be bragging.

Terry looked impressed, sucking in his breath. I continued as we all entered Terry's van. "I bet a reduced eighteen-dollar progression, instead of my normal thirty-six-dollar starting bets. I wasn't sure I could adjust my toss to the longer table length. Guess I should have used my normal opening bets."

Joe said, "Ray's turn looked like most of his practice sessions. Maybe it lasted a little longer."

Terry's eyes grew large. "Fantastic shooting, Ray. A good long roll and a healthy cash-out amount for a single turn." He turned in the driver's seat, so he could view me better. "Doctor Bones says more than fifty percent of your throws came up sixes or eights, and that's phenomenal for such a long turn tossing the dice. I'd be mighty pleased to have you be my craps-shooting partner, anytime."

He reached over and shook my hand, patting my arm with his free hand.

A few seconds later, we headed back to the dealer's school.

Terry smiled. "Ray, You're going to have to show me your modified ice-tong grip and explain its fine points. I might take it for a test spin myself."

Wow! I paid these guys for coaching, and now they're pumping me for information and asking me to teach them how I toss my dice. Unreal.

We'd been in Vegas for not quite twenty-four hours. I had won about $1,500.

Terry stopped at a light. "I guess from now on we're all going to have to call you The Ice Man, because of your unique ice tong grip and because you remain so cool under pressure."

So much for being Robot Ray. Ice Man has a nice ring to it. Getting my ego stroked built up my self-confidence.

******

Upon arriving back at the dealer's school, students divided into two groups for additional practice table time. After a while, Terry told everyone to huddle up: he had something to say.

"We all witnessed Ray's fantastic tosses this afternoon. I found it nothing short of sensational. He tossed forty-two numbers with twenty-four of them being his targeted sixes and eights. This is what dice setting's all about—as fine an exhibition as I've ever seen. I've decided Ray should be known as The Ice Man from this day forward by all dice setters. Let's give Ray a big round of applause."

A standing ovation greeted my ears for more than a minute. My face reddened. I could feel the heat rising from my neck up.

I took it in stride, as being a nice roll, nothing more.

What trouble can we get into tonight?

Chapter Eight — Saturday Night

On our way to supper, I wasted no time calling our parents. I had to tell them all the good news concerning our day, the long rolls and nice winnings. I became ecstatic, relating everything to let them share in the excitement and thinking I might have convinced them that coming here to test my skills was a better idea than they'd first thought.

Joe said, "I'd say Mom and Dad have relaxed a bit, now you've seen major success in our first twenty-four hours here." We each decided to finish off a rack of barbecued ribs at the rib joint inside the Fremont.

"I sure hope so," I replied, still chewing. I licked barbecue sauce from my fingertips. "Mom says she's rooting for me. Dad wished me luck."

"I don't want them worrying themselves sick over how we're surviving out here, especially while we're having a ball."

We didn't go back to the Trop, since I would be shooting craps again soon in the Fremont Street Experience, a four-block-long pedestrian area with no vehicular traffic. We just enjoyed being tourists until it was time to join our team at Binion's Horseshoe.

A pretty young stripper stood outside a little striptease joint, giving away Mardi Gras beads and flirting with every guy who passed by. She stopped us, gave us each a necklace of beads, flirted a little, and talked us into going inside. We found her refreshing and cute, so we needed to please her by doing what she asked. Hormones may have influenced our decision, too. At our age, they are sometimes hard to keep in check.

We came out of there half an hour later with a skip in our step, whistling a happy tune, grinning from ear to ear, and a hundred dollars each lighter in our pockets.

Joe was all smiles. "That's money well spent."

"I can't argue with that. We might even have to go back again later in the week."

Joe remained red faced. "We could never experience that back in Iowa."

There's one thing Mom and Dad'll never find out. Shame on us.

The more we cruised in and out of various downtown casinos and tourist-type souvenir shops, the more I appreciated the atmosphere and felt welcome.

I bought a tourist map that showed the location of everything important in Vegas. I figured this map would come in handy, helping us travel around town and decide where to go and what to do. I put it in my hip pocket, with the idea of studying the map during some down time, should we ever find that in Vegas.

"Joe, do you find the Downtown experience more laid back than on The Strip yesterday? I know I do."

"It feels like we belong here, doesn't it? I feel like a home-town boy here."

I knew we weren't home boys, but maybe Fremont Street had adopted us? It sure felt that way.

We found everything Downtown grouped tighter together, so we strolled everywhere. The tourists' pace proved a lot more relaxed here, too. On The Strip, everyone hurried to be somewhere else. Downtown made us feel we'd arrived. Less flashy than The Strip, Downtown looked older. This added nostalgic charm, but it had plenty of glitter, too.

We played a few penny and five-cent slots at each casino we visited. They provided cheap entertainment, and we both enjoyed their flashing lights, spinning reels, and the sounds of coins falling into the metal hopper when we won. We drank in the music the slots played on each spin, too.

After a while, Joe whispered to me, "Ah, Slot Therapy. Got to love it. Comforting to our souls."

We both belly laughed over the crack, like we were sixth graders breaking wind in class.

"What we need is for these slot machines to accept dollar bills," I said, "so we don't have to carry these buckets of coins around all the time."

"Ray, that's a million-dollar idea. You need to work on that one."

"We wouldn't have to get our fingers dirty from the coins, either." I deposited another coin in the slot and pulled the handle: the wheels spun, lights flashed toward the top of the machine, and the brief burst of music and distinct sound effects played. The wheels stopped one after the other and the machine went quiet. No coins fell into the coin tray.

"Someday they'll have these slots rigged so you insert a credit card and play." As soon as Joe said it, I had all kinds of horrible images running through my mind of people losing their homes to these monsters.

"Oh, don't wish for that. It would be the absolute ruin of a lot of good people."

We both noticed a bedraggled, scruffy-looking young fellow sitting two slots down from us, inside the main entrance. He had his bedroll stashed under his feet. Every few minutes, he'd put a penny in the slot and pull the handle, then he'd sit there again, looking forlorn.

After a while a security guard came up to him. "I'm going to have to ask you to leave. You camping here isn't good for business. Go camp somewhere else and don't come back."

The guy looked like someone had stomped on his world. He cringed, but didn't argue. He gathered up the bedroll and started out the door. Security shadowed every step.

I popped to my feet and chased this man down as he reached the sidewalk outside. I put a hand on the guy's shoulder.

"Are you going to be all right?" I asked.

"Probably. I'm just stuck here, broke and down on my luck. I wish I could go home."

"Let me help," I said, going for my billfold and giving him several bills.

He looked like he might cry. "Oh, thank you. Thank you. Thank you. I'd just about given up all hope."

We shook hands and hugged. The guy tucked the bedroll under his arm then headed on down the street with a new invigorated swagger in his step.

I returned to the slot machine and sat down. "I can't stand seeing someone down on their luck."

Joe nodded.

******

Our small group met up in front of Binion's Horseshoe, which I'd learned online was known affectionately to old timers as *The Shoe*; right in the heart of the old, original Glitter Gulch that had made Vegas famous. We had to wait for about ten minutes, because according to Terry's head count, a couple of our fellow seminar students were running late.

When they arrived, Terry gave us our game plan. "We'd better show up one at a time, to appear like we're not acquainted. I'll enter first and find us a table where we'll all play together. You should put at least a minute between each of your arrivals. Their craps pit is inside their main door, to your right."

After taking in a breath, Terry continued. "If there's no room at our table when you arrive, take up a position at a nearby table, then join us when a spot opens up. Pay attention to what numbers your teammates are rolling, and bet them when their game is on. Perhaps we'll all profit off each other, if we achieve some long rolls."

He reminded me of a quarterback calling signals. It tempted me to call out "Hike!" I decided I shouldn't.

We all joined up again inside at the same craps table with chips in our racks, ready to win money. Joe bought in, too. Before he did, he asked if it'd bother me if he bet on me.

"Nah, go ahead, Joe. Shouldn't bother me." I then winked, giving him a double thumbs up.

Joe said he'd pass the dice whenever they came to him—that he'd be a random roller if he rolled.

They raise smart boys in Iowa.

Terry and Joe flanked me. We stood shoulder to shoulder, which allowed us to chat over the gambling sounds. The floor in the craps pit sported two-inch-deep sawdust and wood shavings. *Maybe the last throwback to old Vegas? How much tobacco juice is in that sawdust?*

None of our group won much money in the beginning. Half lost money on their own turn. Even Terry tossed an early seven. I made my offsetting five-dollar pass and don't-pass bets, to warm up for free.

I started with a five, followed by a hard six, a nine, and a hard ten. I rolled an eight, another nine. On my next toss, the dice jumped up high at the table's distant end, coming to rest in the chip rail.

"Too tall—No roll," the stickman announced. He gathered the dice and returned them to me.

"Dang, this table is bouncy," I complained. "Did you see how high those dice bounced? I thought they'd fly clear off the table."

"I've never seen your throw do that before. Another two inches and they'd be calling out 'lost dice'."

Terry chuckled at Joe's comment. "'Dice down' is what they yell when the dice hit the floor."

Being newbies, we'd never heard the term. But at a craps table, nobody stays a newbie for long. There's always someone nearby willing to educate new players.

I ended my turn, tossing a seven. The other non-team players at our table made all kinds of crazy bets on the layout. They talked their own naming lingo for their favorite bets, calling out things like 'Horn', 'Yo', 'World', and 'Hop eight'.

Terry leaned toward me. "Most bets that casinos advertise on their betting layouts are bad-odds sucker bets—they're there to get you to lose money on them."

Some of those guys made four or five crazy bets before each of their rolls. They then picked up their dice, shook them up in their hand, wished for some luck, and threw them any which way down the table.

Joe said, "Those must be the random rollers you warned me about, shooters I should never bet on?"

"Yup." *They don't raise dumb boys in Iowa.*

Terry took a quick restroom break. He covered his chips in the chip rail with a handkerchief before he left the table—doing so not only protected his chips but also saved his table spot for his return.

The second circulation of the dice showed another zero win to minor loss for everyone on our team. I bet my offsetting warm-up bets again and rolled eleven numbers, with three tosses being my targeted sixes and eights.

I held pretty true to my belief in betting only on myself, too. I risked a single five dollar pass-line bet on Hard Way, a New Jersey teammate, after he began by throwing back-to-back nines to win the first come-out bet. He came back with a ten, then threw a seven out.

"Maybe I jumped in there too soon with my pass-line bet?" I asked Terry.

"Nah, he showed you his number twice in a row on his first pass. It's wise to wait till a shooter hits his numbers twice before betting on them, but Hard Way hit 'em on his first pass. Wait too long, and you might miss getting to cash in on betting a long roll."

Receiving the dice again, I called out, "thirty-six dollar place bets on both six and eight, place bets work on all my come-out rolls."

I opened by tossing a hard six and an eight. I threw a couple non-winning trash numbers that failed to advance my progression. I came back with another six and a two and then popped a six, with the dice again almost climbing that railing at the distant end of the table.

I glanced at Joe and shrugged, then kept quiet and allowed the dealer to pay me off for my fourth hit on a six or eight. Now, even if I failed in the attempt to win my progression, I would at least show a tidy profit for the effort. I added $252 in winnings to my rack.

My dice again tried to jump off the table, producing an off-axis six-one, seven, when they fell back to the table surface. I only lost fifty-seven dollars of my own money, even though $276 in place bets remained in play. 'House money' comprised more than $200 of my bets I hadn't claimed yet in the quest to run my progression. I still showed a $199 session profit, but was dissatisfied with the results my toss was achieving.

"This table's too bouncy," I whispered to Joe. "I'm done shooting here. My toss isn't normal on this table. Let's go shoot somewhere else."

I understood everything concerning my own toss, and now something about shooting on other tables, too.

I gathered my chips. "Let's go to the Fremont. Their tables are supposed to shoot true there. It's next door, across the street."

I told Terry we'd be moving on. We colored up, handing in our chips to the dealer who had placed our bets. I turned in my small chips for mostly black hundred-dollar chips, then took them to the cashier's window and cashed them in for folding money. Joe did likewise.

Before we left *The Shoe*, we stopped long enough to have our photo taken next to the million dollars on display there for that purpose. *Tourists, again.*

******

Happy tourists strolled the Fremont Street Experience. The large overhead several-city-blocks-long canopy LED light-show attraction fired up at the top of the hour, in a dazzling animated display set to music. It froze us in our tracks.

We cranked our heads skyward and witnessed their six-minute light-show display comprised from 12.5 million colored LED lights set to the driving rock of George Thorogood singing "Bad to the Bone." It flashed and changed visual displays in rapid succession, showing: race cars racing, playing cards edge to end, animated ghost figures, flying guitars, motorcycles, and flames going down the display. "Who Do You Love" then played while spaceships, cacti, oil wells, a collage of moving road signs, more motorcycles, and spaceships appeared. It ended with animated versions of all the Downtown casinos' neon-lighted signs showing on the full length of their several-blocks-long overhead canopy.

Yup, we're tourists: I feel it now in my bones.

Yet, we blended in. Everyone else had stopped and gawked, too.

******

Inside the Fremont, I grabbed the end-of-table spot, the sole unoccupied spot in the entire craps pit area. Saturday night found this joint jumping.

Joe said he'd take in the action for a while, maybe even slip away and minister to himself with another dose of slot therapy.

Most players there appeared to be Asian, or perhaps Hawaiian. Everyone looked middle aged, or older. I soon discovered they threw long rolls with the dice, too. Everyone around this table had their chip rails overflowing with high denomination chips. They were happy, because about everyone there threw twenty or more numbers during their turn. It took forever for most shooters' turns to end, and everyone cleaned up. Each player might get a turn tossing the dice once every ninety minutes. No one complained about the slow play on their hot table—better that than a fast-moving cold table where everybody lost.

Wow! If it's this way all the time here, I could earn a full-time living betting on these shooters every day.

I noticed women comprised a third of the players and they nailed their numbers, tossing long rolls right along with the best of the men.

The Fremont featured an LED counter on each table that the dealer advanced each time the shooter threw a number. I asked another player why it was there and learned the Fremont, being dice-setter friendly, encouraged it by tracking how many rolls each shooter achieved. The pit crew rewarded all shooters who exceeded thirty rolls with long-roll certificates that bore the number of rolls they'd managed to toss.

Those certificates were cashed in at Fremont's Rewards Center for a variety of desirable souvenir prizes. The longer your roll, the nicer the prize you got to select. There were separate prize sections for thirty-plus rolls, forty-plus rolls, fifty-plus rolls and super-deluxe prizes for sixty-plus rolls. Recognition of their long-roll feats gave everyone bragging rights, too.

We stayed at our table more than three hours, giving me a couple of chances to shoot. I ended up winning my progression twice on my second round, with a thirty-one roll turn. I produced a wide variety of numbers but still got the mission completed twice, taking my place bets back down to thirty-six dollars each after I completed the first five-step progression bet.

I emotionally detached myself from my play. I didn't get overly excited when I won and didn't celebrate much. I let others do that for me. I tried to run it a third time, but bombed while going for my fifth winning number. I colored up and showed a $1,300 session profit, due to dropping about sixty dollars of my own money.

We saw a tall young guy at the next table, dressed in full drag. He wore a miniskirt to show off his cute but hairy legs and had on a long blonde wig. Everyone around him acted like it was the most natural thing in the world for him to be there shooting craps in drag. I wondered if maybe he was an actor in a stage show in the area.

Guess you can see anything in Vegas.

At the Fremont Rewards Center, we waited while the guy ahead of us redeemed his four long-roll certificates for a variety of prizes. He'd apparently had himself quite a night of winning. His final certificate had 62 written on it, winning him one of those super-deluxe prizes. He chose a blown-glass chess set with an inlaid playing board.

"That prize had to set the casino back a few hundred bucks," Joe said. I agreed.

"Would you like us to ship your awards to your home?" the lady behind the counter asked him.

"Yeah, I'd have trouble carrying all that around and getting it home," said the immaculately dressed man who emitted the pleasant manly scent of a light-musky cologne and talc. The counter lady collected the shipping info.

I redeemed my bottom-tier long-roll certificate, selecting a three inch by two inch solar-powered pocket calculator shaped like a little black leather briefcase. It had *Fremont Hotel & Casino, Las Vegas* stamped on its front in gold letters. It even featured tiny functioning metal closing clasps on top and a little metal carrying handle.

Cute. I still have it, too. I even included two photos of it, because it is tangible proof of my truthfulness

******

We enjoyed another cheap session of Slot Therapy, then went to find ourselves something to eat and drink again.

We ate the ninety-nine cent shrimp cocktail special offered by the Four Queens. We both went back for seconds, and polished them off, too. Late at night, they hit the spot. The portions were big, and the price couldn't be beaten. We ate them standing around one of the many small circular chest-high stand-up cocktail tables that had no chairs. It gave us an opportunity to do a little people watching and mellow out for a while.

******

On the hoof again, I looked up at the spot-lit twenty-plus-story-tall Plaza Hotel and Casino that anchored Fremont Street Experience at its northern end. Something about it looked inviting to me. It reminded me of an art-deco style train station or one of those skyscrapers out of Ghostbusters.

"Let's check out the Plaza," I suggested.

"Sure, why not?"

We walked past the Golden Gate, where Old Blue Eyes and the rest of The Rat Pack used to hang out during their hay day when not performing, crossed the intersection, and entered the Plaza. The tiny stage located on the right inside the front door distinguished it from other casinos in the area. A five-piece rock-and-roll house band made up of older somewhat oriental-looking guys played and sang '60's oldies. They rocked their songs, too.

For some unknown reason, I'd always been drawn to the rock music of the 1950's and 60's. Maybe I'd been a hippy in another lifetime? I always wondered...

We ordered up a couple of Coors and pulled up chairs to take in their free show. The crowd gathered in front of the small intimate stage. The band played to the crowd and had a ball doing their songs. They were good and went out of their way to entertain and please their audience.

We were soon enjoying our third beer, while continuing to enjoy the rock music. When the band took a break, we checked out the rest of the casino.

Cruising through the table games area, Joe saw a dealer standing behind the blackjack table. He had arms folded and cards all fanned out on the table in front of him, waiting for someone to come to the table and take him on. He looked bored.

"Won't nobody play with you?" Joe asked in a pouty voice.

He grinned back. "You want to play?"

"Nah, just kidding." Joe had tried to be cute and it had fallen flat. Nobody ever got his sense of humor. He can't help it if it's odd.

The casino area felt old and dark, and somewhat uninviting. Their craps tables were almost thread-bare, with cigarette-ash and dried-up-spills-covering the surfaces. The great house band remained this casino's one redeeming feature. We moved on.

******

Once back out on the street, we saw Main Street Station Casino a block or two up the side street. It stood out among all the neighboring casinos with its low-slung brick structure, which looked newly-built.

Joe told me, "I've read online they have the loosest video poker machines in town. Care to try your luck?" I hadn't been the only one to research online to discover what Las Vegas had to offer. After he learned we were going, he'd jumped online, too.

"Never played video poker before," I replied, "Care to teach me?"

"Sure, I've played it a lot on my phone. I'll coach you to get you started."

On our way there, we passed the California Casino, with its big bronze plaque outside the main entrance marking it as the site of the world's longest craps roll, lasting three hours and six minutes.

"I read online that the California brings in lots of package tours from Hawaii and caters to them."

Joe pushed the door open. "Let's take a peek."

Inside, we encountered lots of patrons who looked Hawaiian. They stood around some of the longest craps tables either of us had ever seen.

"Looks tempting," I said after a couple of minutes. "But I'm in no mood to toss on long tables tonight. Let's go on up to Main Street Station, like we planned."

We noticed Main Street Station's antique train resting alongside the sidewalk. According to the plaques there, it included Buffalo Bill Cody's and Anne Oakley's private rail cars. The casinos in the area imported everything of historical value they could find to attract tourists, from pieces of the Berlin Wall to the bullet-sprayed brick wall where Chicago's St. Valentine Day Massacre happened in 1929.

Inside the casino, we admired the many historical antiques on display as we found our way to long rows of video poker machines. Even this late at night, most were taken. We located two unoccupied machines next to each other to play.

Joe spent about ten minutes coaching me. I soon figured out which cards to hold without coaching. When I reached this point, Joe started playing a machine, too.

"I read online that some of Main Street Station's video poker machines are supposed to be positive-expectation machines. They're said to have more than a hundred-percent payback rates, if you're a good enough player to be able to play what they call *perfect basic strategy* all the time."

"Yeah, and I bet you'd have to spend about as much time as I did learning craps to do that, right?"

Dropping in another coin, Joe replied, "You can play a long time for your money, even without being perfect. I've read the one real way to stay ahead over the long haul at video poker is to hit some royal flushes, because their monster payoffs more than make up for your frequent small losses."

It proved to be a good way to spend an hour or so. I found it entertaining, even though I found myself down about ten dollars.

Joe sat the now-empty coin bucket aside. "I've had enough." He pointed out the craps tables. "Let's check 'em out."

I grabbed my favorite end-of-table position and bought in. My turn to shoot soon arrived.

"I feel invincible right now for some reason." I skipped the warm-up bets and plunked down seventy-two dollars in chips for thirty-six dollar place bets to try to run my progression. I opened with a nine, an eight and a hard six. I tossed back-to-back sixes and a ten. My next roll showed a hard eight to win the progression bet.

Joe slapped me on the back. "Invincible, indeed. Way to go, Bro." Cheers rang out from the other players.

I took the bets back down to thirty-six dollars each and repeated the feat in nine more rolls. My next roll showed a six, then came a seven. "Color me up."

"You make it all look so easy, Ray. Fantastic shooting."

I took winning matter-of-factly. I didn't get excited or celebrate much, because I'd done this hundreds of times in practice. I'd learned to expect the wins I was getting. The only difference was the casino gave me real chips for my accomplishments. I'd divorced myself from feeling the thrill of winning money. It kept me from feeling the pressure to win and allowed me to be my best. Those traits help make a pro gambler a success. I wondered how I'd act and feel, though, if the winning suddenly stopped.

If Joe won big, he'd probably be jumping up and down and celebrating his winnings like crazy. He'd be loving every minute of it. And I'd be a lot more excited he'd won than when I won myself.

Another player at the table caught my eye. He motioned toward the door with his head, as if to message me. I wasn't sure if I'd actually seen it or imagined it. Then he did it again. I chose to ignore it, but when we hit the street that guy walked right behind us, trying to catch up. He called out, "Wait, guys, I want to talk to you."

I pulled up and waited for him, while Joe tried to encourage me to keep walking.

"Hi, I'm Ivan. I saw your session in there. Great shooting."

"Thanks, name's Ray. I got lucky."

"Well, Ray, are you going to be in Vegas long?"

"'Till next Friday, why?"

"How would you like to step up to the big time with your play?" asked the sharply-dressed guy. "If you're interested, Ray, I'd like to finance your play. How would you like to be shooting for table-limit-size bets?"

I didn't answer.

Ivan scuffed the sidewalk with the tip of his shoe.

"Your skill and the way you bet blows me away. I'd like for you to win some big money. Your talent and my money would make a dynamite combination. Interested?"

I was curious. "How would we split the winnings?"

"Fifty-fifty. Your talent—my money. We could both really clean up."

I looked the guy up and down. "Look, I can afford to do that using my own money, if I wanted to shoot for big money—which I don't." I rubbed my chin. "I'm turning you down. What I won in there satisfies me."

Ivan looked crushed. His expression became a frown. He took out a wallet and removed a business card. "If you ever get down on your luck or change your mind, call me. Okay?"

I took Ivan's card. "Don't hold your breath. You're barking up the wrong tree."

As we turned and walked away, I shot Ivan another look over my shoulder. He didn't look happy.

"Blood sucker," I said just loud enough for Joe to hear as I glanced at my watch. "It's 2:20 a.m. and I'm worn out. Let's call it a night."

"Ha. I told ya so. Vegas fever strikes again."

The topic change pleased me.

"You can't keep burning your candle at both ends and get away with it. We've got youth on our side, but it's better not to try to run on the rim too long. That can ruin you."

I was ready to drop, could've gone to sleep standing up. "Let's head in."

******

We hopped a cheap open-air trolley back down The Strip to our hotel and called it a day. All this fun wore us out after a while. Our trolley ride gave us a chance to view how long The Strip was and gawk at all the lavish lighting and huge casinos along the way. I dozed off a time or two.

We'd been in Vegas less than a day and a half, and I had won enough money to pay for the dice-setting seminar, our trip out and back, and our expenses for the week-long stay in Vegas. A remarkable beginning for a total novice with the dice.

Doing the math in my head, I found I had won something like $3,680 during those brief hours. It was more than I had brought, and six days remained for us in Vegas.

******

When we returned to the Trop, we went straight to our room, too late to call home and bring Mom and Dad up to date on our adventures. That call could wait until morning.

I unloaded a few one-dollar chips from my pocket and put them on the nightstand.

"Why do you have those, Ray?"

"I'm starting a souvenir collection—a dollar chip from every place I shoot craps."

"You going to mount them in a display frame over the mantle back home, after you have several?"

"Haven't thought that far ahead."

It made me wonder how many others out there might have their own personal chip collections. *Do casinos lose money when someone takes home a dollar chip, or do they make money?* I guessed that would depend on how much it cost the casinos to have them made.

I locked the money in the wall safe, set the wrist alarm, and drifted off to gentle sleep, with visions of cute strippers and dice floating through the air plying my dreams.

What unexpected adventure awaits us tomorrow?

Chapter Nine — Sunday

We got an early start back to the dealer's school Sunday morning. On the way, a small locals' casino caught my eye. Something about it looked inviting, so I had the taxi let us out there.

We hit their restaurant first, where we ordered up hearty breakfasts and coffee. I called the waitress over. "Can you bring me some ketchup?"

She returned with the ketchup bottle. "Here ya go, hon."

I slathered my eggs with ketchup.

"Man, I can hardly see your eggs, Ray. You cover everything you eat with ketchup. I expect to find a ketchup bottle with 'Ray Juice' on the label. Maybe I should buy some shares of Heinz stock?"

"You can't do that. I already own all the available shares," I retorted. *Smart ass.*

When we finished, we were leaving the restaurant through the casino when I spotted an empty craps table with two dealers and a stickman standing around talking. They needed a player to open up their game. I decided to see if I could win. I dropped my normal $400 session buy-in onto the table and received chips, took a couple warm-up rolls, then put the normal bets down and tossed lots of sixes and eights. I stayed in the zone and completed the first progression bet in record time. I took the place bets back down to my starting level again and racked the $699 in winnings.

I next rolled two sixes and an eight. I tossed a five and an easy six then finished off my second successful back-to-back progression on a single turn when I tossed a final easy eight. The curve around my end of the table had all its chip rails full, with each row of chips stretching out a yard long, or longer. Seeing all those chips made me catch my breath and smile.

I looked at the dealer. "How much do you think I have?"

The dealer remained expressionless. "At least $1,700, maybe $1,800."

I thought for a minute, weighing the options. I tossed the dealer a couple of green twenty-five dollar chips for a tip. "Color me up, and include some of those orange pumpkins, too." I needed to satisfy my sudden desire to own some pumpkins.

The dealer traded all my small chips for three $500 pumpkins, two black $100 chips, and two green twenty-five dollar chips. He instructed me to toss him two more dollars in folding money, to create amounts that came out right for the chips he gave me.

The dealer glanced up at me. "Like shooting fish in a barrel, huh?"

I inspected the pretty pumpkins and relished having them. "Nah, got lucky."

Everyone remained ultra quiet.

Later, Joe told me an eerie feeling came over him when it sank in what I had accomplished and how easy I'd made it look. The double-progression win had taken less than ten minutes without anybody doing anything special to celebrate. The pit crew handled my roll like an everyday occurrence, but my welcome here was wearing thin. I chose to forgo finishing my turn tossing the dice.

Joe said, "Unreal. How long could you have stretched your turn, if you tried?"

I couldn't answer. It didn't matter.

After we left the table, he said, "Fantastic roll, you ran your progression twice and never tossed a single seven. Congrats, Bro. Big time."

I took my chips to the cashier's window to cash out. The older homely-looking redheaded cashier scrunched up her face into a dirty look, showing only the slits of her eyes.

"Where did you get those $500 chips? What table did you get them off of?"

I recoiled at her insinuation. "I won those pumpkins shooting craps."

Her eyes grew to silver-dollar size and her face grew red to match the color of her bottle-dyed hair. She snatched up the phone and called out urgently over the public-address system, "Manager to Cashier Cage. Manager to Cashier Cage."

I shot her a dirty look. "Hey, I won those chips. Cash 'em in. They're your casino's chips. Either they're good, or they're no good. Which is it? Cash 'em in."

The casino manager appeared and saw my pumpkins in the cashier's hand. "What table did you get those off of?"

Before I could answer, the manager reached in and grabbed up the phone. His loud voice came over the public-address, "Security to Cashier Cage. Security to Cashier Cage."

Panic gripped me. I swallowed hard, thinking all this had turned into a nightmare.

How could this be happening?

"I won those shooting craps. I want them cashed in, please."

"I was with him when he won them," Joe said. "Give my brother his money."

Two security guards approached and stopped short, ready to jump us both.

The manager picked up the phone again and dialed the craps pit. We could tell by the look on his face they had confirmed a young fellow looking like me cashed out three pumpkins there.

I received my winnings.

The manager's face turned red. "I need to apologize. I jumped to conclusions without having all the facts. I made a mistake. Sorry." His heart wasn't in it, though.

I scrunched my shoulders. "Whatever. It doesn't matter much to me."

Walking away, Joe said, "I would have said the same thing."

******

We took another cab and headed for the dealer's school.

I laughed. "God, if I'd thought there'd be such a stink over having some pumpkins, I never would've asked for them. I guess they believed I somehow stole them off one of their tables."

Joe looked relieved. "It was funny. Her face was so red, I thought she'd crap her panties."

"The manager's forehead was so red I could have fried an egg on it."

We both laughed, seeing humor in the situation. It would be etched in my memory forever.

Being it was a small casino that catered to locals, I bet nobody had tried to cash a pumpkin there in years.

As we rode down the street, I looked at Joe. "Have you ever looked real close at the chips casinos use?"

"I've glanced at 'em. Why?"

"Wonder how easy it'd be to counterfeit them and how often it's been tried?"

"Really? How?"

I shrugged. "They're made out of clay, with simple markings that look like they're painted on, and there's printed paper stickers on them.

You could take a few of their chips to copy them. How hard would that be to counterfeit?"

Joe thought about it. "Easier than trying to counterfeit paper money, I guess."

"You've seen people bet stacks of chips at one time at table games, haven't you?"

"Yeah. So?"

"They could have a real chip on top with counterfeit chips under it," I said. "Nobody would be the wiser. All they'd see would be a normal-looking stack of chips, and they'd place the guy's bet."

Joe's eyes lit up. "Once those counterfeits got mixed into the table's chip supply, they wouldn't know who'd done it, once it got discovered."

"Or they could buy-in big, getting mostly hundred dollar chips, wait a few minutes, then take the real chips with them to the bathroom, switch in the counterfeits, go back to the table and gamble with them."

"You thinking about going into the chip-making business?" Joe asked me.

"Nah, thinking 'bout what's possible. Of course, you wouldn't want to cash any counterfeits in at the cashier window. They'd probably spot them there. That's where they really eyeball the chips before giving you cash for them. You'd have to be sure to remove any counterfeits from the real chips and cash in the good ones."

Joe asked, "Wouldn't they catch on pretty quick when someone else at the table got one of the counterfeits in their payoff and took it to the cashier?"

I shook my head. "I'd never want to try it. After a while, they'd be lying in wait for you. That wouldn't be a pretty sight."

"Besides, it's illegal and not right," said Joe.

"Yeah, but it's an interesting thought, isn't it?" I asked, steepling my fingers.

******

Everyone crowded together in a small room at the dealer's school for our seminar. It featured a world-famous author on gambling, Arnold Moore. I remembered having purchased one of his No-limit Texas Hold 'em books.

He told details about how he and a couple of precision-shooting buddies teamed up to take down the Mirage last night for about

$30,000. He asked Terry how his group's team-play had gone the night before.

"We failed to get anything started, and lost a little money in our attempts."

Moore looked around the group. "How did everyone else do? Any individual wins?

Henry stood. "I had a pretty good win at the Golden Nugget, with a nineteen number roll that made me about $500."

Everyone applauded. When he sat back down, Joe surprised me when he stood up.

"Ray's won about $3,000 since we left here yesterday. He won his progression bet at the Fremont and twice at Main Street Station. A guy approached us there last night and offered to finance Ray's shooting so he could shoot at the table-limits level, but Ray turned him down." Joe paused for a second to let all that sink in. "On the way to class this morning, with about ten minutes of table time at a small locals' casino, Ray won his progression twice in a row on one turn and quit, never tossing a seven."

I blushed and looked down at my shoes. "Well, I had a craps-shooting class to get to. I didn't want to be late." Joe had embarrassed me.

Everyone roared with laughter. They appeared even more amazed by Joe telling about my shooting than they had been about this author's giant take down at the Mirage. Joe could probably sense I wasn't about to tell the group about my successes. He knew I was probably satisfied enough with having won and didn't need to blow my own horn.

Doctor Bones got up and made an announcement. "Hey, guys, I'm having a private get-together at my place tonight. Everyone's invited. I've got my own craps table there we can shoot on. We'll barbecue some burgers and hot dogs, swim, toss back a few and swap war stories. It'll be a great chance for everyone to get better acquainted. Anyone who wants to come, see me for directions before you leave."

Joe rubbed the back of his neck. "You want to go?"

"With all that Vegas has to offer, I think I'll pass on the weenie roast. We've got the *Folies Bergere* tonight, too. Besides, he might be using the shindig to promote his dice-coaching business to the students."

A brief question-and-answer session followed the lecture. Everyone went to put in their practice time again, with additional individual coaching and advice.

My turn came. On the fifth toss, Terry pronounced me 'Good to go, in no need of further coaching'. We were free to leave and begin the rest of our week in Vegas.

Gonna knock 'em dead.

******

Riding in the taxi's back seat and headed for the Trop, I balled my hands into fists. "Dice setters who clip casinos for $30,000 in a single session might screw things up for everyone else. It concerns me—I'm never going to let myself get greedy by winning too much. If you don't milk your cow too hard, the milk will always be there."

We chatted as we rode, watching the outside pass by. I sensed something odd. We'd been riding in the cab through residential neighborhoods for a lot longer than it should take to arrive back at the Trop.

I looked at our cabbie. "Hey, this is the third time we've passed this same street corner! You..."

I noticed those tall hotels—visible through the tree tops and located at the distant end of The Strip—failed to grow any bigger while we supposedly approached. Our cabbie had taken us for the tourists we were, and he was taking advantage by riding us around to rack up a larger fare on the taxi's meter.

The cabbie ignored my complaints, mumbling gibberish we didn't understand, but he drove us straight to our destination.

I'd put a twenty-dollar bill for our ride in my shirt pocket. I'd intended the cabbie have it, even though I knew from previous rides that the fare shouldn't be much over ten dollars. That would have been a generous tip for our cabbie. Now, when we arrived back at the Trop, our cab's meter read nearly twenty dollars, anyway.

I handed him the twenty. "Here, keep the change. You burned up your tip riding us around and wasting our time."

Joe pointed out the lush tropical setting around the huge swimming pool outside the Trop on our way back up to our room.

"Hey, let's go for a relaxing swim right here."

I nodded. "I'm with you, Bro."

It was hot out, and a cool dip would be refreshing. I wanted to slow things down. We'd been going full bore since our arrival. We changed into swimming trunks and headed down to soak up a relaxing afternoon dip.

******

A huge tropical waterfall completely took up one end of the pool, and a forest of tall palm trees surrounded the entire pool area. It even offered swim-up blackjack tables, where people played without getting out of the pool. I noticed a pair of alluring curvaceous bikini-clad women sunbathing together on loungers at poolside.

The pool water relaxed and invigorated us when we swam up under the waterfall, allowing the plummeting warm water to cascade over our heads and shoulders. We swam for a while, then sunbathed beside that pair of exquisitely feminine and gorgeous women we'd eyed earlier.

"Hi, I'm Suzy." The cutest one looked us over. "You two look a lot alike. You twins?"

"Nah, I'm a couple years older. My name's Joe. We get asked that a lot, though. It's usually the first question asked when we meet new people."

Suzy pointed toward her companion. "Well, Beth and I are twins, not identical. That's why I asked."

"Your parents didn't name you similar-sounding twin's names?" Joe adjusted his glasses. "Like Sienna and Savanna, or Allison and Ashley?"

I wiggled my eyebrows. "The Tandy twins and the Jones twins from back home."

Beth ran her long slim fingers through her blonde hair. "Nope, not at my house. We've never dressed alike either."

Suzy sat forward on her lounger and turned toward me. Her movement accentuated the curves of her ample breasts struggling against her tiny bikini top. "Our parents say they really wanted each of us to grow up thinking of ourselves as an individual—not a twin."

"But in school," Beth said, "other students treated us special."

"It really boosted our popularity. On our first day at school, we became the center of attention—like we were really on display—like freaks in a freak show." Suzy smiled at me. She ran her eyes up and down my body. "Yeah, whether we wanted to be or not."

I raised my eyebrows, letting her know I'd caught her checking me out.

Unlike her sister, Suzy wore no makeup. No eye makeup, no lipstick, and nothing on her cheeks. Her self-confidence about not needing makeup fascinated me. None of the girls back home would dare be seen in public without it.

Suzy's drop dead gorgeous.

She had no ugly to hide.

Suzy retrieved her Coke. "There was really only one other set of twins in school, so we were a novelty, really. The other twins were boys a couple of years older."

Beth eyed Joe. "By us looking somewhat different, people could tell us apart. Being mistaken for each other could be a hassle and get old quick."

"I don't really know," Suzy said. "Might be really fun. We could really pull pranks and get away with it."

Yup, Suzy talked kind of funny: she said "really" all the time. I noticed it right away, but she was so sweet, beautiful, and good-natured I overlooked her one minor bad habit without a second thought.

Suzy glanced at me. "We're from Indian Hill, a suburb of Cincinnati, Ohio."

"W-W-Where do you work?" I asked her.

"I work part time at a really upscale consignment shop—'From-Me-2-U Boutique'."

"Any hobbies?"

"I really like writing children's stories."

"How about you, Beth?" Joe asked. "Tell me a little about yourself."

Beth applied sunscreen, without taking her eyes off Joe. "I'm studying art and I teach second-grade at Indian Hill Elementary School."

"Home of the Braves, really." A quick stolen glance down Suzy's long, slim, shapely thighs indicated she must be quite tall.

We talked on for more than half an hour, getting acquainted. The reason behind our trip to Vegas grabbed their attention.

"Wow. Really? A professional gambler?" Suzy gave a low whistle, lowering her sunglasses enough to peer over the top at me.

"N-N-no." I said, my face growing red. I froze. I had stuttered as a child but overcame it and now seldom became tongue-tied.

Joe touched both lips with his fingertips, probably hoping I could get my stutter under control.

I swallowed hard and looked at him, shaking my head. I paused, then began again. This time I spoke slower and with more purpose.

"I'm so new to gambling that I'm a wannabe like everyone else. I've only begun to test my skills. But I have high hopes."

Suzy looked at me, lowering her chin and raising her eyebrows.

"I'm applying my skills—not gambling. I've given myself an advantage when my game's on." My speech gained speed as I regained confidence. The more I said without becoming tongue-tied again, the more I relaxed.

Suzy arched a single eyebrow, dipped her chin and looked sideways at me. "Really? How've you really gained an advantage?"

Just as I started to speak, a muscular teen did a cannonball off the diving board, splashing water in all directions and soaking me from the waist down, breaking my train of thought. I got it back a couple of seconds later.

"The w-w-way I line up the dice and toss 'em produces twice as many sixes and eights as normal. That's all I bet on."

"Ray tosses losing sevens half as often as expected, too," Joe said.

I wiped off with a towel. "M-My goal is to never be a loser. Most people get ahead a little bit during their gambling session, but their desire to be entertained doesn't allow them to quit while still a winner. They stay too long and lose it all back, along with the rest of their money."

Suzy pursed her lips, then a smile lit her face. She looked at me through her eyelashes and asked, "Maybe... you could really teach me how you do it?"

"S-Sure thing."

Suzy returned the attention I showed her by shooting me flirty shy glances. She locked gazes with me, causing my heart to beat harder.

I found myself not wanting to look away. My face grew warmer, and the sun wasn't causing it. I couldn't take my eyes off Suzy, but I made sure to keep my gaze on her face so she wouldn't take me for a pervert.

"Together," I said, "everything falls into place, giving me a consistent winning combination. T-T-Three things determine my success..."

Suzy smiled and took my hand, "It's okay. Take your time. You'll do fine."

I gathered myself and let out a sigh. "One, I modified my dice grip... so it creates enough rotation to make the dice stay on my desired rotational axis at the same spin rate—winning results. Two, I refined my toss to be repeatable. My dice get the exact same launch each time. Three, I learned to slip into a trance-like mental zone... my forearm's trained muscle memory becomes a robotic dice-tossing machine."

I continued drinking in Suzy's beauty. "I've practiced every day for about eighteen months to master my throw."

What I learned about conquering my stuttering may have even made it easier for me to wrap my brain around what I needed to know to master my dice throws. It taught me to fight for control over what I wanted to do.

"Impressive," Suzy said, twisting her long blonde hair around her finger and then letting her silken hair spring to life when it uncurled.

My breath caught in my throat when she did that.

She again locked her attention on me. Her little flirty smile spoke volumes, and I liked what it said.

Joe said, "Ray's belief in his ability adds to his success. Seeing consistent results adds positive reinforcement to the mix."

"Uh... Yeah... w-well." I punched him in the arm. Hard. I looked away for a moment. My attention returned to Suzy. "You girls ridden the Big Apple Coaster atop New York-New York yet?"

"No, but we really want to! We've seen it and heard the people screaming." Suzy flashed a provocative smile, showing her even, white teeth. "We love roller coasters."

Joe stood up. "Want to have some fun, girls? Why don't we get dressed, mosey across the intersection, and do a little coaster riding?

"Yes. We're really thrill-ride junkies." Suzy couldn't get her answer out fast enough.

"Always have been, even as kids." Beth gathered her things. "You've made my day."

Joe motioned toward the hotel. "Let's all go get dressed."

We exchanged room information, learning their room was in the same tower but on a lower floor. We'd regroup in front of the Trop's check-in desk when everyone was ready to roll.

Chapter Ten — Sunday Night

We showered and changed as fast as we could. I nicked myself with the razor, I was so distracted with thoughts of Suzy. Ten minutes after we reached the check-in desk, the girls appeared out of the crowd. They looked stunning. Suzy looked like she'd walked off a runway. Beth could have been on the cover of a western magazine, with her tight jeans and cowboy boots. Joe and I headed out on our unexpected double date with a couple of cute chicks.

Vegas luck, I guess.

We took the skywalk across Las Vegas Boulevard, then crossed Tropicana Avenue at street level and scoped out New York-New York. Inside, various parts of their casino recreated different famous New York City neighborhoods. The details were accurate down to the authentic-looking steam that rose out of their metal man-hole covers embedded in the middle of the recreated streets we walked on.

Joe and I each had a sharp lady on our arm and a warm glow on our face. A big dose of unplanned happiness had dropped right into our laps. We'd hit the jackpot, were on a roll, and maybe even on the verge of something big—maybe the most exciting thing I'd ever experienced. I'm sure Joe agreed.

Now we had to be cool and not blow it. Opportunities like this didn't happen every day. I made a habit of not getting excited over gambling, but I couldn't control my excitement over Suzy.

"Hey, Ray," Suzy cooed, "I bet New York-New York has craps tables. Can we watch you shoot some craps? It sounds really intriguing."

I blushed and squeezed her hand. "Let's stroll around a little and ride their coaster. I might take a run at craps later. I'm relishing being with a super cool lady." I winked at her.

We all went to the second floor, where they sold us expensive ride tickets and loaded us onto the Big Apple Coaster. It had four cars, each built to resemble a small cartoonish version of a New York City checker cab. Soon we were swooshing through the air and getting flipped upside down. The girls screamed at the top of their lungs.

I took this opportunity to slip my arm around Suzy's waist. She appeared glad I had, and shot me warm glances between screams.

The Big Apple Coaster proved to be amazingly fast, and it featured all kinds of unexpected surprises. It left everyone breathless, especially during its twist and dive inversion. During our brief times spent upside down, I came close to losing the tiny notebook from my shirt pocket. Keys in my pants pocket jabbed into my thigh three or four times when we got slammed against the side of our coaster car.

As we exited the ride, I heard Beth exclaim, "Let's ride the coaster again!"

"Oh, yeah," Suzy agreed. "Really."

Can't deny a lady's request.

Suzy and Beth both pulled out inch-thick coupon books with tons of discount and freebie offers in it from casinos, attractions, shows and restaurants all over Las Vegas.

Suzy waved her booklet. "We got these for joining the Las Vegas Advisor Website for thirty-five dollars a year. There's a coupon in here for a five-dollar second ride on the Big Apple Coaster."

Beth pointed. "There's even a slew of free gambling coupons. This little book'll probably save me several hundred—"

Joe had become interested. "May I look through it?"

Beth handed him her booklet of coupons. He and I examined it. The front cover read, "Las Vegas Advisor: Member's Reward Book."

We leafed through it. Two-for-one buffets at the Mirage, the Fremont, the Golden Nugget, Ellis Island, and about forty more casinos and restaurants. Two-for-one offers on show tickets for at least a dozen shows around Vegas. Coupons for ten-dollar match-play and other gambling offers, including some free slot play from about twenty casinos, and two-for-one or reduced rate ride offers on several thrill rides around town.

"Wow," Joe said, "This thing's loaded with value."

"I know." Suzy replied. "That's why we're LVA members."

Beth said, "It's more than coupons. There's their website, forums, and newsletter to keep us up-to-the-minute on everything happening and about to happen in Vegas."

They both found their five-dollar-second-ride ticket for the coaster and used them.

This time I put the little notebook in my hip pocket and held the keys in my free hand, wishing I hadn't even brought them to Vegas with me. They were useless here. The coaster's thrill was as intense as the first time we rode it. When it stopped, we helped the girls get out. I took Suzy's hand in mine and squeezed. She raised her eyebrows and returned the gesture.

Suzy and I walked with our arms around each other's waist. She leaned her head against my shoulder. I tickled her ribs and she giggled.

On our way back down to the casino level, I told her, "Later on, Joe and I are going to have to cut out for a while. I bought tickets weeks ago for the topless Folies Bergere at the Trop tonight."

Suzy shook her head. "Boys really will be boys. I guess we can't fault you, since you bought your tickets weeks ago."

Beth huffed and pouted. "You're leaving us for a bunch of Vegas showgirls?"

Everyone chuckled at her remark.

"I bet almost half the audience will be women, so it's not a guy thing." I said. "I think people want to see what they consider the old-Vegas-style shows."

Suzy wrinkled up her nose. "Next thing, you'll be trying to tell us you're going for the nostalgia."

As we reentered the casino, I said, "Let's shoot some craps."

We'd seen the craps tables on our first pass through the casino, so we knew where to go. I took up my normal shooting position. Everyone else bought in for some chips of their own to bet with.

"We've never played craps before," Beth said. "May we toss the dice, too? It looks like fun."

I taught both girls how to put down small bets on the pass line when their turns to throw came around.

Suzy won her pass-line bet and tossed a five for her point. She won her point, throwing another five. She squealed, jumping up and down, then threw a come-out roll of seven for another win. She followed with an eight, then the losing devil seven.

I enjoyed seeing her having fun. I kidded her. "Keep your day job."

She punched my shoulder. "Rats."

Beth threw the dice and established a point on nine, then came a seven to end her short turn.

"Too bad," Joe consoled her, giving her a hug.

With my own rooting section in place, I picked up the dice. Since I'd never shot on this particular table before, I told everyone to hold their bets. I made offsetting warm-up bets, then popped an on-axis double-pitch four-three seven on the first throw.

The dealer took my don't-pass bet, which I replaced. The dealer then paid off my winning pass-line bet.

Suzy squeezed my arm. "Is that good?"

I nestled her closer and whispered, "No. I'm wanting sixes and eights—not that number." I gave her a little smooch on her cheek. I avoided saying 'seven' because it's deemed unlucky to say that word at a craps table, lest the losing devil sevens show up to end your turn.

I took another offsetting warm-up toss. Out came a five-four, to establish the point on nine. I tossed a hard eight and an on-axis hard six.

"Okay, ladies, go ahead and place six and eight."

We instructed them how to put out twelve-dollar place bets on six and eight. They did, and so did Joe. I sat seventy-two dollars in chips on the table, called out my bets, and tried to work my magic. The dice found their mark in their landing zone again, stopping with an eight showing.

"Take your winnings when the dealer gives them to you, but leave your place bets at risk—so you can keep winning," I told the girls. Joe followed suit.

My next two throws encountered a slight problem and resulted in trash numbers, an eleven and a four. A new player took the end spot at the other end of our table and started putting his pass-line bets right where I wanted to land the dice. They hit his chips and bounced off on both previous tosses.

Joe slipped away to talk to the guy.

"I can put my chips wherever I want." The guy shouted, slurring his words. "I'm not moving 'em for anyone."

Joe returned to our end of the table. "Doesn't want to cooperate," Joe told me.

"Okay, I'll move my aim over then. Thanks for trying, Joe.

"I now aimed the dice a foot farther left for the next roll and let them fly. The dice missed the guy's stack of chips this time by a good six inches. My roll showed an eight. Again, they took their winnings but left their bets up. I continued to go for the progression-bet win. A ten showed, then a six for another win for our peanut gallery.

The trouble-maker at the distant end of the table bet on Don't Pass—betting on me to fail. He lost.

The girls whooped, hollered, and jumped up and down, excitement lighting up their faces.

Suzy yelled, "Go, Ray, go! Really."

I tossed the dice, but when they rolled back and stopped at the other end of the table, a four-three seven showed.

"Seven-out." The stickman scooped up the dice. "New shooter. Get your bets down."

Joe looked at me.

I shrugged. "Hey, I'm not going to win 'em all." I looked over at the girls. "Sorry girls, I'll try to do better next roll." I was down seventy-two dollars because of that short roll.

Fifteen minutes later, I got the dice again. Everyone's turn had ended in a couple of rolls each. Without hesitation, out went my place bets again. Another seventy-two dollars risked. "Always working," I told the dealer, who moved my bets into place on the betting layout.

My dice sailed smoothly through the air. At the end of their roll back, a hard six showed. I upped the bets and tossed again. A nine came next, then another six showed. I tossed a five, then another hard six. I upped the bets with each win, inching closer to winning my progression bet. Everyone else put their pint-sized bets out, too.

The Ice Man assumed his role, and cranked out an eight. Again, everyone rejoiced. The peanut gallery took in their small winnings.

Joe told the girls, "One more six or eight and Ray wins $700."

I tossed a five, then a hard four, which can happen when one die goes off axis. I next delivered a progression-bet-winning five-three eight. After checking my watch, I ordered my bets taken down, then put all the chips on the table's surface to color up.

Suzy and Beth appeared stunned by what they'd seen me accomplish without apparent effort. The girls bounced up and down.

A grin spread across Joe's face.

Suzy smiled broadly. "Ray, you've got a beautiful-looking toss that's really something to see. Joe, I wondered if you two might be blowing smoke up my skirt when you told me earlier about Ray's skills. Now I see how really fantastic—"

"Ray had to work for that win," Joe told Beth.

"Big kiss for the winner?" I asked.

Suzy granted my request, surprising me with a quick slip of the tip of her tongue between my lips.

Everyone had won money betting on me, even though I bombed on the first attempt.

"Got to love that progression bet." I flipped a green twenty-five dollar chip to the dealers as a tip for the pit crew. "It lets ya win, even when ya lose."

"Yup," Joe agreed. "Lost one. Won one. Up over $600. I'll take that anytime."

I cashed in chips for cash at the teller window. "Joe and I are taking you ladies out for supper." I bowed formally. "If you'll allow us?"

I got my wish. I appeared to be on a roll today with more than $2,000 in winnings and an unexpected date with a stunning woman.

Our girls chose Gallagher's, one of the casino's upscale restaurants. We began with everybody sharing some delicious breaded shrimp.

Joe and I were surprised when Beth took out a cellophane-wrapped package of eating utensils, consisting of a plastic knife, fork and spoon. She unwrapped them and put them down by her plate, then put her napkin on her lap. "I've got this thing about using silverware. I can't stand when metal comes in contact with my teeth. It's like fingernails on a blackboard to me, so I always bring my own plastic utensils."

We nodded.

Okay. Nothing wrong with that. Everyone has their little quirks.

I never pass a cat without stopping to pet it, if it allows me to get close enough. I always pet the cat until it makes me stop, too.

We savored the moistest, most-tender mouth-watering steaks, grilled to perfection with a light coating of black pepper and spices. We talked while we ate. Beth informed us they'd been raised in a quiet suburb near Cincinnati, and appreciated shopping and concerts in Cincy.

Joe wiped his mouth with a napkin. "We're both farm-raised, but we may have difficulty keeping Ray around after his recent success—"

I shrugged. "I guess we'll see. New possibilities are appearing."

Joe asked Beth, "How long before you two have to return to Cincinnati?"

"We fly out next Saturday, she said between bites. "How about you guys?"

"We're booked to fly out at 7:05 p.m. next Friday," Joe said.

Suzy suggested, "Maybe we can regroup again after your show and share more really good times? Would that suit you guys?"

My eyes widened at her suggestion. "Boy, I'd sure like that." I almost choked on my drink.

"Me, too." Joe raised a glass. "To more great times."

Everyone clicked their glasses together, then took a sip.

Beth stared while Joe salted his food. "Joe, Why do you over-salt everything?"

"It brings out more flavor."

I took a shot at Joe. "Ah, he's a saltaholic. He even salts saltine crackers when he eats soup. He salts bacon and pretzels—"

"Ray's exaggerating. That's not true."

I gave him a salute. "Gotcha, Bro." I turned to Suzy. "Got to raise a little hell every once in a while, especially when it's at Joe's expense."

Joe set out to get even. "Well, what about you putting ketchup on everything you eat, Ray?" He pointed a finger at the ketchup bottle. "There's a reason I call ketchup 'Ray juice'."

Joe leaned toward Beth, "He even puts it on mashed potatoes."

"Not true," I protested, knowing he'd told the truth and evened the score.

Suzy and I kissed and put our numbers in each other's phones. Beth and Joe also exchanged numbers. We finished eating, then strolled arm-in-arm with our new girlfriends. The time had arrived for Joe and me to go to our Folies Bergere show.

Upon entering the Trop's lobby, Suzy looked at Beth as if she'd read her mind. "You guys go get your jollies at the follies. We're going to be playing slots, right over there." She pointed to a bank of three-reel slots. "After your show ends, come join up with us again. Okay?"

"You bet," we both answered, thanking our lucky stars.

"I'm glad we met," I told Suzy.

"Why?" she asked, teasingly.

"You're fantastic and fun to be with." I pulled her closer as heat rose in my cheeks. I'd never felt this way about a girl before. My feelings surprised me as they washed over me like waves lapping a beach.

"You're sweet." She locked her hands together around my neck. "I'm glad we met, too."

I paid little attention to what Joe and Beth discussed or did. Suzy claimed my undivided attention.

Joe and I took our leave, with me getting another kiss and hug from Suzy.

Joe settled for a hug from Beth. He probably didn't want to go too fast and scare her off.

Upon entering the show's waiting line, I called home to bring our parents up to speed on the craps-shooting wins in Vegas. I chose to skip the part concerning us meeting a couple of gorgeous women.

Dad wasn't there, but Mom wished us more good luck and hoped we had the times of our lives. Little did she realize how much fun we were having.

We went inside the Trop's theater to see the Folies Bergere. We sat near the stage, left of center. Tall, curvaceous dancers displayed bare boobs while they danced and strutted around the stage in tall feathered headpieces and skimpy sequined costumes.

My mind refused to focus on the show taking place on the stage in front of me. I found myself wishing the show would end, so I could meet back up with Suzy. Joe continually shifted positions in his seat, too. The longer we sat, the more worried I became that Suzy and Beth wouldn't be waiting for us when we got out of the show.

But my worry had no merit. Both girls where right where they promised they'd be and flashed big smiles when we joined them.

Joe and I picked out slot machines to play on either side of the girls.

Suzy winked. "Did you enjoy your show? Did your girly-show charge you up, big boy? Did you find it titillating?"

Sidestepping her humor, I volunteered more than I probably should have. "To be truthful, my thoughts were on you." I slipped my arm around her waist and pulled her close.

"How sweet. Say, are you getting a crush on me?"

"Hmm. That's for you to find out." I replied, avoiding an honest answer and wishing I could be bold enough to nibble her ear.

Suzy's voice was low and flirty. "Sounds like a fun challenge."

Joe and Beth were hitting it off, too.

Suzy suggested, "Let's all explore the southern end of The Strip. Check out Excalibur, Luxor, and Mandalay Bay."

"What do you two say?" I asked Joe and Beth.

Both agreed.

******

We became tourists again, checking out the scene at some of those gigantic casinos we first viewed when our plane slowed down during landing. We spent several hours casino-hopping, sightseeing, and doing everything we found to do. We had dates on our arms, money in our pockets, and the world's adult playground at our feet. I had won about $6,400 over our last two days.

We went to Excalibur first, using the overhead foot bridge to cross Las Vegas Boulevard. Excalibur resembled a medieval castle with appropriate interior decor. They had a dinner theater featuring knights in armor jousting on horseback, but we passed because we'd eaten earlier. We strolled around long enough to get the feel of the place and try out a few of their slots before moving on.

The pyramid-shaped Luxor appeared to be made of black glass, with a huge beacon on top that shot its beam straight up. "I've read this beam is the most powerful on earth and visible from outer space with the naked eye," I said, snuggling Suzy.

Suzy and Beth marveled at Luxor's about-ten-stories-tall sphinx out front. It sported authentic-looking Egyptian pharaoh-type head gear and ornate eye makeup that reminded me of what I'd seen Elizabeth Taylor wear in her title-roll as Cleopatra.

Luxor's interior was open in design, with elevators creeping at an angle up its slanted walls. Its interior motif transported us back to ancient Egypt. The gaming floor resembled those of the other casinos we'd been to on The Strip, offering a wide selection of slots and table games.

After playing a few slots, I said, "I'd like to shoot some craps."

Suzy's face beamed. "Great. I want to see you win again."

"I've been rolling a new idea around and would like to check it out at their craps table."

"What's that, Ray?" Joe asked.

"I don't know if it'll work for me, but Heavy uses the v2 dice set— with twos on top forming a small 'v', instead of threes. The v2 set produces lots of fours and tens for him that pay nine dollars for every five-dollar bet. It also produces lots of fives and nines that pay seven dollars for every five-dollar bet. Both of those are better payoffs than I get for my sixes and eights, because there are fewer ways for a random roller to roll 'em."

Joe said, "Whoa, you're thinking about switching horses midstream? Is that a good thing to be trying right now? I mean, you're killing it with how you already bet and shoot."

We arrived at my choice of craps tables. Everyone bought chips. The current shooter tossed the dice. A group of four young women were playing, too. I studied them. They appeared to be winning, judging from the noise they were making; or maybe they'd had a bit too much to drink? They all had drinks in their hands.

"Seeing Heavy shoot got me curious. I'm going to try my idea for one or two turns, betting cheap to learn what numbers I roll. I may not win, but it'll be educational." I paused. "I'll switch back if I don't get good results, then play around with the idea more when I get back to the practice table."

"Okay," Joe said, "Don't screw up your regular game in the process."

"Don't worry, I won't do that. Don't anyone else bet on my throw while I try this. It's going to be an experiment."

When it came my turn to shoot, I placed five and nine for five dollars each, then added offsetting pass/don't pass bets so I'd be allowed to shoot. On the come-out roll, I popped an on-axis five-two seven.

"No harm, no foul," I said. I hadn't called the place bets working on the come-out roll, so I couldn't win or lose those bets on my first toss.

I then tossed an on-axis three-six nine to establish the point. I collected the winnings and left the cheap bets in place on five and nine. I rolled a string of four straight sixes and eights, much to my surprise. Next an eleven came out, then a hard ten and an on-axis four.

"Darn, those are supposed to be harder to toss than five and nine. Maybe I should have bet on four and ten, instead. They pay even better when you hit them than fives and nines do." I tossed a losing seven, making me have an affordable ten-dollar loss.

"That gives me some food for thought. On the next turn, I'll try betting the higher paying four and ten."

Joe and the girls didn't seem to know what to make of what they'd seen. They lacked a lot of the insight I possessed about such matters. They all waited for my next turn. I used this opportunity to flirt a little more with Suzy, but I believe she might have out-flirted me.

One shooter tossed the dice from near-center-table, aiming them so the dice always hit the back wall up high in the curviest part of the corner. Apparently, he knew something we didn't, because he rolled the same numbers on most tosses. He didn't get a super-long roll going, or he might have cleaned up.

Why would anyone want to aim at such a dangerous and unpredictable spot on that corner of the back wall? I guess that will remain a mystery.

When I received the dice to shoot again, I put out five-dollar place bets on four and ten, then opened with an eight, tossed two nines, a six, a hard eight, and two fives in a row.

"I dodged when I should have weaved, and weaved when I should have dodged." I scratched my head. "Maybe that's why Heavy bets all four outside numbers. But that puts a lot of money at risk and makes it harder to come out a winner, unless you toss a lot of winning numbers before a seven."

I next tossed a six, then an eight and a losing seven.

I pulled Suzy close to my side. "Okay, that's a pretty good cheap education. Enough messing around with new ideas for the rest of our trip. I'm going back to my old, proven ways."

Beth and Suzy didn't toss any winners on their turns, which ended quickly.

When the dice came back to me again, someone flipped a switch. With my normal dice set and progression bets down again, I rolled eighteen numbers and cashed in on the progression bet twice, winning $1,400. Everyone else won money betting on my throw, too.

We moved to Mandalay Bay, a tall, massive building that served as an anchor for the southern end of The Strip. All decked out in a floodlighted light-toned stone exterior, Mandalay Bay featured a sports event center. World championship boxing matches often took place there.

Mandalay Bay also had a sports-booking establishment. The hotel boasted a Shark Reef Aquarium, a huge convention center, and its own shopping experience at Mandalay Place. It also housed half a dozen restaurants, including their famous House of Blues, The Burger Bar, and a Wolfgang Puck restaurant.

After an hour or more of exploring, flirting, and trying out their slots, Beth said, "We should head back up The Strip and give MGM Grand a good look-see and check it out."

Joe yawned, looking at his watch. "It's late and I'm pooped. That'd be a great way to wrap up our day."

Suzy looked up into my eyes. "I don't want the night to end."

"Neither do I."

******

We rode a monorail from Mandalay Bay back up to Excalibur, then crossed over to MGM Grand. It was huge, both on its emerald-green exterior and in its not-so-inviting interior. It proved too big for my liking. I felt lost half the time we were there. It overwhelmed me. At the time it was the world's largest hotel.

We did our usual tour of the casino floor, tried out the slots, and stopped for a couple of hands of blackjack, but didn't win. We grabbed a bite to eat at MGM's tropical rain-forest-themed restaurant. It featured an inviting waterfall, tropical birds, and vegetation. All the exploring and walking we'd done had worked up an appetite that needed to be satisfied. We all ordered breakfast, then took it to an empty booth.

Snuggling closer into Joe, Beth asked, "What kind of careers do you and Ray want to have?"

"I expect to end up taking over our family-farm when Dad retires. Someone's going to have to run it."

Even though my watch showed three a.m., the large restaurant was more than three-quarters full. Free-flowing conversations floated around us, as people at tables around ours discussed what they'd enjoyed doing and were going to do tomorrow.

Vegas never sleeps.

Beth said, "Teaching second graders is rewarding. I also want to see where my interest in art takes me. I'm hopeful of becoming more than a hobby painter someday."

Suzy moved closer to me. "I'm really want to write children's stories, and get published someday."

Beth squeezed Joe's hand. "I want to get my own apartment and venture out into the world on my own."

I changed the flow of the conversation when I looked over at Joe and flashed one of my Ray-grins. "Joe, do your mouse imitation for the girls. I'm sure they'll like it."

He ignored me, hoping the subject would get dropped.

"Aw, come on, Joe. Do your mouse bit," I asked again.

"What's his mouse bit?" Beth looked at Joe in puzzlement.

"Joe impersonates a mouse. It's funny."

Everyone stared at Joe now.

"Aw, come on Joe. Show us your mouse bit," both girls pleaded.

Joe's shoulders sagged. He sighed.

I kept looking at him in anticipation. "Come on, Joe. Pretty please?"

"Oh, all right." Joe held the back of his hands against his chin, wiggling his fingers. He puckered his lips and made sharp, high squeaking sounds in a great impersonation of a mouse. Everyone broke up laughing.

I probably had a cat-that-ate-the-bird look on my face. "Do it again, Joe."

He did, seeming to feel a bit foolish. Everyone laughed so hard and so long they wiped tears out of their eyes.

"Where did you come up with that?" Beth asked. "That's the funniest thing I've ever seen."

"My sides are really sore from laughing," Suzy added.

I flipped him a fingertip salute. "I knew you girls would get a kick out of that."

It took a couple of minutes for everyone to regain their composure. Everyone at the tables near us looked at us like we were all crazy with their mouths open, shaking their heads in disbelief. One guy even hid his eyes in the crook of his elbow on the tabletop. His whole body was shaking violently with laughter. Joe probably swore to get even with me.

"Joe's a pretty good guy. Back in high school, one of the girls in his homeroom had to undergo chemo. When she returned to school, Joe shaved his head. He confessed he didn't want her to feel so weird and alone about being bald. He didn't care if others thought he'd gone weird on them, but the girl most likely understood and appreciated the gesture."

"Is that true?" Beth asked.

Joe's face reddened. He shrugged. "Yeah, I remember something like that."

Both girls were impressed. That's why I mentioned it.

Everything gradually returned to normal and the conversation drifted back to Vegas.

"Every time I walk into a different casino, I get an adrenaline rush, like when we go to a fair, carnival or circus," I said. "Anyone else notice that, too? Every place promises such potential for fun, they ought to call this Fun City."

"Look at Circus-Circus," Suzy said, "that's carrying the idea clear out to it natural conclusion."

"Who doesn't love a circus?" I asked, then added, "Good point, Suzy girl. That new adrenaline rush is what makes casino hopping so much fun. You get a new rush every time you switch casinos."

Joe was deep in thought. "These casinos know how to let tourists enjoy themselves while they empty their bankrolls."

Suzy chuckled. "Next thing you know, they'll be putting ATM machines that take credit cards right out on the casino floors."

"I know if I wanted to start a pawn shop," Beth said, "I'd want it located next to a casino."

"If the mob still ran the casinos..." I took a sip of Coke. "there'd probably be pawn shops attached to them."

Joe commented on the foreign-looking card flickers, the rolling billboard trucks, and the free curbside newspaper dispensers we'd encountered on The Strip.

"That's free speech," Suzy said. "The Las Vegas Advisor website says the city's trying to get rid of the card flickers and such, but the ACLU's defending them being there as using their free speech rights."

Everyone rolled their eyes.

"Money talks," I said, finishing my Coke. "Let's call it a night and get some rest."

Suzy gazed into my eyes. "Say, Ray, where did you get those beautiful blue eyes?" She looked even closer. "Wow, your left eye has tiny flecks of greens, browns, and golds mixed in among the blue."

I blinked rapidly. "It's always been that way. Nobody ever said why. It doesn't feel any different to me."

Suzy sighed. "Oh, but your eyes are so beautiful. I've never seen anything like them."

"It's what gives him super-human powers," Joe kidded. "He's Wonder Boy."

"Yeah, sure," I shot him a dirty look.

Suzy cradled my chin in her hands, then ran her fingers through my hair. "I may have to take you home with me."

I pulled her toward me and we kissed, oblivious of all those seated in our area.

Beth and Joe looked at each other.

We finally headed back across the intersection to the Trop, where Suzy and Beth exited the elevator on their floor. Suzy planted a sweet, romantic goodnight kiss on my lips, igniting my face and making my ears burn.

She whispered, "You guys stop by at seven in the morning. We both enjoyed your company and would like to spend tomorrow together, again. Okay?"

I'd been ready to voice that same idea, but she beat me to it. I agreed, giving Suzy another kiss and hug. I was anxious for tomorrow to get started, so we could be back together again.

After going to bed, I became aware of a weird feeling suddenly coming over me. I couldn't explain it or pin it down, but it was there none the less; a thought buried deep within my brain decided to surface. We'd had everything going our way ever since hitting Vegas, even our love lives. Now a nagging feeling that something bad might be heading our way was making itself known.

I shrugged it off, rolled over, and went to sleep.

Nah, nothing to worry about, right?

Chapter Eleven —Monday

We woke to my wrist alarm, showered, got dressed, and soon found ourselves knocking on the girls' door. It opened a crack, then Beth stepped out to join us, then Suzy followed. She wasn't all that cheerful for some reason.

Beth smiled up at Joe. "Yesterday, people at the pool said the San Remo, next door, has a fantastic and affordable breakfast. Want to go?"

"Let's eat a light breakfast and save room for a couple of buffets later on."

"Great idea," Beth said.

Joe's back in non-stop eating mode again.

"I remember Doctor Bones commenting on San Remo's craps tables. Maybe we should check them both out."

I tried to pull Suzy closer as we walked toward the elevator, but she pulled away. Something was clearly bothering her. She fidgeted and shook, about to cry. Joe noticed it too as she pulled away from me.

Joe asked Beth, "What's wrong with Suzy?"

Beth lowered her eyes and bit her lower lip. "Suzy broke up with her trouble-making boyfriend, Tony, before we came to Vegas. We just got a call from home."

"What about?"

"Tony called Mom, asking where we were staying in Vegas. He's coming here to find her."

We hadn't heard about a breakup, or even about a boyfriend being in Suzy's past. It caught me off guard. I reeled back at the news. "That son-of-a..." I paused, regaining control. This news struck me hard.

Suzy burst into tears and shook all over.

I pulled her into my arms. "H-Hey, babe, it's going to be all right. I'm here. I'll protect you."

I gave her my handkerchief to dry her tears, held her close, and stroked her hair. "I'll never let anything happen to you, babe. I'll keep you safe."

We waited until Suzy regained control of her emotions. She stopped crying, dabbed her eyes, and regained her composure. I cupped her chin with my hand and lightly kissed the tip of her nose.

Joe asked Beth, "Is he what you'd consider a loose cannon?"

I bundled Suzy close, offering her protection.

Beth said, "He gets pretty crazy. That's why Suzy broke up with him."

"I'm sorry for being such a mess and involving you guys..." Suzy took a deep sigh, then forced a smile. "I don't really know what he wants, or what he'll do when he finds me."

"Suzy and I moved our vacation up a week to get away from him," Beth said. "Mom didn't tell him anything."

"But, he's a cop, so he'll really know how to find me." Suzy drew in a deep breath.

I smacked a fist against the palm of my other hand. "He's not a cop out here. If he shows up and causes any trouble, I'll take care of it, Suzy." I took her hand in mine.

I locked eyes with Joe. "Why don't we trade rooms with the girls, right now? That way Tony'll get an unpleasant surprise if he shows up at what he thinks is their room, looking for trouble."

Everyone said that was a great idea.

"That'll add an extra layer of protection," Joe said.

"Oh, thank you both. That really means so much to me. I've been scared since Mom's call." Suzy leaned in and gave me a sweet, appreciative kiss. "You're my man, Ray." She embraced my body while I encircled her in my arms.

"Let's go back upstairs and trade rooms."

We all turned around right then and there and went back to our rooms and gathered our belongings. Twenty minutes later we had switched rooms with the girls. Heading back downstairs, everyone was in a better mood again.

"Hey, girls. We're going to Riverdance tonight at the Mirage. Want to see if we can buy you tickets, too?"

I wasn't thrilled at the idea of leaving our ladies for a second time to attend another show. We might not be so lucky this time. They might not be around after the show.

"Sure," Beth said, "but we won't be able to get seats beside you, if we can even get tickets."

"But," Suzy added, "if we bought an extra pair of tickets seated together, we could really sit as individual couples."

"Sounds like a winner. You girls are smart." I lifted Suzy off her feet and kissed her.

Joe squeezed Beth. "We'll try to buy another pair of tickets."

"Okay, but we're paying for them, Suzy and I insist."

I shrugged. "We're glad to treat you, but if you insist, we'll agree."

We soon were next door at the tiny San Remo, which sported a stuccoed Italian exterior. Low mood-lighting bathed its interior, rather than the bright glitzy lighting most bigger hotels featured.

I noticed a woman passing back and forth throughout the restaurant, calling out "Keno. Keno." She carried a small circular tray in her hand, upon which sat a jar full of blank wagering tickets. People in a booth across from us stopped her and placed a Keno wager, using one of those blank tickets. They gave her twenty-five cents.

Observing this piqued my curiosity, so I asked our waitress about it. She pointed out monitors positioned on their walls in several locations throughout the restaurant. They were broadcasting live; showing winning Keno balls being selected for a game that had closed to betting.

"The locals are into Keno, big time," she told us. "You try to guess the winning numbers for as little as a dime, and if they all hit, you could win some serious money. It's a constant ongoing instant lottery that customers play in-house. A new game goes off every few minutes."

Her saying that reminded me of the quiet background-level announcements over their public-address system informing those listening of a Keno game ending soon, or another one soon starting.

It amazed me a casino collected such chicken-feed bets, so I looked up info about Keno on my phone. I learned odds on winning Keno are the absolute worst bet in Vegas.

I had difficulty believing people who resided in Vegas could become so hooked on such a bad bet. Then again, if you lived in a gambling mecca, what better way to keep your gambling under control than to keep it at the ten to twenty-five-cent level?

"Let's find San Remo's craps tables," I said.

They proved to be within fifty feet of where we ate breakfast. Their tables resembled whaling boats rather than craps tables. They looked longer than twenty feet.

"Dang," I commented, "That's one long table. We'll see what I do. Don't bet on my throws until I tell you."

I bought in, and rolled. The dice failed to touch the back wall on some of my throws, which casinos require. The crew here didn't warn me about the short tosses. Instead of the numbers I sought, I threw large and small numbers, throw after throw.

I took thirty tosses with offsetting warm-up bets. I was the only player at any of the tables at this early morning hour, so I kept shooting. I neither won money nor lost, staying even.

I shrugged. "I'm not going to attempt to swim upstream. I'm done here."

The stickman colored up my small value chips for big value ones. "Man, you missed out on cleaning up by not betting the large and small numbers. I've never witnessed that many twos, threes, elevens and twelves tossed at one time before." He seemed amazed.

With flawless hindsight, I guess I might have adapted my betting to win on my string of high and low numbers, but I'd rather get away from shooting on such a long table. There's a ton of much shorter, better-shooting craps tables in Vegas, and I hadn't had much luck trying to roll more-difficult outside numbers last night, either.

"Let's go back to the locals' casino we played at on the way to dealer's school yesterday. I'd like to play their tables, again," I said.

******

Our cabbie spoke little English, but understood the casino's name. When our taxi entered their parking lot, a car, hidden from view, materialized from a row in the parking lot and sped up. It T-boned our taxi. Crunch. That other driver must have hit the wrong peddle with his foot.

Airbags in both vehicles inflated, and everyone in our car pitched violently sideways before we came to rest. The other car's horn stuck and blew loudly. Steam, or smoke, rose from under the hoods of both vehicles. A rank choking smell filled our taxi from its airbags inflating. I found myself on the cab's rear floor, with Suzy on top of me. We both got back up and dusted each other off.

Our taxi driver complained in broken English about his back and neck hurting. He looked to be in a lot of pain.

Beth asked, "Is anybody else injured?"

Suzy replied, "I'm okay. Really."

"Same here," Joe added.

I rubbed the back of my head and neck. "I feel strange. I'm okay, but my head's foggy."

Everyone exited, trying to shake off the wreck. Several people, including security personnel, came running toward us.

The irate other driver rushed the cab shaking a fist. "That bozo cabbie came out of nowhere... drove in front of me, speeding." He pounded on the driver's window.

We stayed inside the cab until someone had him under control.

Casino security officers informed us that since our accident occurred on private property and involved a taxi, they wouldn't be calling the police. The Las Vegas Taxi Authority got called to handle our wreck instead. Everyone had to stay put until they investigated and released us.

An ambulance whisked our taxi driver away to a hospital, with siren blaring and lights flashing, because he kept repeating in broken-English, "Whiplash. Whiplash."

After finally getting the hood forced open, casino employees disconnected the other car's battery to silence the constantly blowing horn. I pulled Suzy close and did my best to comfort her. Joe hugged Beth.

We stood in the hot morning sun on the casino's parking lot for about an hour before a uniformed female Las Vegas Taxi Authority investigator arrived. Our wreck became the parking lot's main attraction, with in excess of forty gawkers present.

Nobody could leave the scene—not even to visit the restrooms inside the casino—until she told us she was done. Time slowed to a stop while the investigator worked. Everyone became over-heated and wanted out of the hot sun. The taxi's engine refused to start. Without air conditioning, we couldn't even consider spending more time sitting in the taxi.

My head still felt strange. I tried to act okay, but I knew it would be hard to fool Joe. He knew me too well. I wanted to avoid them worrying.

"Ray, are you really sure you don't need to be checked out at a hospital?" Suzy asked several times.

I kept saying, "I'll be okay. I'm just a little groggy."

Wreckers arrived, and after an eternity the investigator said, "I'm done now. You all can leave. Do you want me to call you another taxi?"

"This is our destination," I said. "We're going inside now."

Everyone headed straight for the restrooms. When we regrouped, I said I needed something cold to drink and to rest a few minutes to recover my bearings.

As we took up seats in the restaurant, Suzy's phone rang. She answered it, listened for a minute, and then hung up with a worried look on her face.

Her voice shook. "Tony called. He's really coming to Vegas. He said, 'I'm going to find you, bitch' and hung up."

Beth struck the table with clinched fists.

Everyone shook their heads.

"Leave Tony to me." I winked to Suzy and held her hands in mine.

Our trip had been a total lark up until now, but the lightheartedness of our previous day had disappeared. We sat in the restaurant for a long time. Nobody talked.

Joe asked me, "You up to shooting craps again?"

"Let me try. Winning money might put everyone back in a good mood again."

The same pit crew recognized and greeted us again when we joined their three-fourths-full table. Due to lack of room, Beth and Suzy stood behind us, observing the action from a few feet away, but they were still close enough to talk.

After a couple of tosses by another player, our dealer turned to Joe. "Tell your friend there to bet on the other shooters." He motioned a finger toward me.

Joe and I ignored his comment.

After another roll of the dice, our dealer again turned his head Joe's way. "Tell your friend there to bet on the other shooters."

I asked, "Don't I get to choose who I bet on?"

"We want you to bet on all the shooters."

I glared at him. The comment pissed me off, since I had tipped him well yesterday morning. In true Ice Man fashion, I placed canceling-out five-dollar pass/don't-pass bets on the shooter.

More than one way to skin a cat.

Joe said, "Strange they asked you to bet on each shooter—they ignored me. They must be hassling you for clipping them for so much yesterday."

"Management must have chewed them out over such a large loss?" This was, after all, a small locals' casino.

Finally, it was my turn. I put down my warm-up bets. My first toss brought a six-six, boxcars. I lost the pass-line bet, and replaced it. A random roller expects to toss boxcars once every thirty-six throws. Boxcars weren't one of the things I should have been tossing. I only did that when one die went way off its rotational axis. A snake-eyes two appeared next—again unwanted trash from the other end of the spectrum. Snake eyes were expected with the same frequency as boxcars. My next eight tosses showed no sixes or eights, most being outside numbers. I tossed a seven out. I found myself five dollars down on my first turn and was less than pleased with the results.

I shook my head. "Our car wreck must have affected my game. Maybe I'll do better on my next turn."

Our dealer no longer hassled me over not betting on other shooters. Everything at our end became pretty quiet while the dice worked their way from shooter to shooter, until they once again arrived back in my hand.

My second turn results stunned me, being similar to the first attempt, but ending in only four rolls. I lowered my head. "Oh buddy, The Ice Man's left the building."

I colored up then went to convert the chips I hadn't lost from my buy-in back into cash at their cashier window.

"No pumpkins today?" the smug cashier from yesterday asked me, smirking. Her hair looked even redder today.

"This casino must sweat losing their money, like the guys say the Barbary Coast does." I rubbed my chin. "Girls, we're going to be tourists for the rest of today. My game's off. I believe that wreck screwed up my toss or mental game; my psyche might have gotten bruised. Let's try buying more Riverdance tickets and do fun things."

Our girls responded by giving us hugs and kisses.

Everyone entered another taxi.

"I hope this one doesn't wreck," Beth said.

We were on our way to the Mirage. Nobody talked much, except to encourage me in believing my abilities would soon return and my winning would continue like before. Deep down inside I hoped our wreck hadn't somehow undone my abilities for tossing sixes and eights. Time would tell if the answer to that question would be the one I hoped for.

After standing in line for twenty minutes, Suzy and Beth purchased their own pair of Riverdance tickets.

While there, Suzy and Beth chose a restaurant, where we all sampled the fresh seafood buffet. Beth used her plastic silverware. Joe over-salted everything. I asked for ketchup, and Suzy "really" liked her meal.

Joe and I ate the crab legs and beer-battered shrimp. Beth enjoyed broiled scallops. Suzy liked both the beer-battered shrimp and peel-and-eat shrimp.

******

"Let's head over to the Gamblers General Store. I've got their address in my billfold. I need a few extra sticks of dice and some more gaming chips for practice."

I spent half an hour shopping. The Gamblers General Store stocked everything gambling related, specializing in books on all forms of gambling. I loaded up by buying twelve foil-wrapped sticks of five casino-quality dice for less than twelve dollars each and a generous seventy-five dollars' worth of betting chips in various denominations to use on my table back home.

I had ordered from the Gamblers General Store website for a year and a half, and had been anxious to visit their store in person. Like a kid in a candy store, I examined various slot machines for sale and cruised shelves full of books on every form of gambling.

A two-sided view of a stick of dice,
containing five dice,
all with matching three-digit numbers
between pips on the six die face.
Matching numbers are utilized by casinos
to prevent dice switching
or tampering during play.

"Where to now?" Joe asked the girls while I wrapped up my shopping trip. "It's three hours till show time."

"We'd really planned on riding all the coasters in Vegas..."

Beth finished Suzy's thought. "Let's ride *Speed - The Ride,* at the Sahara."

"Sounds like a winner." Suzy pulled me closer.

******

We walked over to the Sahara, dropped five dollars each on ride tickets, and boarded Speed when our turn came. An out-and-back coaster, Speed began at sixty miles per hour and reached a top speed of more than seventy miles per hour during about a thirty-second ride in each direction.

We might as well have been strapped to a rocket sled, except we took our ride facing forward then backward. We got flipped sideways, went from ground level through a tall overhead loop, paralleled Las Vegas Boulevard outside on their sidewalk for passersby to witness, and then dove underground.

"Oh, my God," I said weakly while we waited to be freed from our coaster seats.

Suzy shouted, "That's what I like!"

Beth showed a calm, pleased expression on her face. "Let's ride *Speed* again."

I was probably green, with bulging eyeballs.

We rode Speed three additional times, to our girls' absolute delight. I worried we'd never get Suzy and Beth to quit. I'd ridden Speed enough, at least for now. Each ride scared me out of a year of my life.

The girls' LVA coupon books held a free gambling coupon for the Sahara, so we went inside and cruised their Moroccan-market-themed boutique-shopping area. We then hit the casino, where Suzy and Beth each used their coupon to receive a ten-dollar free spin on the roulette wheel.

"What do we do with these?" Suzy asked at the roulette wheel.

The dealer took her coupon book and tore out the coupon for the ten dollars' free play on any even-money bet. He handed back her coupon book.

"Put it on red or black, or odd or even."

Beth said, "Red," placing her coupon.

Suzy said, "Let's really make sure one of us wins. Black." She used her LVA coupon to cover the other half of those options. The little white ball spun, and after about ten laps around the roulette wheel, the ball slowed and bounced around then came to rest on eleven.

"Eleven, odd, black," the dealer announced. He swept away all the losing bets and then paid off Suzy and the other winning betters.

Beth frowned and looked up at Joe with an exaggerated pout on her face. "I lost."

"Darn, you're so cute," he told her, giving her a kiss.

******

Our foursome strolled arm-in-arm back over to the Mirage, catching their volcano's fiery eruption outside on our way in. We killed time playing some entertaining three-reel slots, losing a few dollars.

Four towering, beautiful women suddenly appear at the end of the next bank of slots. Three tall, overly-handsome, rugged-looking young men soon joined them. After a few minutes a couple of guys wearing suits appeared with a photographer in tow carrying two big cameras.

He spend twenty minutes photographing different combination groupings of his beautiful models from several angles at the slots, as they simulated winning. Each time he would say, "Big smiles, throw your hands over your heads."

After a while the entire group moved to an out-of-service blackjack table nearby for more photos. The photographer gave one stunning blonde beauty a double-handful of simulated casino chips. He snapped her beautiful smile when she looked skyward and tossed all the chips high into the air. The chips were gathered up, with the event being repeated twice more.

After a few more minutes the photographer and his models went a different part of the casino.

Great, even the advertising Vegas uses to draw gamblers isn't real. I was disappointed.

When show time came, we lined up for *Riverdance*. Beth and Joe took the seats for the tickets the girls purchased. Suzy and I used the tickets I brought with me from home.

The show featured fantastic Celtic music and dancing. Onstage pyrotechnics livened everything up when they went off near their finale. The dancer who amazed me most took a short three-step run at an onstage wall, planted both feet head high on the wall, and flipped himself over backwards, landing again on his feet. My jaw dropped open the first time he did that.

******

After the show, the girls asked to walk down to the Bellagio to take in the dancing-waters display, because like Suzy said, "The spotlighted fountains would really be stunning and romantic at night."

The air smelled fresh. Warm mist from the fountains kissed our faces, bringing light whiffs of the scent from blooming desert flowers our way. Those dozen fountains danced back and forth while water cannons shot varying water streams high into the air in rhythm to the music.

Suzy's nearness made the scene super romantic. I cuddled her firm body, with the delicate scent of her fragrant shampoo wafting over me. As we stood cheek-to-cheek, time became suspended. This had to be the world's best sensation. We stayed long enough to see the water display dance twice.

Before we left, we went inside the Bellagio and checked it out, more out of curiosity than anything else. No one was anxious to gamble, so we didn't. We strolled around inside, taking in the interior in awe. To me, it was what the inside of the richest man-in-the-world's house would probably be like. Its beauty overwhelmed, but being poor all my life made me feel uncomfortable there, like I didn't belong. I was glad to leave.

******

Beth said, "The Las Vegas Advisor website says the Station Casinos have more than a half-million-dollar progressive jackpot that's guaranteed to be won before this coming weekend. Anyone like to take a shot at it?"

"How does the casino guarantee it'll be won before a certain date?" Joe asked.

"Beats me. The LVA website says teams of dedicated slot players are all converging on it. They play on machines non-stop around the clock, working in shifts to never give up their machines. I guess they figure it's a good risk for them to take. They feel like they'll win it, so they keep pumping coins through the machines as fast as they can."

"It might be fun trying," I said. "But let's put a hundred-dollar limit each on it, so we don't go crazy and blow a lot of money."

When we arrived, the big marque outside the Palace Station Casino advertised what the girls had read—half-a-million-dollar-plus progressive jackpot, guaranteed to be awarded by Saturday.

We were soon seated inside at the progressive slots, with each of us carrying a big bucket of 400 quarters to try our luck. I looked around, wondering which players around us were pro slot players camping on their favorite progressive machines.

Each of us fed coins into the hungry monsters. Suzy hit a small win that let her play a little longer than the rest of us. The money each of us had set aside to try to win half a million dollars with soon disappeared.

Joe turned his now-empty cardboard coin bucket upside down. "We gave it a valiant try."

"I guess it wasn't meant to be," I added. "It was fun trying and something we can tell our grandkids about someday."

******

Suzy said, "I'd really like to go to the Rio."

"Isn't that the shiny-green casino with the top cut off on a slant?" I asked.

"Yup. 'Bout half way up The Strip, on one of the other roads."

"We're gone," I said, hailing a cab to get us there.

The party atmosphere almost knocked us down the second we entered, with South American style music playing throughout the entire casino. We looked up to see a series of about a dozen Mardi-Gras-type parade floats snaking their way high above the gaming floor. They were all full of a mixture of tourists and Vegas showgirls. Everyone on the floats waved to the spectators below and tossed them strands of Mardi Gras beads. Many danced around on the floats.

Everyone on floor level got into the spirit and enjoyed themselves, too. Most people had some kind of drink in their hand. Party time. The parade going on, known as The Mardi Gras In The Sky, lasted another ten minutes before they wound it down.

Joe saw a cocktail waitress nearing us and asked her, "How often do they do that thing in the sky?"

"Every hour, on the hour. Can I get you all something to drink?"

"We might get something later, thanks," I said, not knowing where we'd be by the time she returned with any drinks we ordered.

We hadn't eaten anything in quite a while and were hungry, so we headed over to their World Wide Buffet and paid for meals. Once inside, we found it consisted of about ten individual buffets. Each offered food from a different country of the world.

"I don't know where to start." I looked around. "Looks so good. Can't wait to get at it."

We decided to tour each of the buffets to see what they had to offer before deciding on anything. Everything looked and smelled fantastic.

We faced difficult choices. We finally settled on putting a taste of one thing from one buffet, then a dab of something else from another on our plates. There must have been fifty different types of meat dishes to choose from throughout the different buffets. And about anything else your heart could desire. Eventually, we'd all made the circuit. Joe and I had been pigs, with plates heaped so high with food that I feared losing part of it on the floor. The girls had taken lesser portions and had been more selective.

We all put our plates down at an open table, then went to get our drinks. I was so stuffed by the time my plate was empty that I had difficulty justifying going back to get dessert, but I somehow managed. I topped the meal off with an oversized piece of lemon meringue pie.

After drinking coffee at the end of the meal and talking, we headed out in time to get in on riding the floats above the floor as the celebration started all over again, with everyone joining in. I'll say one thing for the Rio—they know how to throw a party.

******

When it got time to head in for the night, I told Suzy, "After we see you ladies back to your room, Joe and I are going to rent a car for the rest of the week. I'm tired of messing with cabs."

"I wondered why you ever messed with taxis in the first place, really."

The news excited Joe. Getting a rental car hadn't crossed my mind until now. We'd have wheels under us for the rest of our stay in Vegas.

Joe and I went to the airport, because we knew they had a lot of car rental places there, and the airport was near the Trop. I completed the paperwork at Hertz and gave them my credit card. We got the car, a nice looking nearly-new Toyota Corolla, and parked it in the Trop's parking garage then went to bed.

Will things improve for us tomorrow? How could they get worse?

Chapter Twelve — Tuesday

At breakfast at the San Remo again, I said, "I want to take another shot at some craps tables and see what happens."

Joe munched toast. "Why don't we try the tables at the Trop? We haven't tried them yet."

I stood up. "Okay, let's go."

"Whoa. I've still got toast and coffee to finish."

"Well, hurry."

Sitting back down, I drummed my fingers on the table. By the time Joe finished, the girls were more than ready to get underway, too.

After a short walk back to the Trop, I picked a table to play on. They all stood back and watched me buy-in. I got the dice right away, because the guy to my right had tossed a seven to end his turn.

I put out offsetting warm-up bets, selected my dice, then set about to see if I could work my magic. My hopes were riding high. I tossed a five, a three, and an eleven. Then I tossed a three, a two, and a nine. Next came a five, a ten, and a twelve, then four, six, nine, and finally a seven.

"That was pure torture. Did you see that?" I looked at Joe. "One lousy six in about a dozen rolls. A random roller tosses more sixes and eights." I seethed, but didn't give up. I took two more turns tossing the dice. The second turn was a little better, three target numbers in nine tosses. My final turn produced two target numbers in ten tosses.

I felt destroyed. "I'm done. Cash me in."

No magic today.

I wasn't ready for this. This wasn't supposed to happen, but it had. I didn't have a clue what to do next. I wasn't throwing sixes or eights. The one bright glimmer of hope? I wasn't tossing very many sevens, either.

"Come on everyone. We're going for a ride."

"Where to?" Joe asked.

"I don't know and don't care. I've got to clear my mind."

We all piled into the car and aimlessly rode around Vegas for about an hour while I sulked and thought. I finally broke the looming silence. "You know what? That table felt weird. I've been trying to figure out what went wrong and why I bombed so badly back there." I hung a left at the next corner. "I think the actual table-top was a couple of inches higher than normal. My release didn't feel like it always does. I had to start the dice out from too high a position for my toss to work."

"It will all work out, Ray." Joe said. "You've got too much talent for these things to hold you back. You'll come out of it. I've got faith in you, Bro."

An epiphany. It hit me out of the blue. I slammed both hands hard against the steering wheel.

"I think I've got it. I know what I can do to put my game back on track." I grinned one of what Joe calls my Ray-grins.

Joe's face sprang to life. "What is it? Come on, tell us."

"I did real well at Green Valley Ranch on our first night in town, right? By zoning in on that waterfall. It had such a positive and mesmerizing effect on me. We're going back there. That's gotta help."

"Fantastic idea," Suzy said.

Joe nodded as his spirits seemed to lift. "Glad you're thinking positive again."

A short while later, I pulled the car into Green Valley Ranch's valet parking. We all went inside. After getting my mojo loaded up by getting positive vibes from that waterfall, I went back to the same craps table I'd played before. Suzy, Beth, and Joe stood a few feet behind me on both sides.

One of the other players there was the one who'd won Terry's long-roll contest that first day of the dice-setting seminar. Apparently we weren't the only ones who had stuck around for an extended chance at the tables in Vegas. He acknowledged me with a brief wave.

My first offsetting warm-up rolls showed that yes, indeed, Ice Man might again be ready to take over the table. I now saw an abundance of sixes and eights in the numbers I tossed. After rolling four good numbers out of my first seven rolls, I got my usual progression bets down. My throws continued to find their mark, peppering sixes and eights.

My spirits now danced happily and my mind went wonderfully blank. I flashed Joe my most-mischievous grin. "I might have a new trick up my sleeve."

"What?" Joe asked.

"You'll see."

The stickman said, "Three-three, hard six."

Beth and Suzy clapped and cheered.

I threw an easy six, a couple of trash numbers, then hard eights, twice in a row. I won the progression bet with a follow-up six.

Welcome back, Ice Man.

I revealed my new trick by collecting the winnings, but leaving up the $216 place bets on both six and eight. Out came five and another winning six. I took the chips I won and racked them, but kept those same $216 place bets active on six and eight.

Nine rolled, then a winning eight. Again, I took the chips and racked them, but kept the $216 place bets on six and eight working. Three sixes showed in a row and an easy eight.

"Divide my winnings up and add them to my six and eight." I racked the few surplus dollar chips the dealer tossed me.

"Oh, my God," Joe said. "How did you ever come up with such an idea?

"What's he doing, Joe?" Beth whispered.

"I don't know. He mentioned something about a new trick he wanted to try."

There it was, another eight, winner.

The girls whooped and hollered, cheering me on even though Joe tried to shush them. He'd never seen me shoot with this kind of money on the table.

I threw two sixes back to back, one hard, one soft. I almost ran out of room in my chip rack. I filled one chip rack completely with the winnings while my string of sixes and eights continued with three more, interspersed with a couple of trash numbers.

The hammer fell when a devil seven appeared. My turn ended after I'd cleaned house. A large crowd now surrounded our craps table, taking in the big win. The way I counted, I won my $216 place bets six times, upped the bets again to $342 on each six and eight. I won at that betting level six more times. I had won about $4,500, in less than thirty minutes.

Everyone fortunate enough to have gotten an opening at our now-crowded table cleaned up by betting on my sixes and eights, too.

Joe said, "Man I wish I'd gotten an opening at the table and bought some chips, too, so I could have been betting on you."

The whole craps-pit area erupted in cheers, shouts, and an ovation for my feat. Players and spectators high-fived and patted me on the back. I lost the $684 in chips out there working on my place bets by rolling seven, but I had locked up such a humongous win that what I left on the table meant nothing.

Risk it to win it.

Besides, all the money on the table had come from the casino, not from my gambling bankroll. I'd locked up a tidy profit by a fourth of the way through my turn, taking all the pressure off my shoulders. I'd let my talent take me on its own wild ride and just hung on, relaxed, and allowed it to happen.

Pretty decent for a country boy from Iowa.

Joe exclaimed, "Wow! Some new trick."

He pumped my arm vigorously, slapping me on the shoulder.

"I'd been wanting to make those wagers for a long time, but I waited until I gained a little experience," I said.

Suzy kissed me in celebration.

I flipped a black hundred-dollar chip to the dealer. "For the boys in your crew."

"Thanks, man." The dealer tapped the black chip's edge against the crew's tip box, then dropped it through the box's slot.

The game stopped while security brought in a fresh supply of chips to restock the house's depleted supply. They counted all their newly-acquired chips, signed for them, and placed them in the house's chip rack on our table's backside.

Suzy hugged me and rubbed my back. Joe went into stealth mode and slipped around our table, talking to each of the other players.

I finally got to hear what Joe was saying when he reached the guy nearest to me on my right. "Let's pass the dice right back to Ray and allow him to shoot again, right away, and win us all some major money while he's on a hot roll."

An open conspiracy was afoot at the table. Sure enough, each player stated I should shoot again, waving the dice away when our stickman offered them the chance to shoot.

I found myself being given the dice again right after the game resumed.

"Everyone's waiting to witness a repeat performance," Joe said slyly.

I grinned. "You're behind this. I saw what you were up to."

Okay, let's do this thing.

I then showed Joe another new trick with my betting. Instead of the usual thirty-six-dollar opening bets, I made place bets for $240 on both the six and eight.

Out came an opening eight. I took the $280 in winnings. Now I rolled a six and racked another $280 in winnings. I relaxed, being in the black for the rest of my turn. I had racked $560 on the first two rolls, verses $480 I left at risk. I had taken my game up a notch.

Three trash numbers appeared, then a winning eight.

"Split the winnings between the six and eight."

"Okay, I need you to toss me a dollar chip to make it even," the dealer said.

I tossed down the dollar chip. Both bets now increased by another $200 each, to $480 each. I completed the pass-line bet with a soft six, winning another $560 I put in my chip rack. I left the place bets in play.

I established my new point by rolling another six. I ordered those winnings again added to the six and eight bets, increasing them by another $280 each, making each now $760. A nine appeared, then a hard ten. I tossed an eight and racked another $910 in winnings. A six appeared, and I ordered the winnings split and added to my six and eight.

The dealer told me, "We can only take each of your bets up to the $1,000 table limit."

"Fine, take 'em up." I remained emotionless and super clear-headed while racking the $480 surplus after increasing my bets to their betting limit.

$996 in chips now rested on each six and eight, to allow correct payouts be paid at seven dollars for each six-dollar bet.

I won twice, winning $1,162 on each. On my second win, I took the bets back down to thirty-six dollars each.

I leaned over to Joe and whispered, "Damn. I refuse to leave $2,000 in danger all day. Never. For right now, that continued risk is outside my comfort zone."

I threw an eight, then tossed an on-axis seven.

Ice Man delivered again, winning $8,332 on my second turn with the dice. In an hour, I had won $12,832. Everyone within thirty feet of the table went absolutely crazy. The scene became an instant party.

"Color me up." I unloaded my mountain of chips upon the out-of-play area of the table's surface.

The pit boss stepped in from nearby. "The casino manager will either cut you a check for your winnings, or hand-pay you in cash. Since your winnings this session are more than $8,400, you'll need to sign a Form W-2G for the Internal Revenue Service, first. We'll have to withhold Federal Income taxes."

I tossed the dealer a couple of black hundred-dollar chips. "For the boys in your crew."

"Great shooting," they all said together.

"Lucky, I guess." I waved to everyone to acknowledge their support. The most serene feeling in the world washed over me—one wave after another. I exhaled and let all my muscles go totally limp. Like a descending air balloon, I returned to Earth.

The girls sprang up and down, clapping their hands, yelling, "Our hero!"

The pit boss said, "The dealer will color you up with large denomination chips and move them out of everybody else's way. You can wait beside them. I've already called our manager and informed him of your win. He should be here to pay you in a few moments."

The table's supply of chips once again got replenished, then the dice passed to a new shooter, and the game continued. The air around the table still felt electrified and I felt serene and calm.

True to the pit boss's word, their casino manager soon arrived, with IRS Form W-2G on top of the papers on the clipboard.

"Congratulations on your win. May I see your driver's license and get all your contact info?"

He filled in all the required info on the form, giving me my own copy.

I noticed twenty-five percent of the winnings were being withheld for Federal income taxes. I let out a low whistle.

"I'm glad I pulled my $2,000 down when I did. It'll help offset the taxes they took out." I groaned.

The manager asked me, "How should we pay you? Cash? Check? We can deposit your winnings into your bank, or we can hold your winnings here at our casino for you to gamble with in the future."

"Cash will do."

"Okay, follow me to our cashier's cage, please."

We all did, like ducklings behind their mother.

The manager spoke to the girl at their VIP cashier window, passing in the required paperwork. She counted out ninety-seven one-hundred-dollar bills, plus a few smaller bills, quickly counted them again, then counted them out to me.

I took the money and quickly kissed it. It was the most money I'd ever held at one time.

The manager spoke. "Congratulations, Ray. Nice win."

We shook hands.

"How long will you be in town?"

"Until next Friday, why?"

"May we put you up in a deluxe comped suite for the rest of your stay in Vegas?"

"No, but thanks for the offer."

The girls and Joe continued to watch.

"Here's my business card. Call me when you plan another trip to Vegas. Green Valley Ranch would be delighted to put you up in a comped suite."

"There is one favor you might be able to do for me. Could you score me two tickets to *Santana* at The Hard Rock Thursday night?"

"Probably. If I'm successful, I'll call you. They'll be on us, and you'll be able to claim 'em at Hard Rock's Will-Call window any time before the show."

"Thanks. I like shooting craps here. I'll be back."

"You're welcome here, anytime."

We shook hands again.

As we all left the VIP cashier window, I stuffed my pocket with the half-inch-thick stack of hundred-dollar bills, to hide the money from view. I had no desire to get robbed.

I skipped a couple of steps. "I turned down the offer on the comped suite because I thought it smart for us to remain back at the Trop with the girls for the rest of our trip. Besides, the inconvenience of repacking and moving out here didn't appeal to me."

Suzy's arms encircled me. We walked on a while.

"I wasn't aiming to win that much money today, all at one casino. I guess I got drawn up into the excitement for a change and lost track of my total. I was shocked when I realized I'd won so much. Got to learn to keep the wins on the small side in the future—or I'll become a two-faced hypocrite about wanting to keep my wins on the small side."

I waited no longer, whipping out the cell phone to call home.

"Guess what. I won about $13,000 shooting craps for an hour. I had to tell you!" I exclaimed to Mom when she answered.

"Great. That much? We're sure proud of you, Son."

"Keep on winning," Dad encouraged. "I wish I'd gotten to see it."

A few minutes later, I hung up. "You gals ready to do something touristy?"

"Yeah, provided I'm touristy with you at my side," Suzy said to me. "Maybe we can drive out to Boulder Dam, or the Grand Canyon?"

"I'm flush with newly-won money." I clapped my hands together. *This win does need celebrating. Dang.* "We should celebrate by taking a helicopter tour of Vegas and the Grand Canyon. How does that grab everybody? Big winner treats."

Everyone jumped on my offer. Now I had to deliver. I got on the phone and called three different tour companies before I found one that would let me make arrangements for a helicopter tour on such short notice.

"I'll pay extra if you can take us up right when we get there—in a little over an hour," I said into the phone. "How much? Fine. We'll be there. Thanks. The name? Ray Hitchcock."

We stopped by the Trop long enough to unload most of the cash into our new room's wall safe.

As instructed, we soon arrived at North Las Vegas Airport and took off in one of the twenty-six helicopters hangered there.

Our pilot acted as our tour guide. She pointed out points of interest on our headsets as they came into view. We flew over Hoover Dam and Lake Mead, which delighted Suzy and Beth. We reached The West Rim of the Grand Canyon and descended 3,200 feet to land on the canyon floor, where we appreciated the much cooler temperature.

Beth exclaimed, "Wow. Is this cool, or what? Who would have ever dreamed we'd be standing on the floor of the Grand Canyon after getting here by helicopter? Unreal."

"Champagne for everyone." The pilot passed out glasses, then popped the cork on the bottle of bubbly and filled everyone's glass.

"To good times," I toasted. We all clicked our glasses together and took a sip.

A few minutes later, Suzy finished her Champagne and handed her empty glass back to the pilot. "Thanks, Ray. Really. This is super."

Both girls planted kisses on my cheeks. Joe nodded thanks, too.

"You're all welcome. I'm liking this trip, myself," I said over the low whir of the idling helicopter engines.

I'll always remember how minuscule and unimportant being deep in the Grand Canyon made me feel. Time ceased. I experienced what I might feel like if I were a grain of sand on an ocean beach. The breathtaking, stark, multi-layered, colorful canyon walls surrounded us, and the Colorado River rushed by.

I imagined I'd get even more in tune with these strange sensations if I'd come down to the canyon floor on a mule train ride, or arrived floating on a raft from upriver.

We took in our brief glimpse of what others likely enjoyed when they hiked or rafted through these wild surroundings.

Right then and there, as I viewed the immenseness of the Grand Canyon, was the first time I actually appreciated having the ability I'd cultivated with tossing the dice. The canyon humbled me enough to realize what I'd accomplished. I'd actually done it. Long-felt hopes had finally become reality.

"What's wrong, Ray?" Suzy asked, wiping a tear from my cheek.

"The realization just hit me like a ton of bricks—that I've actually made it. That's all. That feeling's so freeing."

We hugged a really long hug. "You sure have. I haven't known you very long, but I'm really proud of you. I mean it."

We kissed and then hugged again as I held back another tear.

******

On our return trip, we cruised at low altitude right up Las Vegas Boulevard, taking in that spectacular view while all those casinos and hotels passed below us. People walking on The Strip below looked a few inches tall. When we landed, Beth said, "Find us a great restaurant. This time we're treating you guys, no arguments, either."

I laughed. "Someone request Mickey D's?"

Suzy punched me hard on my right shoulder. "They really have names for people like you."

"Such as?"

Suzy scrunched up her nose as she stuck out her tongue. "A-hole, for one."

"Oh, better watch that," I kidded, wagging a warning finger at her.

Our interplay caused Joe and Beth to chuckle.

Man, life sure had improved again today, especially when compared with how down everyone had been yesterday.

We drove up Las Vegas Boulevard again in our rented car. At the girls' suggestion, we went to Ellis Island Casino on North Koval Street, which paralleled The Strip a block away. It was a small locals' casino, restaurant, and microbrewery.

Beth said, "They offer a super steak dinner special for locals—which is off the menu. You have to know to ask for it to order it. The Las Vegas Advisor website and newsletter call it one of the best bargains in Vegas."

The girls directed us over to the bar at the microbrewery there. They got out their LVA Members coupon books and used them to start us each off with a free glass of beer. We then went to Ellis Island's restaurant, a friendly little place with two separate dining rooms. Their food and service proved outstanding. We ordered the steak specials the locals liked so much. The meal prices would never bust your budget either, and we loved the friendly atmosphere.

"This place could fast become one of my favorites," I told Suzy. "I'm glad you had us come here."

A karaoke bar with three small booths and a short bar sat less than twenty feet off to the side of the restaurant's seating area. We had no choice but to listen to the singers while we ate. Some of their voices could curdle milk.

Toward the end of our meal, Suzy glanced over at Beth and shot her an inquisitive look. She received a slight head nod in return, then excused herself to go to the restroom.

Suzy returned to our booth, then the guy on the karaoke bar's PA announced, "Now here are twin sisters Suzy and Beth, from Cincinnati. They'll sing "Stairway to Heaven."

My jaw dropped open. I whipped my head around, looking first at the bar area where the announcement had come from, then back at Suzy and Beth.

So this is what the little look between the girls was all about?

Our ladies rose and moved those few feet to the bar area and picked up microphones. We moved to where they were, looking first at each other, then at them. They belted out a great-sounding rendition of one of my favorite oldies rock songs.

We listened and clapped along while they sang. We couldn't help but be amazed at how good they were and how well they harmonized. By the end of their song, Joe and I wore ear-to-ear grins. Everyone in the area kept time to the music by clapping their hands. Joe and I silently mouthed the words as we listened to the girls sing. Thunderous applause erupted when their song ended.

Suzy and Beth took their bows and threw kisses to the small group who had enjoyed their performance.

"Bravo! Amazing!" I exclaimed, still clapping as the girls returned to our sides.

Joe put two fingertips in his mouth and blew out a loud shrill whistle of appreciation. "Beth, you never even mentioned you could sing. What a surprise. You're fantastic."

We both gave big hugs and kisses to our ladies—a couple of times.

Beth bowed. "Thanks, guys. We always sing together at parties and family gatherings."

Suzy added, "That's really one of our favorite songs. Glad you liked it."

They got out their LVA two-for-one meal coupons and used them when they paid for our meals.

"Those things come in handy," I said.

"Wouldn't be without 'em." Suzy gave me a flirty wink.

"We thank you girls for the meal."

Giving us kisses, the ladies took a for-real restroom break. Joe and I used the opportunity to wander out onto Ellis Island's casino floor in front of the restaurant. We examined the little eight-foot craps table Doctor Bones had discussed at dealer's school. It wasn't in use. They told us it would open up later in the evening when the locals got active.

Joe asked, "Can you win on it?"

"I doubt I'd be able to adapt my pitch to work at such a short range. A softer toss would translate into less dice rotation, so the dice would probably go off axis. If I tried, I might screw up my play on normal tables. Besides, we need to put a larger dent in the supply of full-size tables in town."

The girls rejoined us.

Joe asked them, "Anyone up for casino hopping?"

"Sure," they said.

I asked Suzy, "Have you been downtown to check out the Fremont Street Experience?"

"Nope. I read it's supposed to have more the flavor of Old Vegas." She took my hand.

"That's the idea. I did well shooting craps there earlier this weekend, and we soaked up the friendly atmosphere there." I pulled her nearer. "Should we go? Or would you rather check out some of those flashier casinos on The Strip?"

Joe said, "Let's take them downtown. They can shoot some craps again, and we'll be the ones watching. Would you girls like to toss some dice?"

Beth said, "Fantastic. Let's go."

Suzy added, "We're really going to be craps stars, like Ray. Yeah, baby."

"Um, results never guaranteed," I said, "We're going to do this for fun. And please, gamble only with money you can afford to lose, okay?"

Both girls agreed.

******

We soon pulled into the valet parking at the Fremont. Once inside, we found a half-full craps table and bellied up. Both girls bought in for fifty dollars each.

Suzy shot first. Her first throw showed seven—which, to her delight, won her come-out pass-line bet. I told her to rack her winnings and shoot again. She threw a ten.

I said, "You need to throw another ten to win. Your best hope for winning is having me plant a good-luck kiss on your sweet lips."

She informed me—with her devilish look and scrunched-up eyebrows—she disbelieved me regarding that kiss, but she kissed me anyway. She threw a few trash numbers, then an easy ten to win her bet. She hopped up and down ecstatically.

I asked, "Are we having fun?" I gave her another kiss.

"Loving it."

"You've won ten dollars. Great." I said. "Congratulations, win again."

She tossed a seven again, for another come-out five-dollar win. She established five for her point, but then threw another seven to end her turn.

Beth proved less lucky. She established her point on nine, then threw another nine for a win. After getting a five to establish her point, she threw a seven out.

"Aw, heck," she protested when her dealer took her five-dollar bet and she learned she had to wait to shoot again.

"Your luck may turn." Joe pulled her closer, kissing her.

She pouted. "Yeah, but I wanted to throw the dice some more."

"Be patient. You might win a little money betting on a competent shooter, if we spot one."

I added, "The dice'll work their way around the table and you'll shoot again."

I held Suzy close, appreciating the pressure of her tight body pressing against mine.

The next two rollers were random rollers, so we told Suzy and Beth not to bet. The next player proved to be a precision shooter with a smooth delivery. He set the dice and made his numbers.

I told the girls, "Here's one you can bet on."

After that shooter won his point, we told them to bet five dollars on the pass line for the come-out roll. He tossed an eight. He soon tossed another eight, and our girls each showed a five-dollar profit.

They celebrated.

I told them, "Leave your five-dollar pass-line bet out there."

They both did.

The shooter threw a hard eight and a nine, then another winning eight. The dealer paid off the girls' bets. They won again on that shooter's opening seven. He tossed a four, then a losing seven out.

"He used my favorite V3 dice set. Those two four-three sevens he threw, close to each other, told me one die over rotated by two die faces," I whispered to Joe.

Suzy's turn to shoot arrived again. She put down her bet and tossed a winning eleven. Her dealer surprised her when he passed a five-dollar chip her way.

"Do they toss money each time I throw an eleven?"

"Only on your first throw." I kept the explanation simple.

Suzy winked at me, picked up her dice, and tossed a seven then received another five-dollar chip.

"I'm really doing pretty good, right?"

"You're sensational." I gave her a quick kiss.

Her next toss showed a one-one, craps. The dealer quickly whisked away her five-dollar pass-line bet. He was nice enough to smile when he did it.

"He took my bet," she protested. "Why?"

"Rolling a craps—a one-one, two-one or six-six—loses on the first toss after a point's been won."

"There are too many rules to this game," she complained.

I agreed, stroking her hair.

She threw a nine, then tossed a losing seven.

Beth, a random roller in the truest sense, opened with two winning sevens.

"Baby needs a new pair of shoes," she said, quickly adding, "I heard that in a movie somewhere."

Joe looked at me and rolled his eyes. I stifled a laugh.

She established her point on four, but came right back with a losing seven.

"I guess we aren't exactly burning up the table, are we? But at least we're having all kinds of fun trying. Winning consistently is a lot harder than the illusion Ray creates with his tosses."

Joe said, "It demands you appreciate what he does, cranking out all those sixes and eights."

The girls indicated they'd played enough. We wandered outside for them to view the overhead LED canopy lightshow—the signature of the Fremont Street Experience—which we could tell from inside the casino had begun. They were impressed. Having someone special to snuggle with as I watched it made the light show a lot more fun than when Joe and I had experienced it alone.

After the light show ended, we encountered a spray-can street artist sitting cross-legged on the sidewalk making stupendous 11"x14" spray paintings nearby. He had about a ten-foot-square area roped off to work in and display his wares. We found ourselves transfixed by the speed and ease he used to create the paintings—using only ordinary cans of spray paint.

He modified each application of color—swiping the paint on the surface this way and the other with crumpled-up newspapers. He even blotted the paintings with the newspaper and used it to mask off and control where the paint got applied.

We cuddled together as couples while he produced three or four mini masterpieces over a twenty-minute span. We'd never witnessed anything like what he did. He put on quite a show and kept us entertained.

The painting being created suddenly became recognizable as a dolphin jumping out of the water in back-lit moonlight. I spoke up, "I like the dolphin. What'll it cost me?"

"Forty-five dollars."

"Sold." When he finished, I paid him.

Before he allowed me to claim my painting, he said, "You'll have to wait five minutes for the paint to set up, before you can have it.

When I got it, I gave the painting to Suzy, along with a kiss and a hug.

She didn't restrain her enthusiasm as her eyes beamed with delight. She jumped into my arms, still holding the painting. I spun her around, then kissed her lips and squeezed her tight.

"Vegas is really wonderful," she said, her toes still not touching the ground.

"Anywhere you are is wonderful." I winked. I wouldn't have traded that moment, with her cuddled in my arms, for all the diamonds in Antwerp.

Dare we hope all this will work out with the girls the way we want it to?

Chapter Thirteen — Wednesday

Joe's phone rang at six a.m. Beth sounded alarmed, "Joe, we need you two up here right away."

"What's up, babe?"

"Someone broke into our room during the night and stole money from Suzy's purse. She's upset and crying."

"We'll be there in a flash. Bye."

Joe and I raced each other getting dressed, then waited impatiently for the elevator. After knocking on the girls' door as soon as we arrived, we slipped inside the moment it opened. A hotel security officer was asking Suzy questions and taking notes.

"All my money's really gone from my purse." Suzy appeared upset and on the verge of tears.

"Who are these two guys?" The security officer looked us up and down.

"They're our friends we called before you arrived," Beth said. "We asked them to rush right up."

I went to Suzy's side and embraced her. "We're sorry this happened. You must have been terrified."

"Boyfriends?" the security guy asked, pointing at us.

"Yeah, I guess you could say that." Suzy smiled over at me.

Losing interest in Joe and me, he asked Suzy, "Where'd you leave your purse?"

"On the bench at the foot of the bed."

"You locked your door, with your security chain in place?"

"Yes, we really did," Suzy said.

"Did your door click shut? Did the safety chain get put in place?"

"I really think so," Suzy replied.

"Either of you leave your room after settling in?"

Beth looked sheepish. "I bought Cokes from the vending machine outside and got ice from the machine down the hall. I don't remember if our door clicked or not."

"Always be careful; double check those things," the security officer said. "People called *door pushers* earn their living by stealing from guest's rooms. That's true all over Vegas. They trick an unsuspecting guest into letting them inside the locked complex, then push on each room door, on every floor. When a room door opens, they slip in and steal what they can grab. Usually, they're back out of the room in thirty seconds."

I raised an eyebrow as I listened.

"They often use a pretty girl to gain entry into the locked towers," he said. "She'll arrive at the same time as a male guest and fumble like she's hunting for her room key. The guy, wanting to be a gentleman, holds the door open and lets her enter. She'll go back in a few minutes and let her buddies in."

Studying the clipboard, the security officer added, "The hotels stay silent about door pushers because they don't want to scare guests away, but it's pretty much an open secret all over town."

"They really come inside and steal stuff while you sleep?" Suzy asked, a panicked look on her face. "I've been violated. Wouldn't we be in danger if we woke up and really caught them red-handed?"

"Yup, afraid so." The security officer wrote something on a form. "They're pretty bold and willing to do almost anything to avoid getting caught. Unless we catch them before they leave our premises, there's little we can do to recover what's been stolen. It's gone. Please, be more careful in the future."

The security officer promised to file a report, but told Suzy, "Don't expect to get your money back. You're lucky they stole only your money. They could have taken your purse, along with all your identification and credit cards."

"Oh, God," Suzy moaned, "Without ID, how would I board our plane?"

The security officer shrugged. "Not my problem." He then double-checked their phone numbers and left.

"How much money did they steal?" I asked, snuggling Suzy in the safety of my arms.

"My walking-around money, more than $475," she replied. "The money really isn't important. I'll replace it at an ATM. The idea someone came into our room—as we slept—really scares and angers me."

I took five hundred-dollar bills out of my billfold and gave them to Suzy. "Use this to hold you over until you replace your money." I gave her a strong, protective hug.

Beth took both of Joe's hands in hers and walked him backwards a few steps. I was grateful. Suzy and I needed this private moment. And they needed theirs, too.

"Oh, Ray, you're wonderful." She nestled against me. "I really love you," she declared, smiling, then lost herself in a deeply-romantic kiss.

I held her even tighter. "I'm very much in love with you."

I continued to cuddle Suzy, and did my best to comfort her. Her getting robbed crushed me.

Suzy whispered, "My hero, I'm really glad we found each other."

I rested my forehead on hers. "Me, too, precious."

"I'd love to have caught 'em red-handed. I'd have whopped on them something fierce," I whispered. "Say, it couldn't have been your ex-boyfriend Tony, could it?"

Her face fell.

If I could have stuffed that question right back into my mouth so that I hadn't asked it, I would have. What was I thinking? We didn't need to have Suzy all worked up again over Tony. Especially since there hadn't been anything to indicate it was him.

"On second thought, I don't see how it could have been, this soon," I reassured Suzy. "Tony wouldn't have had time to get to Vegas, track you down, and figure out the room switch we did. If anything, he would have gone to your old room downstairs."

The tension that had been on Suzy's face from my mention of Tony disappeared. The room went quiet.

Gathering my nerve, I looked Suzy squarely in the eyes, drew myself closer, and whispered to her. "You mean the world to me. Am I going to lose you when we have to return home Friday? It's been weighing on my mind. Time here is flying by, and now our going home is rushing right at us. I never want to lose what we have and feel for each other." I sniffled, welling up with overwhelming heartfelt emotion.

"No way." She glanced up lovingly. "I'm yours, now and always." She dabbed her tears away, then demanded, "Let's get out of here. We really have some living it up to do."

Bad things were put aside, and emotions and commitments got declared.

******

Over breakfast, Suzy asked if anyone else noticed the signs posted all around the Trop advertising being able to win $1,000 if you beat the tic-tac-toe-playing chicken at the Trop.

I interrupted to ask Joe to pass the ketchup.

Beth suggested, "Maybe we should take a shot, might be fun."

I whispered to Joe. "Maybe one of us can win the money to replace what got stolen from Suzy."

Beth asked the person at the cash register how to find where the chicken tic-tac-toe game was being played. We received directions and everyone soon stood in a line of twenty people waiting for a turn to play either of two chickens.

I overheard someone standing in line say, "That tic-tac-toe board is rigged to a computer that tips off the chickens on which square to pick. Their computer drops a kernel of corn into the right cubicle on the tic-tac-toe board each time it's the chicken's turn. Then the chicken pecks the corn to eat it, which selects their square."

My ears perked up at hearing that. Maybe beating the chicken wouldn't be easy, after all. I consoled myself. They're probably not in the habit of giving out the $1,000 prize very often or they wouldn't be doing it.

We each took our turn trying to out-figure the chicken. The best any of us did was win a tie match against our chicken, which didn't win anybody the $1,000 prize. I was the last one in our group to try. A young woman standing directly behind me then beat the chicken and won the $1,000. Buzzers went off, lights flashed, and confetti dropped.

I asked, "Why didn't that chicken screw up a few seconds earlier so one of us could win?"

We all missed out on some easy money, by a few seconds. We hung around, curious what would happen next for the winner.

A man wearing a suit and carrying a clipboard appeared out of nowhere. The winner and her friends were moved to a table at the side of the game display to allow play to continue.

They congratulated her and took down her personal information, then told her it would take half an hour for someone to pay her the prize money, because they had to drive all the way across town with her winnings.

"So darned close," Joe said. "Missed out."

I said, "I wish one of us had won. I didn't need it, but I sure would have loved for Suzy to have walked away with that prize money."

"We're in Vegas." Beth said. "Win some, lose some."

I suggested we squeeze in a stunt acrobatic plane ride near Bolder City, Nevada. I called their phone number I had stored in my phone and discovered we'd lucked out due to a couple of no-shows and one last-minute cancellation.

The voice on the other end asked me, "When can you be here?"

"We're leaving from the Tropicana right now."

We all headed off to the address near Boulder City, arriving at a tiny rural two-hanger airport. *Stunt Plane Rides* proclaimed the sign on the side of one hanger. We met our pilot to be.

His stunt plane was a single-prop single-winged two-seater. He piloted it from the front seat, with room for one passenger behind him.

"My plane is the most acrobatically-capable plane flying today," he informed us proudly. "Each ride is under an hour long. I'll need to refuel after our second flight, but I'll work you all in for the rides of your lives."

Waiting around became boring for the non-passengers back at the hanger office, but the stunt ride he took each of us on proved, indeed, to be the biggest thrill any of us ever experienced—something everyone will remember until the day they die. I paid for Suzy's and my rides, while Joe treated Beth to the $185 ride.

We played rock-paper-scissors each time to determine our ride order. Those waiting on the ground watched TV, checked for texts on our phones, or played Solitaire with the deck of cards in the waiting area. We also discussed everything we had done since hitting Vegas.

When my turn came, the pilot taught me how to communicate via our headsets. He then strapped me into the seat, using what he referred to as a five-point restraint.

He assured me, "The restraint will keep you from falling out of the cockpit while we're flying upside down. You're going to swear nothing is keeping you from falling to the desert floor 3,000 feet below, and you'll swear you're hanging in midair—but, in reality, your butt will only be an inch or two off your seat. You're safe in your harness. You should keep repeating that fact to yourself when you believe your life's ready to end."

I rolled my eyes. "Oh, boy. Thanks a lot."

After take-off, we flew low over Bolder Dam and Lake Mead to reach the vast and empty lifeless-appearing Mojave Desert.

"Did you eat a hearty breakfast this morning?" he asked over the headset.

"A light one," I replied, a knot already twisting in my stomach.

"Good. Roger that. You'll find a bright yellow plastic barf bag alongside your left elbow. Use that barf bag if your breakfast comes back up. I'm not too thrilled about cleaning up the aircraft between flights. Roger that?"

"Roger," I squeaked.

"You may've noticed our public showers back at the hanger office, too. Those are to allow you to clean up, should you lose breakfast all over yourself during our maneuvers." A few minutes later he came back over the headset, "Ready for some fun?"

"I'll never be more prepared," I replied, then swallowed hard.

"A video camera is located over your right shoulder behind you. It's recording our flight and everything you experience, along with our headset conversations. You may purchase a copy when we return to the airfield. That video makes a heck of a conversation piece to share with your folks back home on a rainy night. Roger that?"

He announced each aerobatic stunt beforehand, telling me what to expect. He began with a series of 360-degree slow rolls.

"So this is what being inverted is like?" My butt wasn't touching the seat. Blood rushed to my head. It took effort to breathe.

"You'll receive plenty of opportunities during our flight today to figure out if you enjoy it or not. Roger, that?"

Where did he say the barf bag was? My breakfast hovered about two inches below my Adam's apple.

Now we'll be doing a hammer-head stall, where I climb straight up with engines at full throttle till our plane stalls to a complete stop, then dip one wing to bring our plane out of its stall and start diving straight at the ground below." He sounded calm. "But don't worry, I'll try to remember to pull up before impact with the ground."

Oh, boy. A comedian. I swallowed foul-tasting bile

He did the hammer-head stall while my life passed before my eyes as the ground rushed up at us. True to his word, he pulled out of the dive fifty feet off the ground.

I might need to change underwear when we land.

"Now we're going to do an inside vertical loop. I'll take our plane up at a sharp angle, force it over backwards at the top of the circle, and dive back down to complete our loop."

Yup, there we were, diving back down toward the ground again at the end of this stunt.

I fumbled around for the barf bag. *Where is it?*

I somehow controlled my inner beast and resisted upchucking. Everything stopped near my Adam's apple, but I could still taste it. I envisioned the worst before our flight ended.

Every once in a while, after a stunt, the pilot would ask, "How we doing back there? Use your barf bag yet? Want more stunts?"

I replied, "Bring it on. This is the world's best roller coaster."

"Roger that. No tracks or rails up here, though. Stunt flying makes roller coasters appear tame by comparison. Now we're going to flip our plane upside down and fly inverted for a while. Remember, your life isn't going to end. You won't fall through the canopy to the desert floor below, but you'll probably believe you're going to. Roger that?"

The video of our flight recorded me saying, "Holy, S___!" half way through that inverted flight.

I'm going to die! I'm going to die! No way the harness will keep me from crashing to the barren desert floor thousands of feet below. I don't even have a parachute. Nothing but an ultra-thin Plexiglas canopy existed between me and the ground.

"For our next stunt, we're going to do a series of four-point snap rolls. Our plane will be flying parallel to the ground throughout this maneuver. I'll snap the plane's controls to the left to line up our wings perpendicular to the horizon, snap our plane inverted, then snap our wings perpendicular to the horizon in the opposite direction. Finally, if I still remember how, I'll return us to our normal upright flying position."

"If you ever quit your job, you should become a comedian. You must get off by torturing people."

"Roger that. It's good for business."

"Now I understand why you had cancellations and no-shows today." *When is this going to be over?* More bile. *Yuck.*

"Roger that. It happens from time to time."

Our next death-defying stunt promised to be an inside loop with a half roll at the top, so that when we pulled out at the last second—a few feet above ground level to complete our loop—we'd be approaching the ground inverted.

Now when I experienced the ground rushing up at me, I realized we'd be inverted when we pulled out at the last second. I kept the barf bag in hand for this one, just in case. Half way through the maneuver, a chill ran through me to my very bones and didn't release its grip.

"Makes you pray, doesn't it?" I said into the headset while still inverted a hundred feet off the ground as we completed the maneuver. I became light headed.

Whose idea was this? Oh yeah, mine.

"Roger that. Nothing like getting your morning prayers in; except up here, you mean 'em." The pilot chuckled.

After several additional death-defying stunts that commanded my heart to jump free of my chest, he announced, "Well, I'm glad we shared this experience. We've done everything an aerobatic stunt pilot does at air shows. I hope you've had fun and will tell others about us. We can use all the referrals we can get. Now, sit back, relax, and absorb the beauty of the desert scenery below while I turn this thing around—and head us back to our base."

"Roger that." Instant relief flooded me as my stomach settled.

"Darn. I should have put fuel in this thing before we took off."

I couldn't even see him to tell what he was doing, or what was going on. I stiffened in my seat.

After a couple of seconds, he came back on the headset. "Just kidding. We have plenty of fuel for another flight. Roger that?"

"Roger that." Worries were once again relieved. I melted into the seat. "This is the most fun I've ever had while thumbing my nose at death."

Color came back into my cheeks when I planted my feet back on the ground.

Beth took the final stunt flight. We all went outside waving as she took off. Joe turned to Suzy and me. "I bet this adventure will satisfy her thrill-ride-seeking desires for a long time to come."

******

"Say, we haven't shot any craps yet," Joe said when Beth returned to the hanger office. "What are we going to do about that?"

"We're going by Green Valley Ranch on our way back to Vegas. I'm sure they'd appreciate me bringing some of their money back to their table, so they get another shot or two at winning it back."

"That's why they offered you a comped suite for the rest of our stay. They'd like to get some shots at recovering their losses. They're convinced they still hold the long-term advantage over you."

I motioned like I was tossing dice. "If my toss is still on, I want everyone to win some money."

Back again at Green Valley Ranch, I went through my offsetting warm-up bets, judged my toss as working, then won the five-step progression bet in nine tosses. I racked up $699 in chips.

Joe congratulated me. "You're hot."

I shrugged and tried to run the progression again. After decreasing my bets to thirty-six dollars each, I reached the fourth stage of the progression and collected my $161 in winnings at that level. But I fell short and tossed a seven out.

Yet, I was still $788 ahead for the session.

I received the dice back twenty minutes later and ran the progression again. I took my winnings and left my bet up for one additional win, then brought the wagers back down. I threw two sixes and another eight before tossing a seven out.

Everyone congratulated me when I colored up, receiving almost $1,600 for my effort.

"Can we be comped for meals for four, please?" I asked the pit boss, who checked my level and length of play, then scribbled something on a form he handed me.

"Enjoy your meals. Rejoin us when you're done."

"Oooh," Suzy said. "Really, they give you free meals for shooting craps?"

"Yeah, babe." I kissed her. "And a lot more, if you guarantee the house enough betting action."

Beth and Suzy hugged and thanked me, then smooched both my cheeks.

I told Joe when we both visited the bathroom, "I played until Suzy won enough to replace her stolen money. I needed her to be whole again."

The Green Valley Ranch Buffet tasted sensational. Everyone shared conversation and the enjoyable company.

"How about slowing things down for a while? Maybe go for a swim back at the Trop?" I asked.

Everyone concurred. That sounded pretty good about now. Back at the Trop, we put on our swim trunks and headed for a relaxed, revitalizing dip in their splendid tropical pool. After an hour spent poolside, I called Joe aside.

My voice came out sounding mysterious and urgent. "Joe, I need to talk to you for a minute, alone."

We walked a bit farther away from the girls so our conversation wouldn't be overheard.

"Joe, how do you feel about Beth? Are you in love with her?"

"Oh, yes. Head over heels, Ray," Joe admitted.

"I'm going to ask Suzy to marry me tonight. Want to make it a double wedding?"

"You are? A double-proposal? I don't know. That's mighty risky. I'm not sure Beth would say 'yes'. What if she doesn't? I'll be devastated." Joe took a deep breath and got fidgety.

"I don't know if Suzy will say 'yes', either, but they can't if we don't ask 'em. If they say 'no', we'd have to suck it up and live with it."

"How'll we propose?" Joe asked.

"Leave that to me, Bro." I winked.

"Let's do it."

We rejoined the girls. "Joe and I've got a quick errand we need to run. We'll be back soon, promise."

Both girls looked at each other with raised, questioning eyebrows. Suzy locked eyes with me. "Don't be gone too long, okay?"

"Will you wait for us?" I asked.

Beth looked less than totally happy. "We might be here when you get back."

Less than an hour later, we were back again. The girls weren't at poolside, so I nervously called Suzy to see where they were. Them not still being at the pool worried me.

"We're playing slots inside. Come join us," Suzy said.

As soon as we rejoined the girls in the slot area, I kissed Suzy, then reached into my pocket and took out the ring box containing the engagement ring I'd purchased. I dropped down on one knee at Suzy's feet.

"Will you marry me and be my soul mate for a lifetime, Suzy? I love you with all my heart." I opened the ring box and took the ring out, then slipped it onto her ring finger.

Her face lit up as tears became visible. "Yes, Ray. I will." We hugged and kissed.

I looked over at Joe. It was now his turn to propose.

"Congratulations, Beth and Ray." He swallow hard, fingering the ring box in his pocket.

Both girls hugged then began to sob. Suzy gushed in a rush, "Ray and I are getting married!" She cried tears of joy.

Beth's face lit up. "Oh, I'm overjoyed for you, Sis. You, too, Ray."

When Joe shook my hand, I gave him an inquisitive look. He only shrugged.

Guess now's not the time.

We all kissed and hugged, sharing our emotions and feelings of love for one another. Everyone nearby whistled and clapped, while gambling in the area momentarily came to a halt.

Joe told Suzy, "I'm going to be getting myself a sister."

Suzy looked at Joe. "I'm going to have a new brother."

I looked at Suzy. "Care to set a wedding date, babe? The sooner the better, as far as I'm concerned."

Suzy replied, "Friday afternoon, if that's alright with you, Ray—and if we can make it happen by then. Let's do it right here in Vegas."

"Perfect." I flashed her a thumbs up. "This is the marriage capital of the world. I think we can make this happen on Friday. We can find out."

"Should we see if our parents can come to Vegas to attend our wedding?" I asked. "If they aren't too pissed off over us getting married in Vegas."

"Let me be somewhere else when you tell Mom and Dad," Joe said to me. "They might even become pissed at me. They entrusted me to keep you safe and make sure nothing happened to you."

"You were supposed to not let anything bad happen to me. What's happening isn't bad. It's great."

"I hope Mom and Dad see things the way you do."

"Beth, what's your take on how it'll really play out with Mom and Dad?" Suzy asked.

"We need to call them right away," Beth pointed out. "If they're going to be given a chance to attend your wedding."

"There is another possibility," Joe said. "You could get married and tell them later. They're going to be mad, no matter what. A lot of times it's easier to beg forgiveness than it is to be granted permission. Having mad parents here might spoil your wedding."

"You might wait and plan a wedding back home for later on, too," Beth suggested. "That's another option to consider."

Suzy and I whispered back and forth in each other's ear. Joe and Beth exchanged inquisitive looks. Our conversation didn't last long.

"Ray and I both really want to have our wedding in Vegas. It's where we met and fell in love. We really can't stand being apart and not seeing each other, or having to wait to start our lives together. I'm going to be living in Iowa with Ray."

I cracked my knuckles all at once. "We're going to take Joe's advice: get married, then ask forgiveness."

Joe combed fingers through his hair. "Ray, you'd better never tell Mom and Dad it was my idea. They'll never forgive me."

"Let's drive up to one of those wedding chapels," I said, "and learn what we need to do to make this happen come Friday."

Suzy agreed.

******

At one of the smaller wedding chapels on The Strip, they told us a marriage license cost sixty dollars. They went online for us and reserved us a reference number with the Clark County Marriage License Bureau. It would let us proceed to the express service lane there to obtain our marriage license anytime during business hours.

We only needed our driver's licenses, since we both met the age requirement. No blood tests. No waiting period. We could show up anytime with our marriage license in hand and be married when any other wedding going on there ended. We could even get married without ever leaving our car if we wanted to drive up to the chapel's express drive-thru marriage lane.

We all examined their package options.

We decided we'd purchase the "True Love Package" for $239. It included chapel use, music, minister, use of flowers, boutonnieres, a few digital photos, witnesses if needed, and champagne toasts during the complimentary limo ride to the chapel.

As soon as Joe and I were alone, I asked him, "What happened, Joe? I thought you were going to propose to Beth, too?"

"When the time came, I couldn't pull the trigger."

"Cold feet?"

"But that doesn't mean I'm not still going to ask Beth to marry me. For one thing, I didn't want to encroach on your moment with Suzy. You deserved that all to yourselves without me stealing any of your thunder."

"Well, thanks, Bro. I see your point. Any idea when you're going to pop the question?"

"Soon, Ray. I think it'll be soon."

******

"Let's go to the Stratosphere," Suzy said. "It features a couple of really wild rides way up high on top of their casino. I believe they offer the tallest observation platform in town, too. Let's ride the rides there and take in the night view of The Strip from up high."

"Sounds romantic." I kissed Suzy, then she kissed me.

When we arrived at the Strat, we bought tickets and boarded the express elevator going to the top of the structure. While we waited for more passengers to board, Rose, the young female elevator operator, asked, "Any first-timers here?"

We all raised our hands.

"Anyone going to ride the rides up top?" Rose asked.

We all raised our hands again.

Rose punched the button to start the elevator. "We'll be at the top of our 1,149 foot tall building in about thirty-seven seconds."

"Really? That fast?" Suzy asked.

"We're averaging about twenty-one miles-per-hour," Rose said. "We'll be arriving at the 114th floor before you know it. You might want to chew gum or swallow on the way up, to help avoid your ears popping and relieve the pressure."

The elevator proved to be a thrill ride in itself.

We rode Big Shot, which held us all at once and launched us straight upward, similar to an airplane pilot's ejection seat ejecting and then floated us back down again with a few random jolting jerks along its way.

Suzy and Beth insisted we ride Big Shot again. We did, purchasing everyone souvenir photos showing the terrorized expressions at the top of the ride on Joe's and my faces.

The girls didn't look terrorized at all.

Suzy beamed. "Wow, what fun."

Beth said, "Let's ride X-Scream."

Suzy and I rushed into the front seat the first time we rode X-Scream—a new ride that hung out over the edge of the Strat. Its beam extended our car out far beyond the edge of the building. The car lunged down the tilted beam, breaking free four times, each time diving farther down the beam toward the street more than a thousand feet below. It always screeched to a jolting halt when we swore we were doomed.

Beth insisted she get a turn in the front seat, so we rode X-Scream again. Twice proved more than enough for me.

I've tried to figure out how they accomplished the ride's thrilling effects. The best explanation I can come up with is maybe the car didn't move down the beam, at all? Instead, maybe it was fixed in place at the end of the beam? Maybe an extension section got released each time the car broke free—using sections nested inside each other, like on an old-time telescoping car-radio antenna—with each section being quickly extended by hydraulics?

We took an elevator down a floor or two to their 360-degree glass-enclosed observation deck. There, we basked in the sensational panorama of The Vegas Strip lit up in glittering neon glory for young lovers to drink in, nestled in the arms of our mates. We appreciated being surrounded by such a romantic view late at night—with no kids running around to create any mood-breaking interruptions.

We understood words without them being spoken. We drank in the beauty and glitter spread out before us and the nearness of those we loved. Everyone wanted to stay. Right then, no better place on Earth existed.

Joe gathered his nerve, then took the ring box out and opened it before Beth noticed. In one swift movement, he took her hand and slipped the ring on her finger. "Beth, I love you. Will you be my wife?" He kissed her before she could answer.

She looked first at the ring on her finger then at him. She froze stiff. Looking him in the eye, she sighed and slowly shook her head no.

"Joe, I love you, too." She lowered her head. "But I can't answer that question right now. I'm not ready for marriage. I don't want to hurt your feelings, but that's the way things are right now. I'm so sorry." Then she took the engagement ring off her finger and handed it back to him, with a tear running down her cheek.

She had probably torn his heart to shreds. "Okay then, can we pretend I never asked and go on like I never had?"

She kissed him as another tear ran down her cheek. She looked up into his eyes. "Sure. If you want to. That would be fine with me."

Joe wiped away the tear and pulled her close and hugged her tight. She returned the hug. They shifted their attention again to the panorama of twinkling light that lay before us, as Joe handed her a handkerchief to dry her eyes. They remained in each other's embrace cheek to cheek for quite some time.

I felt terrible for Joe. I wanted to disappear right into the floor. I didn't think they even realized Suzy and I were within earshot and heard and saw everything. We silently stepped away, putting distance between us and them so they wouldn't suddenly realize we'd been privy to their scene.

Joe, why didn't you ask her in private?

When they rejoined us, I broke the silence. "I believe the Strat has some craps tables on the casino level. Let's find out if they're friendly."

Suzy and I strolled together behind Beth and Joe over to the elevator door. Back at casino level, I bellied up to my choice of craps tables. My first turn tossing the dice showed a nine, then a quick off-axis seven-out.

"Not what I hoped for," I said. "At least with offsetting warm-up bets out, my first turn cost me nothing."

My second turn began with both dice jumping straight left upon impact.

As the dice came to rest, our stickman chanted, "Six-one, seven. Winner seven on the come-out roll."

No win with the offsetting warm-up bet in place.

"I've never witnessed my dice jump sideways together on impact." I shook my head. The next toss kissed off the back wall and rolled back together to establish five as the point to make.

Our stickman yelled to me, "Throw the dice harder."

I threw again, this time producing an eight.

Again, the stickman shouted, "Throw harder."

I protested, "I'm hitting the far end wall on every toss."

Our stickman ignored what I said.

I popped a nine.

"Throw harder." the stickman again yelled, pointing his stick at me.

I launched the dice with extra force. One die landed in the empty chip rail at the distant table end. The other die cleared the back rail, disappearing somewhere into the darkness under the craps table behind ours.

"Dice down," the loud-mouthed stickman called out.

Everything stopped at both tables while everyone scrambled to find and retrieve the missing die.

I locked eyes with our stickman and asked him, "Hard enough for you?"

A couple of minutes passed while casino personnel hunted for that missing die. They made darned sure nobody ever walked out of their casino with a house die from one of their live games. The Nevada Gambling Commission probably required that kind of protection.

The dice again passed to me when they'd found their lost die. This time our stickman said nothing about me needing to throw harder. My toss again found both dice hopping straight sideways to the left upon table impact—producing a hard eight. I had somehow completed my point.

"Tell ya what," I said to the dealer, "Color me up. I'm through trying to shoot here." We went to change our chips back into cash.

"I've never seen my dice both bounce straight sideways together, in the same direction. I have a sneaking suspicion they might have one corner of their table jacked up a bit to warp the surface. There's no other way to explain the dice's behavior."

We all agreed to return to the Trop and pull the curtain closed on this day, which had been crammed with excitement, joy, and disappointment. Beth had rejected Joe's proposal. I had won about $1600 shooting craps, and my game seemed back on track again. What put my day over the top was Suzy saying "Yes" to my proposal.

Beth's old boyfriend Tony crossed my mind again when I thought about us all going back to different rooms tonight.

******

Once back at the Trop, we all strolled down by their outdoor pool before going to our rooms. Suzy and I cuddled near Joe and Beth. I was looking over at Joe to see how he was taking everything when I heard him say something to Beth.

"I'm going to have to call the police first thing tomorrow." Joe cuddled Beth and brushed back her blonde hair and kissed her lips.

"Why, what's wrong?"

"I've checked around everywhere for it, but it's lost." He gazed deeply into her eyes.

"What have you lost?" She flashed Joe her flirty smile and gave him a tight hug. They kissed again.

Joe whispered just loud enough for me to hear, "My heart. You've stolen it."

"Oh, Joe, I feel that same way about you. I hope I haven't hurt you too bad." She rested her cheek on his chest then kissed him deeply.

I suddenly felt like a peeping Tom again.

Damn, I'm going to have to teach that boy how to court in private.

Mom and Dad, please forgive us.

I thought of what all to avoid telling them when we called. '*We met some girls. Oh, by the way, I'm getting married. Hello, Mom? Hello, Dad? Anybody there?' Yikes.*

Will Joe ever get a chance to change Beth's mind?

Chapter Fourteen — Thursday

Joe and I'd had plenty to discuss before going to sleep last night. Suzy and Beth probably did, too. Everyone was excited. During breakfast, we all were full of ideas concerning Suzy's and my upcoming wedding.

"Let's pick up our marriage license this morning," I suggested.

Between bites of bacon, Joe asked, "If Suzy's coming to Council Bluffs with us, how are we going to get her there? We won't be able to book her on the same flight we're on. It's tomorrow."

"Beth and I really discussed it last night. Let's use our rental car to drive there."

Beth sipped her coffee. "It's a twenty hour drive. We could break it into two days."

"We'll leave right after an early morning wedding tomorrow," Suzy suggested.

Beth said, "We should come up with something to tell your parents to avoid them worrying when you guys aren't on your flight."

"Possibly, you're really extending your stay for another day?"

Joe asked sarcastically, "We're going to show up back home, unannounced, with a new bride in hand?"

"Any way you slice it," Beth said, "there's got to be a wee-tiny fib told if we're going to pull this off without much bloodshed."

Suzy and I nodded.

"Maybe we should tell Mom and Dad right after your wedding," Joe suggested, stifling a yawn. "The more honest we are with them now, the better for everyone."

"It'd allow them time to settle down before we arrived." I simulated a big explosion with my hands, complete with sound effects. "I'd like to avoid seeing them explode right before our eyes." Joe shot me a dirty look for being overly dramatic.

"Yeah, extra time might defuse things." Beth nodded.

So much for 'What happens in Vegas, stays in Vegas.'

Joe swallowed another bite of scrambled eggs. "What about Beth? We're not going to leave her alone in Vegas. We should never abandon her. I won't allow it."

"I'm coming along, too." Beth smiled. "Road trip."

Joe smiled broadly.

I mused, "We'd go through part of the country we've never driven before."

"Are you girls punching a clock about getting home?" Joe asked.

Both said, "No."

"If we use the rental car," Joe said, tapping out *Three Blind Mice* on the table with his fingertips, "then we'd better make sure Hertz understands we'll be renting our car longer and turning it in outside of Nevada."

Everyone agreed.

Suzy buttered a biscuit. "After Beth and I meet your family, Ray and I could drive or fly back to Cincinnati and really meet my parents."

Beth raised an eyebrow. "Joe, would you like for us to go on to Cincy, too, so my parents can meet you both at once?"

Joe sighed. "Going along to Cincy might be the most decent thing to do. We could lend Ray and Suzy moral support."

My head swam with too many thoughts, yet no singular clear thought existed.

"I'll do the dirty work," Suzy promised. "I'll call Mom and Dad after the wedding, tell 'em the news, and let 'em in on our plans."

Beth said, "We've already told them we've met a couple of super-charming guys and enjoy your company."

Suzy wished aloud, "By the time we reach Cincy, they might even really be eager to meet you."

Beth completed Suzy's thought, saying, "And, hopefully, welcome you with open arms."

"Are you both sure you still want to get married this quickly?" Joe asked.

"Absolutely," Suzy said.

I added, "Darned tootin'. I love Suzy and want to share the rest of our lives together."

"Ditto, in spades," Suzy declared. "How will your parents react, Ray?"

"No idea."

We'd finished breakfast. After paying the bill, we all headed out to our rental car, and I drove us toward the Clark County Marriage License Bureau.

"Everyone should really wear our street clothes for the wedding. That part of getting married doesn't matter as long as we're wed."

"We could rent tuxes," Joe said.

"No need," Suzy said. "It's being married to Ray I care about; everything else doesn't matter." She smiled at me, covering my hand with hers.

"That'll simplify everything." Beth said.

Suzy voiced agreement, "Right, we really won't spend much time today or tomorrow getting ready."

Joe snuggled up next to Beth in the back seat. "If we're going to leave for Iowa right after the wedding, we should check out of the Trop beforehand and already have our bags in the car."

"Roger that," I said.

We'd pick up our marriage license this morning, have fun the rest of the day, and cap it off up by attending *Santana's* performance. Tomorrow morning, we'd pack, check out, drive to the chapel, enjoy our wedding ceremony, and then start our road trip home.

Our plans were cast. I hoped for the best possible outcome with both sets of parents. I wanted to avoid anybody hating us or being mad.

Joe spoke up from the backseat. "Hey Ray, let's shoot some craps at the Stratosphere."

"Ugh, don't bring that up again."

We arrived at the Marriage License Bureau. There was a newspaper on the counter that caught Joe's eye as Suzy and I waited nearby. He picked it up and showed it to me. We read the Las Vegas Review-Journal's front page headline: *Chicken Beaten At Tic-Tac-Toe, $1,000 Won at Trop: Contest Continues.* I read the first few paragraphs of the write-up and learned one of those chickens had last been defeated six months ago.

Close, but no cigar.

"What now?" Joe put the newspaper back on the counter after we got our license.

Suzy said, "Today really might be your last chance to shoot craps for a while, Ray."

"Let's win some major money," Beth added, rubbing the palms of her hands together.

Joe said, "Pick out where to play. We'll tag along for the ride."

******

We valet parked at the Golden Nugget. On the way in, we eyed their lunch-box-size nugget made of sixty-two pounds of gold: *The Hand of Faith* on display behind plexiglass.

I said, "I heard success stories at our seminar about shooting here. I'd hoped to shoot here before leaving Vegas."

With it being a Thursday morning, the craps tables were almost empty.

"I might log a lot of shooting time here," I said as we all bought in.

I warmed up quickly, then bet normal place bets. The others bet their smaller place bets, too.

A familiar face joined our table. I recognized Willie Nelson, the famous country singer and songwriter. A super tall thin older guy accompanied Willie. The stranger wore a coordinated tan cowboy outfit, complete with hat. Willie wore a red western shirt, faded jeans, beat-up boots, and a semi-floppy black cowboy hat.

Willie acknowledged me with a nod. He viewed a few of my tosses, then started tossing down pumpkins for $246 place bets on both six and eight. Willie looked at me. "Win me some money."

"I'm shooting for fun today." I entered my zone and pumped out lots of sixes and eights, completing the first progression while only tossing two trash numbers. I was smoking. The table and the area nearby had filled with betters and spectators, maybe because of Willie's presence. Everyone there asked me to keep shooting, except for one player who wanted his own turn tossing the dice. Most gave me plenty of shooting opportunities.

I completed the progression bet four more times in forty-five minutes in spite of two failed attempts—by making up ground with multiple successful runs on two of my other turns.

Everyone colored up when I quit shooting.

Willie approached with an extended hand. "You're some shooter. I've never seen that many sixes and eights rolled before in such a short time. You won me some serious money."

He dropped a big handful of gray $1,000 chips sporting red, white, and green denominational markings into a shirt pocket.

I blushed a bit and bounced my left heal up and down nervously, "T-Thank you, Willie."

Willie introduced the ultra-tall fellow beside him. "This is my friend Amarillo Slim, the world's best gambler."

Amarillo Slim shook my hand. "It's been a pleasure watching you work your skills. I've never witnessed anything like you did."

"Big honor and a thrill to play craps with both of you." I introduced the rest of my group to the famous pair. Willie and Amarillo Slim shook everyone's hand in turn. Beth and Suzy didn't seem to be in awe of meeting such a famous pair, but I didn't think too much about it at the time.

"Good luck, kid." Willie touched the brim of his hat, then flicked his fingertips away. "See ya around."

Amarillo Slim tipped his cowboy hat. "Keep up your long dice rolls."

After taking two steps, Willie stopped and turned back toward me. He reached into his pocket and pulled out a $1,000 chip and flipped it to me. I caught it. "For entertaining me with the best show I ever saw at a craps table. You earned it."

A look of astonishment covered our faces. I examined the chip in disbelief, turning it over with my fingers. "Thank you, Willie. You sure I should keep this? It's a lot of money." I felt a surprised look still covering my face. My eyes felt as big as saucers.

"I gave it to you because I want you to have it." Willie formed a hand to look like a pistol, pointing it at me and pulling the trigger. The famous pair turned again and departed, discussing what they'd witnessed as they crossed Fremont Street and headed into Binion's Horseshoe.

I'd read about Amarillo Slim winning the World Series Of Poker a couple of times at *The Shoe* and becoming world famous for winning all kinds of huge, weird, outrageous bets with other gamblers. He specialized in beating world champions at their own specialties by finding a way to change the rules to his favor.

Say, that sounds like me, too—finding an unusual way to win.

Joe and I were star struck at meeting this pair.

I'd give anything to trade places with either one for a week.

It was all we talked about during our comped meal at the Golden Nugget. Our pit boss had given me four buffet VIP-line passes.

"They'd rather get you right back gambling than standing in the food line," Joe said. "Being a big bettor has its perks."

All agreed and thanked me for our meals. After lunch we checked out the gift shop. I'd been wanting a souvenir of my Vegas trip that would last. I found a nice tan jacket with *Golden Nugget, Las Vegas* tastefully embroidered in gold. I looked at the price tag. Sixty dollars. I sucked in my breath. It was triple what I'd expected it to be. I decided to buy it anyway. After paying, I put it on and proudly wore it everywhere from then on.

On our trip back through the casino, Suzy stopped in front of the roulette table. She watched the tiny white ball spin and spin around the wheel. The rest of us stopped, too. She reached into her purse and pulled out a ten-dollar bill, changed it into chips, and placed them all on red.

The ball came to rest on five, red.

Suzy won, saying, "Let it ride."

The next spin came up twenty-one, red. She now had forty dollars.

"Are you going to take your winnings this time?" I asked, wanting her to. While three reds in a row happens at roulette, you don't expect it.

"No. I've only got ten dollars of my own money at risk, let's see what really happens."

The thirty-four space on the wheel gave the ball a new home on the next spin. Red, a winner again.

Suzy now had eighty dollars in chips on red.

"Can it really happen again?" she asked.

The roulette dealer started the ball spinning again. In about ten seconds he'd call out, "No more bets." After that, nobody would be allowed to place any more bets or remove any, either.

Suzy chewed on a fingernail and squeezed my hand. She made her decision without saying a word. She waved her hand toward her chips, signaling she wanted to let her bet and winnings both ride. She then jumped up and down while the ball slowed in preparation for its landing. It struck one of those little raised-metal diamonds spaced around the wheel that guarantees a random result. The ball careened wildly, hopping in and out of several resting places. It came to rest on sixteen.

Beth jumped up and down, clapping her hands together, reminding me of a cheerleader. Suzy had won again. This time she wasted no time pulling all her chips out of play.

I hugged and kissed her. Everybody joined in celebrating and congratulating her.

Suzy demonstrated she had learned the power of making a parlay bet. She had learned the power of a progression bet by watching me work mine. She had the good sense to know when to pull it down, too.

"I want cash for these," Suzy told the dealer, handing in her solid-color chips.

"I'll give you regular casino gaming chips. You'll be able to convert them into cash at the cashier window," the dealer said.

"Now I really know how Ray feels after he scores a really big win." She took the chips, squeezing them tightly in her hand, then kissed me.

******

After all that excitement, we relaxed, sunbathed, and swam at the Trop pool again; everyone appreciated being together. We even tried our hand at the swim-up blackjack table there, with Beth winning $150.

"This is fun," Beth said, while Joe coached her on her best play.

Joe found himself up eighty-five dollars.

Suzy and I played, too. I lost bet after bet, in a string of bad luck. Suzy stayed even.

Joe kidded me, "You'd better stick to craps. You're luckless at twenty-one."

******

Later that afternoon, Joe told me, "When we were leaving the Trop, Beth pointed toward the elevators and whispered she thought she'd glimpsed Tony, Suzy's ex-boyfriend. She wasn't sure because he wasn't there when she tried to get a second look, but it shook her up."

"That's not good, Joe. Let me know right away if she thinks she sees him again."

"It would help if we knew what Tony looked like. He could be three feet away and I wouldn't know it."

I tightened my hands into fists. "Let's not mention it to Suzy. No point in getting her worked up again."

Over supper, I suggested we take things up a notch by experiencing the indoor skydiving adventure near the Stratosphere. I called ahead and snapped up a reservation for an hour from then.

Once there, we watched their instructional video on how to control our soaring using their special soaring suits we'd put on. We also wore ear plugs, helmets, and goggles. Everyone signed waivers before we took turns soaring inside the twelve by twenty-two foot chamber.

We were floating in air. Their 1,000 horsepower jet engine pumped high volumes of rapidly-moving air straight up from below into the vertical wind tunnel surrounding us, keeping us airborne. We flopped in our first few attempts at doing the maneuvers we'd seen done in the video.

The instructor in the chamber employed hand signals to assist us in learning to climb, dive, soar, rotate, and do mid-air somersaults. Toward the end, we might even have fooled someone into believing we knew what we were doing. We experienced weightlessness similar to what skydiving must be like before popping your chute.

Our adventure proved a lot safer, since we flew a few feet off the special flooring material that allowed us to walk on it while letting all the air rush through.

It felt like we were doing those maneuvers on a trampoline, except we didn't need to bounce—we were airborne most of the time. Actual skydiving would be a bigger thrill, but more dangerous. All thrills aren't created equal. We enjoyed our indoor soaring for the fun it gave us.

******

We soon pulled into valet parking at the Hard Rock Casino, then went in to pick up our Green Valley Ranch comped tickets and watch *Santana* perform. Suzy and I used the tickets ordered online back home. Beth and Joe used my comped tickets.

Santana's driving beat rocked The Joint, adjacent to Hard Rock's Center Bar. After their show ended two hours later with three curtain calls, we danced to the DJ music at the casino's Body English Night Club until after one a.m.

As we left, Suzy squeezed my arm. "Beth and I have LVA gambling coupons for over at the Greek Isle Casino on Convention Boulevard. Mind if we stop by and use 'em?"

"Joe, the girls want to swing by the Greek Isle Casino to use their free gambling coupons." I wanted to make sure the girls got to do the things they wanted to do, too.

"Tell me how to get there."

We soon pulled in to their valet parking.

Inside, the game became blackjack at five-dollar minimum bets. The LVA gambling coupon entitled the girls to receive a higher-than-normal two-to-one payout every time either got a blackjack during their first thirty minutes of play.

The older lady dealer examined the gambling coupons. "I'll have to get our pit boss to okay these."

The pit boss gave the coupons a quick glance. "Be sure to write their ending time for the half hour's play on the back and have the customer sign and date them on the back, too. Leave the coupon lying out in front of them, with the half-hour's ending time showing. When their time's up, put it in the drawer."

The pit boss glanced our way as he left. "Good luck, all."

The girls took the only two open seats at the table, so Joe and I stood behind them.

Suzy and Beth signed and dated their coupons and each bought fifty-dollars' worth of chips to gamble with. Both bet the five-dollar minimum on each hand.

The first hand allowed both girls to stand, while the dealer busted.

I rubbed Suzy's shoulders. "All right. Easy money."

Suzy covered my hand on her shoulder with hers. She got her first ten-dollar win on the next hand when the dealer dealt her a blackjack. Beth busted, so she fell back to being even.

"Way to go!" I cheered, delighted with Suzy's luck.

On the next hand, the dealer stood with a seventeen. Beth had two face cards for twenty for a win, while Suzy had nineteen. Suzy was up twenty dollars, while Beth was up five dollars.

"Another win." I gave Suzy a kiss on the top of her head, smelling her hair's fresh clean scent.

On the next hand, the dealer's up card showed six, so both girls stood on their medium-sized hands. They were betting the dealer would bust, allowing them to win. The dealer turned over back-to-back face cards for a twenty-six and a bust. Beth was up ten dollars. Suzy was up twenty-five dollars.

"Way to go, Suzy!" I cheered.

Both girls got aces as their up cards. Suzy got a king for another ten-dollar win with her second blackjack.

Everybody celebrated with high-fives.

Beth received an eight. The dealer ended up getting a face card and a nine, for nineteen to edge out Beth. Suzy jumped thirty-five dollars ahead. Beth was up five dollars.

"Poor Beth. That sucked," Suzy said. "You'll do better next hand."

Suzy stood with two face cards. Beth got a pair of eights. Joe told her to split them into two separate hands. She received a nine and a queen to go with her eights, giving her hands of seventeen and eighteen. The dealer's up card showed three. She dealt herself another three, then a face card and finally a seven for another busted hand. Suzy was up forty dollars. Beth was up fifteen.

Both girls busted their next hand.

Beth gathered up her chips. "Rats." Her jaw tightened and her eyes narrowed.

Joe rubbed her back. "Boy, that hand really sucked."

Suzy surprised me. "I'm going to quit while I'm still ahead. I didn't come here expecting to get rich."

Beth played two more hands, losing both.

"Well, I'm almost back to where I started. Let's play one more hand and make it really count."

She put out twenty-five dollars in chips and received a ten and a nine, for nineteen against the dealer's seven. She stood, sensing she had a winning hand.

The dealer dealt herself a second seven, then a third seven, for twenty-one.

"Ouch." Beth frowned and indicated she'd had enough.

Everybody shook their head, not believing the dealer's lucky draw. We glanced around and didn't see anything else that caught our fancy, so the ladies redeemed their chips for cash at the cashier's window.

We decided it was time to head back to the Trop. Tomorrow would be a big day with our wedding, and we were getting tired. We went to claim our rental car at valet parking and stood around waiting. Then we waited some more.

A hotel employee finally approached us. Her face was red and she couldn't meet our eyes. "We're sorry, but we're unable to locate your car. We checked everywhere your car could be. It's misplaced or gone."

"How's that possible?" My eyes drew into slits.

The attendant shrugged her shoulders and rolled her eyes, but didn't reply.

"Get me your hotel manager," I demanded.

The manager arrived after a few minutes. "I'm Bill Smith, shift manager. I apologize for your inconvenience. Unfortunately, your car is missing from our property."

That news stunned me. "It's a rental car. We're tired and need to return to the Tropicana to get some sleep. We're getting married tomorrow morning, then leaving for Iowa."

"Who rented you the car?"

"Hertz, at the airport."

The manager asked, "Was it rented in your name?"

"Yes. Are we going to be tied up here very long over this?" I looked at my watch.

"No, since you entrusted your car to our valet service, we'll team up with the police and Hertz and solve this. I'll need to copy your driver's license and contact information. We'll handle everything."

I provided contact information and my driver's license. "How are we going to get back to the Trop?"

"One of our limos will take you back. I'll have one here for you after I copy your license. Again, we're sorry this happened. Rest assured, we'll straighten this all out."

I tapped my toe. I needed some sleep. "How will we get another rental car for in the morning? We're driving it back to Council Bluffs, Iowa after our wedding."

"I'll call Hertz and advise their manager of your situation and your need for a replacement rental car. It will be on us. They should be calling you shortly to work out the details."

I asked, "Am I on the hook for any further rental fees on the missing car? Will we be told what happened to our rental?"

"Your obligation to Hertz ended when we failed to return your car. We'll handle this in-house from here on out. I doubt you'll be informed about what happened to your rental. I'm telling you that because you need to hear the truth. This type of incident has never happened here before."

"Thanks for your honesty. I appreciate it," I said.

Beth and Suzy kept shifting their weight from one foot to the other as I talked.

The manager went to untangle this mess.

I asked if anyone had left anything in the car, and fortunately no one had.

He returned shortly, giving my driver's license back.

A stretch limo pulled up. The manager opened their limo's back door, inviting us to enter. "Again, we're sorry for your delay."

******

Hertz called as we rode back to the Trop. "Your replacement rental car should be arriving in five minutes at the front entrance of the Tropicana. It's the same make and model as your previous rental. Will you be able to meet our driver there when he arrives?"

I checked the time on my watch. "Yes, we're only about a minute away from the Trop now."

"Our driver will need your signature on forms he'll have with him. Sign them, retain the pink copy for yourself, and you'll be all set. The Greek Isle Casino has volunteered to cover all your rental charges until you return your rental in Council Bluffs, Iowa by Monday. We're sorry for the difficulties you've had. Thank you for choosing Hertz. We appreciate your business."

Our replacement rental car arrived within three minutes after we left the limo. I signed the forms, then the driver parked the rental car in an empty parking spot, locked the doors, and handed over the keys. They'd made us whole again, in record time, too. The Hertz driver thanked me for the tip, then jumped into the passenger seat of another car that accompanied him.

"What a mess," I said as they drove away.

Suzy added, "At least we avoided getting delayed for hours, like with the taxi accident."

"It's too bad all this happened. At least the casino and Hertz handled everything well," Joe said. "We can be thankful for that."

I sighed. "I'm sure glad it all worked out. It could've been quite messy and drawn out."

Suzy took my hand in hers. "And really screwed up our wedding plans in the morning."

As we walked, I said, "We'll have to write thank-you letters to both The Greek Isle and Hertz."

We all agreed. They'd both splendidly handled an embarrassing, ugly situation.

We escorted Suzy and Beth to their room, kissed them goodnight, and headed down to our room.

Joe and I got off the elevator and walked down the hallway when we saw a man pounding on our room's door and shouting, "Suzy, let me in!"

"Tony," we both said, looking at each other in surprise.

"Flank him." I said. "He's not expecting us."

We quickly closed in.

Without saying anything or even acknowledging his presence, I inserted the room key and opened the door.

"Who the hell are you?" Tony asked in bewilderment.

I entered.

Tony followed.

Joe brought up the rear, closed the door, and flipped the latch.

Tony watched us warily. He was a big man, muscular, and looked as though he knew how to handle himself. I can look after myself, but I had quit being a brawler years ago—and Joe was the opposite of a ninja. My stomach felt hollow and I could feel the prickle of sweat running down my back.

Tony clenched both fists, while his eyes held a threatening glint. I got the distinct impression he was a man not in total command of his actions.

I glanced at Joe. He stood tense and still, suspiciously close to the heavy marble lamp beside the bedside table.

"Where is she?" Tony's was a voice accustomed to being obeyed. There was no room in it for argument.

"Who?" I asked, stupidly.

He gave me a withering look, as did Joe.

"Suzy Snyder. This is her room."

"No," Joe said, "it's ours."

Tony's lips curled into a sneer. "Says you. Where is she?"

I suddenly had an inspiration. "On her way home with her sister, to tell her parents that she's married."

That stopped Tony cold. His eyes almost bulged. "She's what?" The threat in his voice was all too clear. "Who to?"

"Me. We got married this morning." I hoped my voice didn't quaver as much as I thought it did.

Joe was staring at me with a shocked expression.

"Married to a runt like you?" He slid a hand into his pocket. He had a gun. He had to have. I felt my knees wobble and a wave of dizziness made me sway. I was terrified.

"It's true," said Joe through gritted teeth. "I was best man. She told us about you, but you missed the boat. It's too late."

"Kind of sudden?" Tony said.

He raised the gun barrel in his pocket until it pointed squarely at me.

"I don't mess around when I see something I want."

For a few seconds, Tony and I stared at each other, our eyes locked together. I watched the hand in his pocket in fear. It did not move. The moment seemed to hang in eternity…

"My brother and I will be finishing up some business in the morning, then we're off to rejoin them. You don't see the girls around here, do you?"

Tony looked to be getting madder by the minute. His neck grew rigid and the vein on his temple pulsed with every heartbeat. His face turned deeper red. He looked at us suspiciously, walked over to the chest of drawers, and opened each drawer in turn, looking inside. "This is all kind of sudden, isn't it?"

I dug in my heels. *Might as well make this a whopper.* "I never dally when I see something I want, I grab it. You'd do good to go back to

Ohio yourself and put Suzy behind you. I'm sure you can find something else to fill your thoughts." I didn't flinch.

Tony's jaw went slack. He took his hand out of his pocket and huffed, then he turned and let himself out without saying another word.

Relief arrived as my body went limp. I almost melted into my shoes. I flashed Joe an inquisitive look while turning the palms of my hands up.

"It might have been lame, but it was all I could think up at the time." I let out a sigh of relief. "Maybe I bought us some time. Let's call security and let them know Tony's been sneaking around our room."

"Should I call the girls and tip them off about Tony being here? I'd hate to upset them, but they should probably know."

"Yes."

Joe sat down on the edge of his bed. "Do you think Tony believed anything you told him?"

"Your guess is as good as mine, Bro. I'm calling to alert hotel security, Joe. Alert the girls and tell them not to answer their door or leave their room until we're with them."

Joe said, "Since we're leaving in the morning anyway, all we'll have to do is figure out a way to give Tony the slip in the morning, should he stick around and cause trouble."

I began talking to the front desk. "Listen, we want hotel security to escort the four of us safely from our rooms tomorrow and stay with us while we check out, load up our car, and leave. A guy named Tony just threatened us with a gun, and I don't want this Tony guy to have any more opportunities to cause trouble. He's dangerous, I tell ya. I don't want to take any chances. There's no telling what this guy might do if we run into him again."

Joe phoned Beth and brought her up to speed. "Security will see we get underway safely in the morning. Don't do anything risky tonight. Call us if you feel threatened. This will all work out." After a deep sigh, Joe told Beth. "You should have heard the whopper Ray told Tony while he was here..."

Man, what else can go wrong?

Chapter Fifteen — Friday

Joe got out of bed in the dark about four a.m. and stumbled toward our bathroom, and there was a loud noise.

Thud!

He stopped in his tracks. "So stupid," he chided himself.

I sat up in bed, now fully awake. "What's wrong, Joe?" I flipped on the light between our beds. "Are you hurt?"

He sucked in a deep breath and continued hobbling on toward the bathroom, pain written all over his face. "I broke my toes, Ray. Forgot where the furniture was and kicked it." His voice was two octaves higher than usual.

I asked, "Do they need x-rayed?"

Joe didn't answer immediately, being otherwise occupied. Returning from the bathroom, he hopped across the room, attempting to avoid putting weight on the injured foot. He flopped onto the edge of the bed and raised his aching foot to examine the damage. The toes nearest the little toe were already red and had started to swell.

I'd broken toes before more than once and knew he'd live through it—sucking up the pain—until it eased up weeks from now.

"What a rotten way to end such a fabulous vacation," he grumbled, trying to get back to sleep.

After we got up and showered, Joe did his best to dress. I packed our bags and called the front desk for security, waited for them, then went down with them and put all our stuff in the car. I checked us out and turned in our plastic room keys at the front desk. I kept checking to see if Tony was around.

The girls embraced Joe when he showed up hobbling in discomfort. I told them what happened.

"My poor baby. I'm so sorry you hurt your foot," Beth comforted Joe, running her hand through his hair. "Is there anything I can do to make it better?" She had a cute pout on her face.

He shook his head, giving her his best brave smile. Beth gave him a kiss and hug, resting her cheek on his chest.

With hotel security still shadowing my every move, I took the girls' luggage down and stowed it away with ours. We managed to get safely away from the Trop with no signs of Tony anywhere.

We took a zig-zag route full of unneeded turns to Ellis Island Casino, constantly checking the rear-view mirror to make sure nobody tailed us.

Joe asked over breakfast, "Did anyone sleep well last night?"

Beth added, "This Tony shit kept me awake half the night."

"I really slept like a worn-out baby." Suzy stretched her arms over her head. "I'm not going to let Tony hold any power over me anymore. If he shows up and causes trouble, his ass is going straight to jail."

I nodded between bites. "I slept good, until someone woke me up about four o'clock."

Joe groaned. "My shoe's squeezing my broken toes. It hurts."

"Let's really go have our wedding, Ray."

"Roger that." I replied.

My comment scored me a kiss. Soon, I was easing our car into traffic; our destination being the wedding chapel again. I kept an eye on my rear-view mirror, looking for any signs that Tony might be following us.

As we drove up The Strip, Joe sang, "We're heading to the chapel—and Suzy and Ray are going to be married." He paused. "Say, there ought to be a song written about that."

******

Wedding music came from the chapel as we entered their front office. I gave the manager, Mr. Prescott, a nicely-attired gentleman with a handlebar mustache, our marriage license.

"We're here to get married."

"You don't say." Mr. Prescott's eyes twinkled as he spoke.

Joe handed over a credit card to Mr. Prescott. "Here's my wedding present to you guys. I'm paying for your wedding."

"Wow. Thanks, Joe," I said as Suzy and I hugged him. "It's not necessary, but we sure appreciate the gesture."

"It's the least I could do for my little Bro. My duty's been to help you stay out of trouble, but from here on, I'm passing that torch to you, Suzy."

"Joe, you really are the best brother-in-law a girl could ever have."

"Suzy, I'm glad you'll be my sister-in-law." Joe gave her a big hug.

Mr. Prescott said our ceremony would take place in five minutes, then escorted us into separate waiting areas: guys in one room, gals in another.

146

He pinned boutonnieres on our shirts and gave us a brief run-down on what to expect and what we should do during the ceremony. After a short wait, they escorted us into the chapel, showing us where to stand. The officiate joined us.

Wedding music played as the rear door to the chapel opened, and in came Beth, carrying a small bouquet of flowers. She looked stunning as she walked down the aisle in time to the music. She stopped long enough to kiss Joe at the altar, then took up her position opposite him. We all turned toward the back of the chapel again when the Wedding March's volume increased.

The door opened again and there stood Suzy, carrying a larger bouquet of flowers. I smiled as she walked the length of the aisle, coming to a complete brief stop after each step in time to the music. She handed her bouquet to Beth and turned to me, placing her hands in mine.

"Dearly beloved, we are gathered here today to unite Ray Arnold Hitchcock and Suzy Ann Snyder in the holy bonds of matrimony." The minister looked at each of us as he spoke. "Do you intend to marry each other here today? If so, say 'I do'."

We both said, "I do."

Beth shot a sweet smile at Joe, who acknowledged it with a quick nod.

"If anyone knows of any reason why this couple should not be joined together in holy wedlock, let them speak now or forever hold their peace."

Silence.

I noticed Joe looking over at Beth. He was in love all right.

"Do you have rings?" the minister asked.

My face reddened. "Uh, we forgot to buy them." I looked at Suzy, hoping she'd forgive me.

She smiled and stroked my hand. "Don't worry, Ray. We'll get 'em later. No biggie, really."

The minister took in a deep breath. "Ray, take Suzy's hand in yours and repeat after me. I, Ray Hitchcock, take you, Suzy Snyder, to be my wife."

"I, Ray Hitchcock, take you, Suzy Snyder, to be my wife."

"I promise to love you and be faithful to you through good times and bad."

I squeezed Suzy's hand in mine, then winked. "I promise to love you and be faithful to you through good times and bad."

"…through poverty and wealth…"

"…through poverty and wealth…"

"…through sickness and health for as long as we both shall live."

"…through sickness and health for as long as we both shall live."

I took in a deep breath and winked at Suzy. My heart skipped a beat.

The minister turned to Suzy. "Repeat after me: I, Suzy Snyder, take you, Ray Hitchcock, to be my husband."

"I, Suzy Snyder, take you, Ray Hitchcock, to be my husband."

"I promise to love you and be faithful to you through good times and bad."

"I promise to love you and be faithful to you through good times and bad."

"…through poverty and wealth…"

"…through poverty and wealth…"

"…through sickness and health for as long as we both shall live."

"…through sickness and health for as long as we both shall live."

I could see a tear running down Suzy's cheek, so I leaned over and wiped it away as the minister continued.

"By the power vested in me as an ordained minister in the State of Nevada, I pronounce Suzy and Ray to be man and wife. What God has joined together, let no man put asunder. Ray, you may kiss your bride."

I bent Suzy over backwards in my arms for a passionate kiss. A flash indicated that the staff photographer had captured our romantic wedding kiss for posterity.

Beth and Joe congratulated us with hugs, kisses, handshakes, and back thumps

The chapel's photographer had taken a few more wedding photos when the chapel door crashed open with a loud bang. There stood Tony, wearing an expression of absolute hatred. "Bitch! I'll teach you to dump me." He then glared at Joe and me. "Liars. I'm going to kick your asses."

Chapter Sixteen — Later On Friday

Tony charged, pulling out his gun. Joe and I tackled him before he could aim. Bullets buried themselves in the ceiling. My ears rang from the gunshots. Pieces of ceiling rained down.

The girls screamed, scattered and dove for cover.

I grabbed the gun, but Tony was strong.

Joe hit him with a hard right to the chin. Tony head-butted Joe, sending him reeling. I landed a hard right cross to his gut, while bullets sprayed where the girls had stood.

Tony yelled obscenities. He honked back a huge load of spit and launched it all over my face, then belly-bucked me backwards, but I didn't fall.

"Get him, Joe!" I yelled.

We all struggled for the gun and forced it over Tony's head. It fired.

Tony kneed me hard in the groin.

I collapsed in a heap. Intense pain ripped through me.

Seeing that Tony's gun hand was free, Joe tripped him.

I struggled to my feet and rejoined the fight.

Tony's brute strength took over. Supercharged with anger, he tossed me aside.

Joe pounded on him.

Tony leveled the gun at Joe.

Joe knocked it sideways, but a bullet nicked his ear.

Tony's gun now pointed at my head.

Click. Click.

We both were on top of Tony, who slugged my jaw, making my teeth ring. Blood trickled down my chin.

We were three snarling, fighting dogs struggling for control. High-pitched screams filled the chapel.

I bent back Tony's thumb and wrenched the gun free.

Joe's hard upper-cut clipped Tony's chin.

We were all near exhaustion. We wrestled Tony to the floor.

Only adrenaline, panic, and anger drove me on. Everything switched to slow motion.

I knocked Tony out with a gun-barrel chop to the temple. He went out like a busted light bulb.

After sitting up, Joe struck Tony in the mouth. A front tooth went sailing across the floor.

I got to my feet and looked to see if the girls were okay. I had a strange taste in my mouth. Was it the taste of fear?

Blood trickled down the edge of Joe's ear.

Tony wouldn't be waking any time soon.

The girls emerged from hiding.

"Call the cops!" Beth yelled.

Mr. Prescott mopped a brow with a handkerchief. "They're already on their way. I called them when all this started."

Joe and I continued guarding Tony. Our breathing came easier. Less than two minutes later, the police arrived in force with their guns drawn. I handed over Tony's gun and drew in a deep breath. A couple of ambulances arrived with lights flashing.

I went to Suzy's side to comfort her and help settle her down. "Sorry for all the excitement." I stroked her hair.

Pain thumped and burned where Tony had connected with several blows, including one to my crotch.

Suzy clutched tighter against me than she'd ever done before. "Maybe now we can really put this Tony thing behind us for good."

"I sure hope so," I agreed. My mind spun.

Joe pulled Beth close. "God, I love you." He pulled her even tighter against him.

Hands still shaking, Beth rested her head against his chest. "I love you, too." Her eyes wandered to the side of his face. Seeing blood, she yelled to one of the medics, "Hey, can we get Joe's ear looked at? He's been shot."

Two medics made Joe sit, then examined, sterilized, and dressed his ear.

"You'll be as good as new in no time," one of them said. "Only a scratch."

Joe looked like a one-eared elephant with his ear bandaged. "Can I skip going to the hospital?"

"You're okay. I've seen cat scratches worse than that," the medic said.

"They tell me I'll live." He looked to be deep in thought. "It's funny, but my toes felt just fine during the fight. Now they're hurting again.

"Your tenacity surprised me, Bro," I said. Joe had risen to the occasion in spades.

The second team of medics tended to Tony, after the police handcuffed him.

Suzy sat next to me and held hands. "How's my favorite hubby?"

"We're leaving immediately to go home to Iowa," I told the police. I pointed to Suzy. "We just got married. We don't want to stick around to file charges."

"Well," said Mr. Prescott, "I'm pressing charges, so haul that thug's ass to jail. I can't have this kind of behavior in our chapel. No one would want to come here anymore. Besides, look at all the bullet holes and those two broken chairs."

"In the meantime," I said, "file a claim and send me a bill for any damages insurance doesn't cover."

Mr. Prescott's face beamed. "Thank you, Ray. Most people wouldn't have volunteered to pay damages."

The policeman asked, "Will any of you be available to testify against the assailant at trial?"

I thought for a moment. "I don't know. We'll see when the time comes."

Mr. Prescott swallowed hard. "I believe we've got the whole thing recorded on our security cameras. That should be enough evidence for a solid conviction."

After Tony had been placed in the ambulance and taken away and the police had recorded our statements, I picked up our now officially-signed marriage certificate and thanked everyone at the chapel.

I shook Mr. Prescott's hand. We'd put him through a lot. "Sorry all this had to happen here. That guy is a real jerk."

"I know," Mr. Prescott said, pulling his hand away to swipe his forehead again.

Joe turned to me. "It's crazy, but do you realize we'd have never met the girls if it hadn't been for Tony?"

I scratched my head. "How's that?"

"The girls said they moved their Vegas trip up a week to get away from Tony. If they hadn't done that, they would be arriving in Vegas right about now and we'd be leaving Vegas on a plane in a couple of hours. Our paths would have never crossed, except maybe to see each other in passing at the airport. Tony changed our lives for the better."

I laughed. "I'll be darned."

Suzy flashed a smile. "I never really thought about that. I guess we owe Tony our thanks after all. Now can we get out of here? Please?"

We left the chapel. Five minutes later, I had us back at the Fremont, whipping our car into valet parking without saying anything in advance to anyone. I declared, "I wanted to surprise you. I'm going to take another crack at their craps tables before we leave town. It's my call to duty."

Everybody clapped their approval. Spirits seemed to immediately soar.

"Consider it done." I still had something I needed to do.

I bought in for my usual $400, skipped the warm-up bets, and opened with back-to-back sixes, then an eight and a nine. I came back with a hard six, a five, and another eight to win the progression bet.

Joe offered a high-five. "Way to go, Bro."

I left my bets up, racked the winnings, and came back with a hard ten, then repeated with a winning six. I left my bets up again, racked my winnings again, then tossed an eight. I won again by tossing a hard six.

"Enough, color me up," I ordered, nine minutes after beginning.

"It's still your turn to shoot, Sir," said the stickman. "Don't you want to keep shooting?"

"Nope. I'm done." I tossed a couple of chips I'd palmed to the dealer as a tip. I moved all my chips onto the table, pushing them forward.

Getting one of Fremont's Long Roll Certificates ranks low on my list of things to do today.

I had won $2,696 in chips. After coloring them up into a more-manageable-sized stack of large-denomination chips, I handed them all to Suzy.

"Here, Hon, about $3,000 to set up housekeeping when we reach Council Bluffs."

Her eyes lit up. She responded with a kiss.

******

We began our trip home to Iowa, with Vegas disappearing in the car's rearview mirror. Now came what everyone dreaded. Both sets of parents must be told about what their kids had done.

With the phone on speaker, I dialed home, growing more nervous as the rings on the other end stretched out into a solemn rhythm. Waiting became torture.

What'll their reaction be? Are they going to disown us over what we did? Will they welcome Suzy into the family?

Everything hung on the next few minutes. And nobody was answering the damn phone.

After about thirty long agonizing seconds, the ringing stopped. "Hello," Mom answered.

"J-J-Joe and I are heading home now. S-Some strange and magical things have happened and our plans got changed. We're driving home in a rented car instead of flying back. We thought we'd let you know, so you wouldn't be worrying when our flight lands without us being on it."

Mom's worried voice asked, "What's wrong, Ray? What happened?"

"Nothing's wrong. Everything's great," I reassured her, swallowing hard. "I'm not sure how best to tell you this, but four of us are coming home, instead of two."

We heard hushed whispering on the other end of the call, then we heard a shuffling sound as Dad came to the phone. "Why aren't you flying home? What's this four instead of two?"

"Hi, Dad. We met a couple of wonderful girls in Las Vegas earlier this week. Joe met Beth, and I met Suzy. They're twins from Cincinnati, and, well, I gave Suzy my heart, Mom, and she gave me hers." I gathered my courage. "Mom, Suzy and I got married. We're very happy."

Silence fell as my words sank in. Then Mom asked, "Ray, you're sure you love her? And she's sure she loves you?"

Suzy and I both shouted, "Yes."

"Is that you, Suzy dear?" Mom asked.

"Yes. I'm really in love with Ray and plan on making him happy. I'll be the best wife possible," Suzy said.

"Honey, that's all we ask. Welcome to our family." Mom was chuckling and sounded happy. "We're anxious to meet both you girls in person and become acquainted."

"Thank you," Suzy replied. "May God really bless you."

"You too, sweetie."

"Hi, Mom. Joe, here." he leaned over the back of the car's front seat to get nearer the phone.

"Hi, Joe. You have a girlfriend, too? You're not married, are you?" Mom's voice went from friendly to concerned.

"Yes, Mom, I've got a girlfriend. Ray and I are two lucky fellas. We're sorry for springing all this on you the way we did. Everything happened so fast."

"This is all great news," Mom replied. "I'm elated Ray and Suzy are so happy. I wish you both a long and happy life together. I'm pleased you found yourself a girl too, Joe."

"Super," Joe said. "I've been worried I'd let you and Dad down."

I could see Joe's spirits rise when he realized our news had made Mom happy. He'd been the world's best wing-man of all time. He'd taken a beating this trip, with broken toes, a shot ear, and a shiner now proudly marking his right eye.

Dad said, "You guys sure grew up in a hurry. Congratulations, Ray and Suzy. When will you be getting home?"

I answered, "Sometime late Saturday night, if all goes smoothly. We wanted to stay together. That wouldn't have been possible if we'd flown."

"Be careful driving back," Dad said.

"We will. Joe and I are going to take turns driving to guarantee there'll always be a fresh driver behind the wheel."

Joe shouted, "We'll stop in Denver tonight and should get home late Saturday night. We love you, Mom and Dad."

I added. "Got to go. See you when we get home."

Our phone went silent.

Man, what fantastic parents we have.

"Whew," I sighed. "That went pretty well."

Indeed, everything had. Couldn't have had a better result. One down, one on deck.

Joe asked Beth, "How will your parents react to our news?"

"I guess we'll find out soon enough." She burrowed closer.

Suzy spoke up. "I'll call them in a little bit. Let me have a little peace and quiet before the shit really hits the fan. I'm really afraid we may really be a lot less lucky on our next call."

"Why?" I asked.

"It's a gut feeling I really have. Dad's a bit of a hot head. We'll wait and see. I'll call them in a couple of hours."

I changed the subject. "We have a solid twelve hours of driving time before we reach Denver. We should be able to get motel rooms by midnight, if we control our stops."

Beth smirked at Joe. "Super, but we should switch up sleeping arrangements, to allow Ray and Suzy to start their honeymoon."

Joe smiled. "Oh, we're going to sleep together tonight?"

Beth pulled him close. "That's all we're going to be doing, too—sleeping. No hanky panky, Mister." She gave Joe a kiss. "Okay?"

"I can wait if you can," Joe promised her. "It'll sure be difficult, though."

Suzy examined the map. "We're going to be going through the Rocky Mountains eastbound on I-70. Towns appear to be pretty remote, with nothing in between. We'll really need to be careful planning our restroom stops, meal stops, and gas fill-ups."

I shot her a quick smile. "Okay, we'll pay attention. I-70 joins up with I-80, which will take us on to Omaha and home."

******

We took our first driving break in Cedar City, Utah at a McDonald's, where we ate, went to the restrooms, and stretched our legs. Our gas got topped off at a gas station there, and Joe took over behind the wheel, with Suzy and me moving to the backseat.

Once we were back on the road again, Suzy dialed Cincinnati, putting the call on speakerphone.

"Hello," came a pleasant older feminine voice on the other end.

"Hi, Mom. Is Dad with you?"

"No, honey. He's out playing golf. Why do you ask? Is something wrong?"

"I'm married, Mom," Suzy blurted, her voice breaking. She fanned her face with her free hand and sucked in a deep breath.

I winced. *Nothing like laying it all out there at once.*

"What?"

"You remember me telling you about meeting Ray and Joe? Well, Ray and I really got married this morning before leaving Las Vegas." Suzy fanned herself even faster now.

"Leaving Las Vegas? You were supposed to leave tomorrow. Where are you?" asked her mom in a worried voice.

"We're driving back to meet Ray's family in Iowa. We'll arrive there really late Saturday. We're really fine, and very happy." Suzy now closed her eyes as she talked, fingertips nervously drumming on her forehead.

"Driving, to Iowa? Oh, my," her mom said. "I'd better sit down." Silence was followed by a quiet thud. "Married?" she asked, sounding like she expected we'd reassure her that she had heard incorrectly.

"Hi, Mrs. Snyder, Ray Hitchcock here. I'm head-over-heels in love with Suzy, and she loves me. I wish we'd found a better way of breaking the news to you, but things happened beyond our control. I hope you'll forgive us."

"I can't believe you've done this, Suzy. Call me back in an hour. I need some time to absorb all this." The phone went silent.

Beth winced and shrugged. "Bombs away. Dad wasn't even there."

"And Mom really hung up."

I sucked in my breath. "We blew it."

Everyone went quiet.

I broke the ice. "Has anyone come up with anything we might say to patch things up with your parents?"

Joe said, "Apologize for the way this all went down and ask for their forgiveness. That's all anyone can do."

Suzy bit her lower lip. "I bet Dad will be there too, when I call back. I bet Mom's calling him now, telling him the news."

"That'll ruin his round of golf, too, which isn't going to help." Beth wrung her hands. "Dad loves golf."

Nobody else offered any suggestions. We drove on quietly, listening to the hum of the tires on the road and waiting for the explosion to occur when Suzy phoned home again.

When Suzy's phone rang forty-five minutes later, everybody jumped.

"Suzy, this is your father," came a booming voice at the other end of the call. "Is what your mother tells me true? Are you married? And on your way to Iowa in a car? Is Beth with you, or still in Las Vegas?"

"Hi, Dad. Love you. Yes. It's true. Ray and I are really married. We love each other very much. We're on our way to meet Ray's parents in Iowa, then we'll be coming home to let you meet Ray."

Beth shouted, "Hi, Dad. Love you, too!"

"Beth?"

"Yes, Dad. We're sorry for interrupting your golf game."

"Never mind. Put this Ray on. Let me talk to him."

I heard pops of static.

Oh, please don't let this call be dropped now. Let's get this over with.

"H-Hello, Mr. Snyder. Glad to meet you." I tried to sound cheerful. "I love your daughter and hope you forgive us for things turning out this way." I massaged the back of my neck with my free hand.

Suzy's father asked, "Do you promise to always put Suzy first in your life? To treat her right, and never hurt her in any way?" He cleared his throat, managing to make it sound menacing.

"I sure do." I kept my eyes on the road ahead.

Silence, then, "Well, young man, I'm unhappy with the way this all happened, but I guess things can't be changed—I'll forgive you both. I care for Suzy's happiness." His voice got low and menacing. "I'll give you a chance, but blow it and you're history. I might even personally kick your butt all the way to Maine, you hear?"

"Yes, Sir. Loud and clear."

He asked, "Say, you like to play golf?"

My voice's pitch rose as I spoke. "M-Maybe we can play a round of golf when we visit."

"I'd like that, Ray, later. Here's your mom again, Suzy."

His last sentence actually sounded friendly.

Suzy's mom said, "I told your father getting angry wouldn't accomplish or change anything that's happened. He replied, 'I guess youngsters need to learn by making their own mistakes and decisions, and by living through the outcome'. Believe it or not, Suzy, we were young once, too."

"I'd have really liked to have been a fly on the wall when you and Dad had your conversation," Suzy said, laughing.

Her mom chuckled. "Oh, no. Your father cussed worse than a Dutchman, until I settled him down and made him admit the reality of the situation."

When the call ended, Joe turned to me. "Ray, you've never played golf. What were you thinking?"

"I wanted to smooth things over." I put my hand in the air and shrugged. "I guess I'd better learn to play golf pretty damn fast. I'll cross that bridge when I come to it." I flipped Joe a three-finger salute then lowered my chin a bit and flashed a big Ray-grin.

Beth said, "I bet Mom's mad over being cheated out of planning your wedding."

"Yeah, probably so. Right now, she must be pretty disappointed in me. Oh, well. I can live with it."

About twenty minutes later, Joe looked in the rear-view mirror. Flashing blue lights were right behind us. I saw them in the side-view mirror, too.

He wants to go around us.

Joe slowed, but the state police car kept on our bumper and made no attempt to pass. Then he hit the siren.

Joe eased the car off the highway and came to a stop. I was surprised when two troopers exited their vehicle.

"Holy crap, what's going on?" I asked.

"No idea, Bro. I wasn't speeding or driving recklessly."

I tried to think of what Joe might have done wrong.

About that time a second trooper car pulled up from the other direction. It screeched to a stop in front of our car, boxing us in. Two more troopers jumped out.

"Everyone in the car, keep your hands where we can see them!" one state trooper yelled from our car's rear bumper. His partner positioned himself on the passenger side of our car.

"Driver, grip the steering wheel with both hands."

We did as told, not having a clue what would happen next or why we were being treated this way.

"What's the problem, officer?" Joe asked the one who approached the car window and indicated for him to roll it down.

"Driver's license and registration, please?" the trooper asked.

"Was I doing anything wrong?" Joe asked. "I don't think I was speeding." He took out his driver's license and handed it to the trooper.

"T-T-The rental contract for this car is in the glove box. Is it okay if Beth opens the glove box to get it for you?" I asked. "I-I don't want her to do anything without your okay."

"Do it slowly. No sudden movements." The trooper rested a hand on the butt of his pistol.

Beth slowly took the rental contract out and handed it to the trooper.

I said, "Are we in any trouble? D-Did we do anything wrong, officer?"

"Did anything unusual happen involving this car in Las Vegas in the last twenty-four hours?" the trooper asked in a voice of authority.

"We rented a c-c-car in Las Vegas..." I paused. "but it disappeared at the valet service at The Greek Isle Casino. Hertz delivered this car to us as a replacement. The Greek Isle Casino is covering the rental cost until Monday morning for us. Suzy and I," I pointed to Suzy, "got married this morning in Las Vegas. We're on our way home to Council Bluffs, Iowa."

The trooper looked back at Joe. "Put both your hands back on the steering wheel and keep them there. I'll be back in a few, after I check this out." He returned to his vehicle and got in. Blue flashing lights on both trooper vehicles continued to whirl, almost in unison. None of the other troopers moved. They kept watching all of us intently.

"Anybody have a clue what's going on?" Suzy whispered.

Joe and I both shook our heads no as beads of sweat broke out on my forehead.

After what seemed like an eternity, the trooper got out again and walked back up to Joe's window.

He handed Joe back all our paperwork. "You can go."

"What was this all about?" Joe asked.

"This car was reported stolen early this morning in Las Vegas, but your rental papers check out, so we know it's not stolen. Sorry we bothered you."

Joe spun around and looked at me. We both must have had the same thought, at the same time, because we simultaneously said, "Tony?"

Is that possible?

"Before you go," Joe asked the trooper, "Will we have to worry about being stopped again because of the theft report on this car?"

"Nope. I don't know what caused the mix-up on this, but dispatch will see to it that the theft report gets deactivated," the trooper said. "Have a good day."

He glanced at the other officers and made a circular motion in the air with a finger. "All clear here. Let's roll." All the troopers piled back into their vehicles, doused their flashing lights, and left us parked on the side of the road.

Could Tony be behind all this? Could he have been behind our original rental car's disappearance from valet parking at The Greek Isle Casino? I bet we'll never know. The important thing is that all this is behind us now, right?

After getting to Denver and getting a couple of rooms, Suzy and I enjoyed our wedding night, thanks to Beth and Joe's sacrifice of letting us have a room all to ourselves to start our honeymoon. I thought that was really nice of them.

Before we went to sleep, Suzy asked me, "Do you buy what Beth told Joe about there being no hanky-panky between them tonight?

"What do you mean?"

"They're in a room by themselves."

"So?"

"Beth's got the hots for Joe." Suzy rubbed my back.

"So?"

"I bet she just said that to Joe for our benefit."

"Why?"

"She doesn't want us to know what they might be up to."

"Think so?"

"I bet they're not sleeping."

"Oh?"

"I'd bet money on it."
"Hum, interesting." My mind danced.
"Night, love."
"Night, hon. Roll over so we can spoon."
"Okay."

Chapter Seventeen — Saturday

We grabbed a few hours' sleep and ate breakfast, then left Denver early Saturday. Beth and Joe seemed mighty chipper this particular morning.

I drove, nosing the Corolla back on the interstate. The radio was on. Joe worked on a crossword puzzle. Beth rested her head on his shoulder. Suzy huddled up next to me as best she could in her bucket seat.

I looked in the rearview mirror. "Oh, no. We've got another cop on our tail."

Joe checked the side-view mirror.

Flashing blue lights closed in.

"What are we going to do, really?"

I pulled onto the road's shoulder and rolled to a stop.

I couldn't believe our luck. I held my breath.

The police car whizzed by us at about ninety miles an hour.

"I thought we were dead meat." I still gripped the steering wheel white-knuckle tight.

Everyone gave a sigh of relief. Suddenly, things couldn't get better.

"We are really going to have some interesting stories to tell our grandkids," Suzy said.

******

We turned in the rental car and then stayed long enough in Council Bluffs to give my parents a chance to get acquainted with Suzy and Beth. When Mom asked what their father did for a living—it was the first time anyone had thought to ask—the girls replied he was self-employed and worked from home.

Ah, I thought. *That's why he can be out playing golf on a Friday.*

******

We headed to Cincinnati to take Beth home. On the way there, Beth told us about their sixteen-year-old brother, who still lived at home.

"Clayton nearly died six months ago from a drug overdose. He's messed up and kind of the family embarrassment. We love him, but he keeps screwing up. He got out of rehab about a month ago."

Suzy said, "God, I hope he can leave that junk alone, before he ends up dead. It scares me to death."

We entered the section of Indian Hill where they lived, and turned onto Sleepy Hollow Road.

Joe looked first left, then right. "I can't get over how big and fancy some of these homes are. Some of these are mansions."

I'd never seen anything as huge as the homes appearing before my eyes. "That's got to be the biggest, fanciest house I've ever seen!" I pointed to the castle-style mansion sitting halfway up a forested hillside.

The girls looked at each other and shrugged. "Ours is in the next block, on the other side of the road," Beth said.

Nah, they're kidding.

Only one house was in that next block. It was humongous!

"That's your house?" I asked, swallowing a lump in my throat.

"Yup, we're really home. Take the driveway that winds up the hill."

I was shocked. Ahead of us was what I'd have to describe as a mansion—three-stories tall—sitting on the hillside behind a huge iron gate that stood open. My mouth fell open as we got closer.

"How many rooms does this place have?"

"Twenty-four, really, and six bathrooms," Suzy said. "Why?"

"It's the most fantastic home I think I've ever seen." I pulled up and entered the circular driveway in front.

"Your family lives here?" Joe asked.

"For the last ten years," Beth said.

I probably looked bug-eyed as I turned off the car's engine. But we didn't have time for twenty questions. Their parents were coming out the door to meet us.

The girls bounded out of the car. They hugged their mom and then the person we knew from the phone call as dad. He was huge and rugged looking, with a full beard and a receding hairline. He could have passed for a professional wrestler.

Suzy introduced us. "Mom, dad, this is my husband, Ray Hitchcock, and his brother, Joe. Ray, Joe, this is my mom, Julie. And my dad, Marvin."

Suzy and her mother hugged. "What happened in Las Vegas, Suzy? We got worried about you—because of Tony."

They stared at us in disbelief as we told the story of what happened in Vegas.

"Oh, no." Julie covered her mouth with her hand as a look of fright swept over her face.

"It was terrible, Mom. Tony emptied the gun, struggling with the guys. It's a wonder somebody didn't get killed."

They hugged again.

Mr. Snyder's eyes narrowed. "That son-of-a-bitch! As soon as Julie told me what was going on, I sent Mory to Vegas, but he got there too late—you'd already checked out of the Tropicana. If I'd only known sooner..."

Suzy saw the look on my face. "Mory is dad's bodyguard, really."

What's going on here?

"Why does your dad have a bodyguard?" I whispered in her ear.

"Tell ya later," she whispered back.

Marvin swept a hand toward the front door. "Well, let's go inside. You can tell us all about it."

I had started toward the back of the car to pop the trunk and unload the suitcases, when Julie spoke. "Leave those. We'll have the butler bring them in."

We stepped through the door and encountered the largest glass-enclosed home office I'd ever seen. There in front of me was an exquisitely-appointed office larger than most homes, with fancy burled wood-paneled walls. My eyes grew large at the sight before me. I couldn't believe what I saw.

"Suzy, what does your father do for a living?"

Marvin looked at Suzy, then smiled. "Ah, I see the girls have been good. They're under strict orders when they meet new guys not to discuss how I earn my living."

I'm sure at that point my face displayed total confusion.

Julie winked at her daughters. "We don't want young men chasing our daughters for our wealth."

Marvin rested a friendly hand on my shoulder. "I started an enterprise in my youth that's grown into a multidimensional international corporation with divisions in almost all segments of the entertainment industry."

Beth wore a nonchalant smile. "He finances movies and manages major entertainers, among other things."

"He's one of those moguls you read about in the tabloids, really," Suzy said.

Joe and I continued to take in the sweep of the view before us and were utterly dumbfounded by what we saw—and what we'd been told.

Joe looked at Beth, "So that's why you weren't swept off your feet when we met Willie Nelson in Vegas? You're used to meeting and socializing with famous people?"

"We've rubbed elbows with rich and famous people all our lives. Even the President visits on occasion."

Suzy said, "Dad and the Prez went to college together."

This was almost too much to absorb. "Really?" I asked, sounding like Suzy by using her favorite word. I couldn't help it.

"Yep, we're rich," Beth said, "but we don't feel different from everyone else. It sure has its perks, but that only makes us want to help others any way we can."

"Dad really does a lot for charities," Suzy added. "Beth and I even volunteer our time to help when asked."

Over the next few hours, we discovered that this was as down to earth and loving a family as any other. Wealth had not gone to their heads or negatively affected their outlook on life. They were truly nice people and didn't put on any airs. They accepted us into their family and did their best to make us feel we belonged. Marvin and Julie had done a good job of raising their daughters.

Guess I'll have to get used to being in such lush surroundings.

Unlike at the Bellagio, I couldn't just leave—my love for Suzy anchored me here. I'd have to adapt to being around people living affluent lifestyles.

How could things turn out so well? Where's all this taking us in the future?

Chapter Eighteen — A Couple of Years Later

Whenever people ask me how I met my wife, I reply; "I hope you can spare a few hours, because I've got a whopper of a tale to tell you."

Suzy and I ended up living near the farm in Council Bluffs. We have a two-year-old beauty of a daughter now, named Cindy. Our family life is the happiest I've seen.

Well, except maybe for Beth and Joe's.

They got married in Cincinnati after a long-distance romance that lasted more than a year, including a few weekend visits together. She still has her heart set on being an artist. She had her own one-woman show at our regional art center last month and sold four paintings. Even got written up in all the area newspapers as being an artist to watch. She teaches school locally too, and revels in the challenges it offers. We just found out Beth's pregnant.

After nearly two years of sending out query letters to publishers and getting rejection letters, Suzy signed with a New York City publisher to have one of her children's storybooks published. They cut her a large advance-against-future-royalties check back at the start of the year, when they signed her. She wrote under a pen name so Marvin's fame wouldn't influence her chances.

******

I probably wouldn't have become successful at dice setting if I'd already been twenty-one when I found out about it. I used those eighteen months waiting to get good and learn how to win before I ever tackled it in the real world. It was a blessing in disguise.

On our Vegas trip, I ended up opening only the first of the seven envelopes I'd divvied up my cash into. I never needed the rest of the $3,000 I'd saved for my dedicated gambling bankroll. I never lost any of the money out of that first envelope, either. No brag, just fact.

Dad didn't object one single bit when I wanted to remove the entire front of that barn stall after I returned home. I added an expandable section in the middle of the practice table to make it adjustable from twelve to sixteen feet long.

******

When I got home from Vegas, I caught up the mortgage payments on the farm. With Suzy's blessing, I earmarked one weekend's craps winnings per month for my new pet project. Over the course of the next two years, I used those special-purpose winnings each month to pay down the farm's mortgage principal.

Two weeks before last Christmas, I walked into the bank one last time. "This is the moment I've been working for. I've got enough cash to pay off our mortgage," I told the vice-president who took my payments.

******

After all the other Christmas presents had been opened, I stood between Mom and Dad, my arms around their shoulders. "I've got one more Christmas present for you two."

I reached behind Dad's favorite easy chair and picked up a brown paper grocery sack I'd slipped there a few minutes before. I pulled out a big manila envelope with a red bow on it and handed it to them. "Go ahead. Open it." Tears welled up in my eyes.

Dad covered his mouth and chin with his fingertips to hide quivering lips. "I think I might know what this is."

Mom looked at Dad, raised her eyebrows, and smiled as Dad tore into the envelope and pulled out the mortgage papers they had signed all those years ago. Across it on a diagonal, big bright red letters said, "**PAID IN FULL**".

Everyone went crazy, then joined in a big group hug, laughing and crying at the same time. Tears streamed down everyone's faces.

Mom let out a war whoop. She wiped tears from her eyes and took in a deep breath. "Thank you, Ray. It's the best gift anyone's ever given us."

Yup, my idea proved pretty good, learning to influence the dice. I kept my promise to Dad: I've never gambled on the practice table out in the barn.

Bonus Section:

So, you think you might like to see if maybe you can make a lot of money controlling the dice at the craps tables, too? The info in this bonus section just might be what you need to know to be able to succeed. I don't guarantee my math or ideas are totally flawless, but they sure make sense to me and I've proven to myself they work.

This bonus section also tells you a lot more about me.

Good luck,
Ray

Ray explains his Five-Level thirty-six dollar Place Bets Progression on Each Six and Eight:

I bet thirty-six-dollar place bets on each the *six* and the *eight* to start my turn by putting my chips down behind the pass line and saying to the dealer, 'Place bet the six and eight for thirty-six dollars each, working on all my come-out rolls'. Since my place bets are working on the come-out roll, if it's a seven, then I'll lose my seventy-two dollars.

I also bet a five-dollar pass-line bet, since it's required to be the shooter. To cover this small potential loss, I also bet an offsetting five-dollar bet on 'Don't pass'.

The first time I roll a six or eight, I drop another six dollars in chips on the table and tell the dealer, 'Make my six and eight $60 each'. He splits my winnings, adding the six dollars evenly to my place bets on six and eight. My place bets now total $120.

On the one hand, if I seven out now, then I lose seventy-eight dollars of my $400 session buy-in money.

However, on the other hand, each time I win a place bet on six or eight, the house pays me seven dollars for each six dollars bet on my winning number. For this reason, I ensure all my bet amounts are divisible by six.

The second time I roll a six or an eight, I tell the dealer, 'Make my six and eight $90 each'. He splits my winnings, adding evenly to each place bet and handing me back the surplus ten dollars in chips. Sixty-eight dollars of my own money is at risk, but $180 is split evenly between my place bets on the six and eight.

The third time I roll a six or an eight, I tell the dealer, 'Make my six and eight $138 each'. He splits my winnings, adding evenly to each of my place bets and handing me back the surplus nine dollars in chips. Fifty-nine dollars of my own money is now at risk, but $272 is in play, split evenly between my place bets on the six and eight.

The fourth time I roll a six or eight, I tell the dealer 'Make my six and eight $216 each'. He splits my winnings, adding evenly to each of my place bets. My winnings from that throw cover those increases. Fifty-nine dollars of my own money is still at risk, but $432 is in play, split evenly between my place bets on the six and eight.

If I'm nervous at this point, or just beginning the day, I might let them pay me my fourth win of $161, leave the bets the same and lock up a guaranteed win at this point, then increase my bets on my next six or eight tossed to reach my final betting level. If I take my $252 payout and then throw a seven, then I lose my place bets on my six and eight but still receive a $193 win for my turn.

When I move on to my final fifth-level progression bets, I tell the dealer, 'Make my six and eight $216 each'. When I roll another six or eight, I tell the dealer, 'Make my six and eight thirty-six dollars each, again'. He hands me back a total $627 in chips, as my winnings. Thirty-six dollars is still in play on my place bets on each the six and eight.

After that, I begin my five-step progression bet all over and attempt to run it again.

If I choose, I can quit instead and take all my winnings from my fifth-level bet, $699 in chips. That's about ten times my initial seventy-two-dollar bet, a great payoff for doing something that's become effortless for me.

Rather than quit, I could press on to a sixth level of progression.

If I did press on, then $342 would be in play on place bets on each six and eight. I'd win $1,096 when I tossed my sixth six or eight before rolling a seven. My sixth hit would win me $399, plus I'd pulled down all my place bet amounts, $684, plus the surplus thirteen dollars in winnings I'd been given back during play.

Not a bad way to bet when you toss tons of sixes and eights and only rare sevens.

Ray's Secret Dice Setting Info

After I completed my craps table, I could be found in the barn every evening tossing dice under the single overhead light in the stall and moving the betting chips around on the official table layout.

To allow me to analyze my results later on and track my progress, after each toss I wrote down in a notebook what I had rolled, recording each die-face result and the total.

I even marked the left die of each pair with a dot from a sharpie pen to tell me which die started out being the left die, no matter where they ended up.

I kept ten pairs of three-quarter-inch regulation casino-quality dice at the table. I made ten throws before I went to the other end to retrieve them. I also numbered each pair of dice, to tell me which two dice went together for each throw when the table was filled up with tossed dice.

And then I got fancy and downloaded a spreadsheet designed to log and analyze my dice-tossing results and spit out statistics to help me improve. I set up the laptop on a small table adjacent to my shooting position to log every toss.

Guess I'm smart, in an analytic way. I never let an idea loose until I explore the subject to its furthest limits. After some initial static, the family overlooked my new, all-consuming interest.

I practiced year-round and never lost interest. I told Joe what I learned and what I was trying to do. After a few months, Joe had become educated too, from listening to me talk. He agreed: the subject was fascinating.

I found out on the net some craps shooters believe you can gain an advantage over the casino by learning to set your dice and throw them a certain way while using a specific grip.

I use what's called a V3 dice-positioning set, always having threes show on the top of each die, with the pips forming an inverted V-shaped pattern facing away from me. A six shows on the left die's back-facing side—facing me—and a two on the right die's backside.

V3 set, rotational axis through outer top-front corners, accomplished by holding the dice at those corners

With my V3 set, I avoid throwing the on-axis one-six seven and the on-axis two-five seven—while my dice remain on axis. Those sevens will always be out of play on the axis sides of the dice—never on top, where they can hurt me.

Instead of rolling an on-axis two-five seven once every thirty-six rolls like a random dice roller would expect, I might roll one once in every eighty to ninety rolls. Same with the on-axis one-six seven.

When both my dice stay on their prescribed rotational axis and spin at the same rate throughout my throw, landing, and bounce-back, the results can only be: three-three six, six-two eight, four-four eight, or one-five six—all sixes or eights. I always win one of my place bets. I toss no losing sevens, when that happens.

Here's proof:

Hot glue two dice together in the V3 configuration and toss them down the table a thousand times. You'll never find a different result, in all those throws. They'll all be sixes and eights.

I discovered that trick online and proved it to myself that way. I was right, only those four results showed on the tosses with the glued-together dice. Joe encountered the same results when he tossed the glued-together dice.

Those results are what absolute perfection in my throw would produce. But, I can be far from perfect and still gain up to a winning edge over the casino. That's my advantage over the casino, as long as my dice stay on axis—even when they end up rotating at different rates.

A random roller, one who does nothing to keep the dice on a desired rotational axis, encounters more ways to toss a losing seven than any other number. That allows the casino to gain its natural advantage over the players.

When my dice stay on axis and I bet on both six and eight, I have eight ways to win vs. only four ways to lose. The odds are two to one in my favor. Of course, a seven loses twice money as much as a single win on either six or eight—so that all comes out a wash.

However, the casinos pay me seven dollars for each six dollars I bet, and that is where the up to sixteen-percent advantage comes from. Divide seven by six. You get 1.166667.

Up to sixteen percent is a bigger advantage than the casinos get on their slots.

When I toss a six or an eight five times before I toss a losing seven, I win my $699 progression bet pay-off. I only lose between fifty-eight dollars and seventy-eight dollars when I fail.

All things figured, I clean up, big time. I succeeded in the barn in practice. I then gave Joe one heck of a convincing demonstration using normal, non-glued-together dice. Almost half my tosses came up totaling six or eight, while I seldom rolled any sevens.

"You're a genius, Ray," Joe proclaimed, flabbergasted.

There are other dice sets that accomplish good results for other shooters. The all sevens set, with a six-one on top and a five-two on the side facing you, is useful for come out rolls where a seven wins for you or when you want to win your don't come/don't pass bets by tossing a seven. Thirteen of the thirty-six possible outcomes of tossing the dice (thirty-six percent) will decide the point on the come out roll—nine produce sevens or elevens and five produce craps.

With the all sevens set, when the dice stay on axis and rotate the same amount, it produces six-one, five-two, one-six or two-five and nothing else, which are all winning come out rolls.

What I call the *don't pass* dice set, with a two-five on top and a pair of ones facing you, is a great come-out set when you bet don't pass. If the dice stay on axis and both rotate the same amount, you stand a fifty percent chance of collecting a thirty-to-one pay off with a bet on two and twelve. If the right die over rotates one die face more than the left die, you have an excellent shot at winning the fifteen-to-one odds on a bet on eleven. Don't be afraid invest a dollar on two, eleven and twelve with this dice set. A few big pay offs on the two, eleven and twelve can make your day.

Four-three and three-four sevens are out of play using the don't pass set by being on the axis and the two-five on top is not likely to appear either, (I know one top shooter who always puts that seven on top of his dice and doesn't seem to ever toss it) so you've cut your potential losing sevens from six down to three.

If the dice stay on axis and either die rotates two die faces more than the other, you've got a fifty percent chance of getting a don't come bet on four or ten, which has the best pay out and highest odds of winning a don't pass bet.

All the craps that win the come out roll with a don't pass bet appear frequently, too—one-one on axis with same amount of rotation on both dice and one-two and two-one when the dice stay on axis and the left die pitches forward one more die face than the right die.

The V2 set with two-two on top forming a small upside down V facing down the table away from you and a four-one on the side facing you is good for winning buy bets on the outside numbers. When the dice stay on axis with the V2 set, it produces two-two, four-one, five-five or three-six. Buy bets on the four, five, nine and ten, made after the come out roll, are rewarding because they pay handsome odds.

The straight sixes dice set with sideways end to end six-six on top and a two-two on the side facing you is good for producing frequent wins on your one roll bets on the two and twelve at thirty to one odds. When the dice stay on axis with the straight-sixes set, the results are six-six, five-five, one-one or two-two.

The crossed-sixes dice set with six-six on top at right angles and a two-three facing you also is good for producing frequent one roll wins on the two and twelve at thirty to one odds. When the dice stay on axis with the crossed-sixes set you results are six-six, two-three, one-one or five-four.

Ray Explains, What Happens When The V3 Dice Set Works Less Than Perfectly:

With my V3 dice-set, when both dice stay on their rotational axis and rotate at the same speed, I win on every toss and get to continue tossin' the dice.

When the right die ends up pitching forward one extra die-face farther than the left die with the dice staying on rotational axis with my V3 dice-set, I'll only toss a three-two five, a six-four ten, a four-five nine, or a one-three four. No winners, but with no losing seven showing up, I get to continue tossin' the dice.

When the left die ends up pitching forward one extra die-face farther than the left die with the dice staying on rotational axis with my V3 dice set, I'll only toss a six-three nine, a winning four-two six, a one-four five, or a winning three-five eight. Two winners out of four, and I get to continue tossin' the dice.

When the right die pitches forward two die faces farther than the left die with the dice staying on rotational axis with my V3 dice set, I'll only toss a losing three-four seven, a six-five eleven, a losing four-three seven, or a one-two three. Either of the two sevens ends my turn and costs me my place bets. The other numbers mean I still get to continue tossin' the dice.

When the left die pitches forward two die faces farther than the right die with both dice staying on rotational axis with my V3 dice set, I'll toss a six-three nine, a winning four-two six, a one-four five, or a winning three-five eight. Two winners, and I still get to continue tossin' the dice.

If both dice fall off-axis by pitching inward sideways one die-face each toward the other but end up rotating forward at the same exact rate, then I'll only toss a one-two three, a six-five eleven, a five-six eleven, or a two-one three. No winners, but I still get to continue tossin' the dice.

If both dice fall off axis by pitching outward sideways one die-face each away from the other but end up rotating forward at the same exact rate, then I can only toss a winning five-one six, a winning six-two eight, a winning two-six eight, or a winning one-five six. All winners, and I still get to continue tossin' the dice.

In order to toss the losing two-five seven that the axis spins around, either:

1) the left die must fall off-axis, pitching inward one die-face while the right die stays on-axis and pitches three die-faces farther than the left die, or

2) the right die must stay on-axis, pitching forward one extra die-face than the left die while the left die also goes off-axis, pitching outward one die face.

Else, I get to continue tossin' the dice.

In order to toss the losing one-six seven that the axis spins around, either:

1) the right die must pitch inward one die-face while the left die rotates three more die-faces than the right die does, or

2) the left die must stay on-axis and rotate one more die-face than the right die does, while the right die falls off-axis, pitching outward one die-face.

Else, I get to continue tossin' the dice.

It's pretty difficult to toss a losing seven.

You can prove all these statements true by picking up a pair of dice, putting them in my V3 dice set, and moving them like I describe above.

Who says playing around with dice has to be boring?

Do you now realize why I toss double the normal frequency of sixes and eights and about half the normal frequency of losing sevens?

Some of Ray's practice dice.

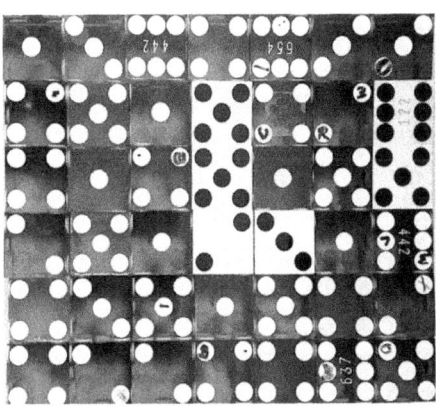

How Ray Figures His Craps Advantage

Casinos obtain their built-in advantage at craps by virtue of there normally being more ways to toss a losing seven than any winning number. I utilize my physical skills and cunning to flip the advantage in my favor.

I have an advantageous combination of:

a) having a current numbers-to-seven ratio of 10.1 to 1

b) getting seven dollars for each winning six-dollar place-bet on six or eight.

This gives me up to a sixteen-percent advantage when my toss is in top form and I'm making my progression bets. Up to sixteen percent is a bigger advantage than casinos have over patrons on slots. It's huge.

Believe me, though: only someone who is as good as me at keeping the dice on axis will ever get to enjoy that huge an advantage to its fullest. I needed to achieve a consistently high-enough number-to-sevens ratio in order to have that advantage working for me. Wannabe dice setters can only strive and hope to ever get this good.

Divide seven by six and I get 1.16667 to 1—that's where my sixteen-percent comes from. That 10.1-to-1 ratio means I should win my progression bets way more often than I lose them. If I consistently throw more than ten numbers between each seven, usually enough of them are going to be either sixes or eights to win my big-payoff progression bet. The stars all align to flip the odds in my favor.

Betting Example: (Non-progression bet)

If I place-bet the numbers six and eight for six dollars each, then I have twelve dollars at risk. I feel I have a two-to-one advantage--eight ways to win vs. four ways to lose on my perfect toss. I receive a seven-dollar payoff for every six dollars bet each time I win. I am ahead when I win twice, racking my winnings each time, before losing once. I get a fourteen dollar win vs. a potential twelve dollars loss for a two-dollar profit.

The only way I will lose money betting this way is if I roll a losing seven before I win two of my bets. Once I pass two winning bets, it is impossible to lose money on that shooting turn. I can leave my bets at risk, having already locked up a profit. The more times a six or eight is rolled, the bigger my winnings will be, because I'll pull down an extra seven dollars every time one of my place-bets wins at the six-dollar bet level.

The Power of the Progression Bet:

I can place-bet thirty-six dollars on six and eight and leave my bets at that level on each roll. When I roll a combination of five winning sixes and/or eights and then toss a losing seven, I win five times forty-two dollars ($210) minus seventy-two-dollars' worth of place-bets lost for a profit of $138.

Here's the sneaky part:

Whenever I'm working my progression bet and my thirty-six-dollar place-bets on six or eight win five times before I roll a losing seven, I am paid $640 for my turn with the dice. I win $699 minus the fifty-nine dollars of my own money still at risk on my six and eight place-bets.

I end up with $502 more than I win with my flat betting. (My $640 progression-bet winnings minus my $138 flat-betting winnings.)

Possible On-Axis Results Listed Below:

With six and eight place-bets made, I get eight ways to win vs. four ways to lose, when my dice stay on axis. Here's the breakdown on each possible toss outcome:

Dice stay on-axis and rotate at the same rate with perfect pitch: four ways to get a winning six or eight vs. zero ways to get a losing seven.

Dice stay on-axis with the left die rotating one extra die-face forward: I can only roll a four-two six or a three-five eight vs. two trash numbers that neither hurt nor help.

Dice stay on-axis with the right die rotating one extra die-face forward: I only toss trash numbers that neither hurt nor help.

Dice stay on-axis with the right die rotating two extra die-faces forward: I can only roll a three-four seven or a four-three seven vs. two trash numbers that neither hurt nor help.

Dice stay on-axis with the left die rotating two extra die-faces forward: I can only roll a four-three seven or a three-four seven vs. two trash numbers that neither hurt nor help.

Dice stay on-axis with the right die rotating three extra die-faces forward: I can only roll a three-five eight or four-two six vs. two trash numbers that neither hurt nor help.

Dice stay on-axis with the left die rotating three extra die-faces forward: I only toss trash numbers that neither hurt nor help.

What Makes Ray's Dice Toss So Special

I used the opportunity when Joe was taking his stunt-plane ride to tell Suzy and Beth how I had modified my dice toss to make it so special.

"Over time, I've eliminated the most significant variables from my toss, making it repeatable. I square up my body and press it against the end of the table and rest my left forearm on the elbow rest to take up my shooting stance. I place my dice in the same location for each toss, with the front edge of my dice touching and lined up with the white line at the back of the pass-bet line. This ensures my dice always start out parallel to the far back wall—which almost always guarantees they'll hit that wall squarely, thereby eliminating an important variable and potential weakness from every toss."

Suzy replied, "Okay, I understand that logic. Tell me more."

"I don't toss my dice the same way other people do. My dice are still sitting on the table surface when I start my toss. I launch them right from the table top with a smooth flick of my forearm upward three feet, with my wrist held stiff. I do everything I can to guarantee each launch is the same. I eliminated another variable in my toss by starting my dice out parallel to the tabletop, since they're resting on the surface when I launch them to my same landing point, two to three feet from the other end."

I showed them my right-from-the-table-top launch using my practice dice and the nearby office desk.

Beth asked, "What's really special or unique about your actual grip?"

"I start out by setting my dice together, side-by-side. I grip them using what's called an *ice-tong grip*, similar to how you'd grip an ice cube with a pair of ice tongs. I lightly hold my dice between the tips of my thumb and first finger, at only the outer upper-front corners on the sides of my dice. This moves my dice's rotational spin axis through the spots where I grip them, instead of being through the middle of the dice. This adds plenty of rotational backspin to my dice that usually makes them remain on my desired rotational axis all the way down the table."

I showed Beth and Suzy my grip with the practice dice I always carry.

"I rotate my wrist an inch to the right while gripping my dice prior to launch. Doing that helps my dice stay on-axis by opening up and leveling my grip to ensure I launch them level and straight. I modified the rotational spin axis point for my ice-tong grip myself, learning by trial and error. Without my modification, the ice-tong grip won't generate any serious spin to the dice, to force them to spin fast around my desired axis."

Bouncing the dice in the palm of her hand, Beth asked, "Do you do anything really special to release your dice?"

"I started out spreading my finger and thumb apart at release; now I find my modified grip releases my dice for me. My dice's takeoff momentum from their initial upward swing into action pulls my dice free from my finger and thumb at the right time," I said, beaming.

Suzy said, "I'm impressed. You've stolen the keys to the kingdom with all your discoveries, research, and practice."

I completed my dice-setting sermon by saying, "The one thing I've noticed that separates me from other dice-setters I've seen is that by shooting over such a long distance and using my modified grip, my dice are given tremendous backspin, vs everyone else's dice having much weaker forward spin."

Ray's Craps Shooting Today

After our initial trip to Vegas, I sat down with a pair of dice and studied each of the different dice sets: V2, straight sixes, crossed sixes, etc. I figured out mathematically what my exact advantage should be—when my game was firing on all cylinders—for each set and how I should bet to take full advantage of each set. It took me an entire afternoon's worth of "hands-on research."

I figured I had up to a sixteen-percent advantage when my V3 dice set produces perfect results with my progression on six and eight. However, those seven-dollar payoffs for each five-dollar place-bet on five and nine would give me more, and the nine-dollar payoffs for each five-dollar place-bet on four and ten are even better paybacks.

I'd quit shooting craps if I couldn't win regularly. Losing doesn't interest me in the slightest.

After some practice, I started hitting those numbers as easily as I had hit the six and eight with my V3 set.

I wanted to quit being a one-trick pony. I felt that always betting on six and eight would make me stand out too much to casino management over the long haul.

Now, I had a new plan.

I'd go to a casino the first time on a trip and show them my V3 dice-set with my six and eight place-bet progression with ninety dollars on each, which would win me more than $1,250 when I tossed my fifth six or eight before a losing seven. Next time I went to that casino, I'd show them my V2 set with a five and nine progression. The time after that, I'd show them my V2 set with a four and ten progression.

It took me a week's worth of practice to get good using my different dice sets and learn the proper progression-betting amounts to make. The casinos can't begin to figure out what I'm doing, if I keep mixing up what I'm letting them see. I can do it successfully because I know what works for me and what doesn't.

I've even used the straight-sixes-set on the come-out roll, where I'm trying to roll seven on the come-out roll to win and then parlay my winnings as odds behind the pass line—like I do with my place-bets. After I finally establish a point, I use whatever dice-set favors the number I have to roll to win my point. That really mixes things up.

I make a practice of not playing any casino too frequently, nor ever winning more than $1500 at a time.

I love to find an empty table to play on, especially in the early morning hours. It lets me get the dice back right away to shoot again, at least for a while. The casinos love me for opening play on their tables. When I step up to an empty table that they can't get any action going on, it's full of players by the time I quit fifteen to thirty minutes later. I bring empty tables to life for the casinos, almost like I'm a shill, a player magnet. Everyone wants to play on a table that's winning. The casinos win more from the new players after I leave than they lose to me for my short session. I guess you could say it's a win-win situation.

I also mix my play up by altering my trips to the casino so they cover all three shifts and all hours of the day and night. This helps because it's not the same staff seeing me all the time.

I'll go to a town like Chicago where they have several casinos, and I'll stay for up to a week at a time. I visit the casinos in rotation and on different shifts, always showing them my different betting styles and dice sets. Nobody complains when I win. Guess they think I'm one lucky son of a gun.

I play here at the local Hollywood Casino, and all up and down the Mississippi River. The games on the river are different from those in Vegas. The casinos on the river are always checking their dice, making sure nobody's messed with them or switched their own dice into the game.

They keep their dice in play a lot longer there, too. Sometimes the dice are handled too long and by too many people, so when I get them, they're sticky and more difficult to control. Imagine that, sticky dice.

I carry a little pouch of talc in my front pants pocket so I can powder my fingers to make them unsticky again. I also play at the casinos around Cincinnati whenever Suzy and I visit her family there.

******

We all journey to Vegas together as often as possible to shoot craps and share adventures. Something in Vegas has changed each time we visit there. Someone's torn down a hotel/casino and replaced it with a bigger one, or a wilder thrill ride has been started somewhere on The Strip.

The worst treatment I ever got from casino management was at the Treasure Island Casino on my second Vegas trip.

I'd started to shoot, when four suits showed up about ten feet from the table. They stood together in a tight-knit group with their arms folded across their bodies and watched me roll. They shot me daggers with their eyes. If looks could kill, I'd have been dead. It made me uncomfortable, so I folded up shop and went somewhere else. Their behavior felt creepy. My game wasn't even working well that day, because I never got out of warm-up mode. Maybe them staring at me had something to do with it.

The worst thing ever to happen to me took place in Saint Louis after I scored a large win on a Mississippi River boat casino there. Two men tailed me when I left the casino. When I stopped to buy gas, they jumped me with guns drawn and stole my winnings. I guess you're bound to be robbed when others watch you win big amounts of money in public.

I gave good descriptions to the police. They showed me surveillance videos from the casino and gas station. The robbers were arrested, but my winnings were gone by then. I had to testify against them in court and wasn't crazy about having to go back to Saint Louis to do that. Both are serving five years each, but they may get out sooner. Guess you can't be too careful.

Can I Hope To Win Regularly,
If I Can't Master Dice Influencing?

People keep asking me: "Is there is a way to consistently win at craps without having to be successful at setting and influencing the dice?"

I believe so. To increase your chances of winning consistently, bet only on shooters who set their dice the same, use the same dice grip and arm movement each toss and seem to have successful results with it—take advantage of their skills to win. You'll want to pay attention to how they are betting, too and what their signature numbers are, then bet on them. Their dice set will give you clues to what numbers you should expect them to toss the most.

When you are losing, reduce your bet amounts or take a break. When you are winning, increase your bet amounts and hang in there.

I'd also avoid the electronic craps games you'll find at some small casinos attached to race tracks known as racinos—play a real craps table. The E-Craps games at racinos provide no way for the shooter to keep dice on axis, since real dice aren't used, so you basically end up with every shooter being a random shooter who's results are being controlled by a random number generator—not a good situation for trying to win.

At our local casino over the last couple of years I keep seeing an eighty-two year-old easy-talking, stoop-shouldered, always-smiling guy named Andy, who regularly wins about eight out of each ten of his sessions—under all types of table conditions and without ever tossing the dice himself.

We've talked several times after getting to know each other. He says, "I let the table conditions tell me how to bet, as I use a different betting strategy for each table condition—cold, choppy, warm or hot. I always quit anytime I lose half my buy-in amount." Andy just watches the play for enough shooters to get the feel for how the table is playing when he first joins the table.

On a really cold table—where nobody seems to be able to roll more than three or four numbers before tossing a losing-seven—after the shooter's second roll he makes lay bets (the opposite of buy bets) across: $40 on four and ten; $30 on five and nine; $24 on six and eight. If the shooter picks off two of his bets, which don't get replaced when picked off, he takes all his bets down and waits for another shooter's turn before betting again. If the shooter rolls a losing-seven rolls immediately after Andy makes his bets—which it often does—Andy wins all six bets and collects $120. If one of his numbers gets picked off first by the shooter, he ends up collecting $100.

On a choppy table—where five to seven numbers roll, without points being won, he waits for the shooter's fourth roll after establishing his point before making a single sizable don't come bet.

On a warm table—where multiple players are rolling more than seven numbers and making a point or two during their turn—Andy place bets all the inside numbers for exactly two rolls after the point is established, then takes down his bets and waits to bet on the next shooter.

On a hot table—where long rolls are coming right and left—he places bets four units on each inside number as soon as a point is established, then reduces each bet to one unit, so that his bets have paid for themselves with that first win. He leaves his bets up until the player tosses a losing-seven. He adds place bets on the four and ten on his third win, then he starts alternating between racking his winnings and pressing half his bets one unit each on every other win.

When Andy bets on my toss—as soon as I put my progression bets down—he bets like the table is hot, but triples the size of his opening bets. "I've thought about making the same exact bets you make," he said, "but, that would probably draw heat to both of us. Instead, I do what I consider the next best thing by kicking up the volume of my bets."

When the table play suddenly heats up or cools down to where he loses two bets quickly, Andy quits betting long enough to get a new accurate read on how the play is changing. He then switches his betting strategy to follow the new way the table is playing. This is something Andy seems to have mastered through years of experience. A word of caution: a complete newbie to craps might not enjoy the same results as Andy by trying to use his betting strategies, because if you get out of sync with the flow of play with your betting strategies, craps can clean your plow in a hurry—that's a good reason to bet really small while gaining experience. There's plenty of time later on to bet and win bigger, after you've grown your gambling bankroll.

Also, a couple of weeks ago while shooting craps back at the Golden Nugget in Vegas, a silver haired older woman not quite four feet tall joined our table. She plopped down the plastic step stool she carried and stood on it, so she could see over the railing better.

After the point was established, she made buy bets on the four, five, nine and ten for twenty dollars each—buy bets are same as place bets, but with better payouts for those numbers after paying a five percent vig. As soon as she won one or two of her buy bets—depending on how she was doing—she called all those buy bets off for the rest of the point and put down a twenty dollar don't come bet. If her don't come bet traveled to a six or eight, she place bet that six or eight for eighteen dollars. I thought about it and realized she must not like betting against the six and eight, so she hedged them in such a way that she made a dollar or three with the nearly offsetting bets no matter whether the number repeated for a loss or a seven showed for a win.

She followed immediately with more don't come bets, each getting smaller than the proceeding bet—twenty, fifteen and then ten dollars. I thought and realized that reducing her bet each time mean she showed a small profit on those bets. Whereas, with equal bet amounts, she would have broken even when the next don't come roll was a losing seven. She used the all sevens dice set when she was the one shooting, to win those don't come bets.

The good thing about don't come bets is that they are even money bets with more ways for you to win them than to lose them after the come out roll. On the four and ten, you have six ways to win with a seven and three ways to lose by repeating the number—that's a two to one advantage in your favor. On the five and nine, you have six ways to win with a seven and four ways to lose by repeating the number—that's a fifty percent advantage in your favor.

After winning a few times, all her twenty dollar bets became forty dollar bets. She used the opening part of the point to win a buy bet or two, then used the middle part of the point to get herself set up with multiple don't come bets, which she won at the end of the point. She worked each point at both ends by using opposite strategies together and cleaned up in the process. In about half an hour, she had over a thousand dollars more in her rack than what she'd bought in for.

Her cleverness won my immediate respect and admiration Good luck at the tables.

Joe and Ray's Formative Years,
For Those Who Want To Know

With my sister, Ellen, Joe and I grew up on a farm near Council Bluffs, Iowa, east of Omaha, Nebraska.

We boys arrived as unexpected late-in-life surprises when Dad was forty-five and Mom thirty-four. I tended to be adventurous as a kid, and ended up looking out for myself. By the time I reached eight, I often ventured off alone to tramp along a nearby riverbank and cross over the foreboding long and tall railroad trestle, with our big red dog, Daisy June, at my side.

She's a sweetie, and we became inseparable. Daisy used to lead me around our yard when I first started walking, while I held onto her collar. She walked slowly with me, and whenever I fell down, Daisy would lie down beside me and put her paws over me. We shared a special bond.

Our neighbor, Mr. Runyon, owned King, a prized black-and-white-spotted bird dog he'd bought, whom many hunters considered the best hunting dog in several surrounding states. Trouble started when King fell in love with Daisy June and always wanted to be at our house with her. Joe and I were six and four at the time.

Mr. Runyon drove up out front and tried to call King to him to take him hunting, but King refused to come. Dad hand delivered King by his collar three or four different times. Mr. Runyon got mad, went on along, and washed his hands of the whole affair, saying we now owned King.

Runyon's two sons, four and six years older than me, took King's loss personally. To them, we stole King, and we must be made to pay.

Over our grade-school years, they did their best to make Joe's and my lives a living hell. If they caught either of us out by ourselves, they swooped down on us on their bicycles, peppering us with rocks or little apples they picked for the occasion. It became open warfare, with us on the defensive or running. Joe ran like hell to get away from them, and managed to stay out of their way.

I fared much worse.

They swooped down on me once, with their cousin joining them, and cut me off from getting home.

When they came close enough, I jammed on my bike's brakes, dropped the bike, and stood there ready and waiting.

The oldest Runyon boy charged.

I grabbed the baseball bat out of the bike's basket and broke my tormentor's arm with a powerful, well-delivered swing of the bat. *Home run! Out of the ball park.*

The oldest Runyon boy could be seen the remainder of the summer, his broken arm in a plaster cast.

Another time, that threesome again jumped me. This time in an alley in town.

I took on the much bigger cousin, chomping down on his wrist, biting him with all my might. I held on for almost five minutes before letting go as I ignored the Runyon boys' pleading. Nothing they did freed him from my vice-like bite. I sent the message to avoid messing with us Hitchcock boys.

Dad caused part of it. He'd told us both to pick out one person attacking us whenever they outnumbered us, and do him maximum-possible damage—no matter how much the others hurt us—because it would instill such fear in that one we centered our attack upon to never have a desire to attack us again.

Long story short, I displayed such tenacity that I won us the war. They never bothered us again. We learned years later how the Runyons and their cousin's parents confronted Mom and Dad, complaining how viciously I treated their much older and bigger cousin, and how he got rushed to the hospital to get stitches and undergo painful tetanus shots.

Dad was proud I stood up to the group of older thugs. He refused to pay any of the medical expenses. Their parents kept their kids away from us and demanded they behave, which brought peace to our valley.

******

Joe's a lot quieter than me and would mentally get lost during the summer by reading books he borrowed from the local library. He read better than a book a week.

He tried his hand at writing his own young-adult science fiction novel in junior high. Back then very few people ever attempted writing a book.

I kept bugging him to let me read it. I viewed him becoming the world's best writer, and couldn't wait until Joe finished another chapter, allowing me to sneak a peek.

I was three years behind Joe in school. I'd been sick often with bad tonsils in the first grade. I'd fallen so far behind in school that Mom had me held back. She said I played hooky, too, by pretending to be sick. It took a while before she caught on to my tricks.

Nobody had created kindergarten back then in our neck of the woods, so our ABCs got taught in the first and second grade. We never learned them at home before entering school, either; therefore, we experienced quite a steep learning curve right out of the gate.

Entering eighth grade proved a turning point in my life. I hated always getting into scrapes and fights, and used this change of venue to become a better person. From then on, I used my wits instead of fists to win my battles.

******

Joe lettered in tennis in high school. Dad taught us how to play. Try as I might, I never made the varsity tennis team, only the reserve team. I also played on the reserve football team and I enjoyed running in the evenings.

Growing up, I became hooked on listening to rock music from the 60s and 70s and own quite a large collection of it. There's something magical about the music from that period of time that drew me to it. I sometimes get the eeriest sensation—like maybe I was a reincarnated hippie from that era. I feel the same way to about the Roaring 20s, sometimes thinking maybe I was a rumrunner or bootlegger in a former life.

******

In high school I teamed up with my freshman class councilor, who laid out a plan for me to graduate in three years. I wanted to grow up and get a taste of the outside world. After the first two years, I entered my homeroom, nodded to my councilor, and asked, "What's my senior homeroom number?"

My mentor said, "Room 206, Mr. Small's homeroom. Good luck, Ray."

I walked into homeroom 206 and took a seat.

Mr. Small glanced up from his desk at the front of the classroom. His shock showed, seeing me sitting there. "What are you doing here, Hitchcock? This is a senior homeroom."

"I'm graduating," I informed him.

Everyone shot their attention toward me, because what I said stunned them.

Mr. Small stared at me, stood up, and left the room. I'll bet he went to check the validity of my announcement. If he did, he found out I'd earned almost twice the needed credits for graduation—fifty-four vs. the required thirty-two—and I had four majors, including a double major in English with majors in math and science, and three minors filled up my bloated College-Prep Curriculum.

No one ever said anything again about me being a senior, but some of those senior boys rode me quite hard, because of the way I joined their senior class. I never felt like part of their class. Nobody got the best of me, though. I always found a way to level the playing field and get even with those who tried to make my life miserable, using my brain now to retaliate.

I chose to skip my own high school graduation, because I considered such affairs boring. The ceremony took place in our school's sunken basketball gym. I stopped by on my run graduation evening, stuck my head in the door, and stood unnoticed at the back of the gym long enough to hear my own name called out when they gave out diplomas. I then disappeared into the night, again, to continue running.

I might have been a little too smart for my own good. When Mom and Dad asked me where I wanted to go to college the summer after I graduated, I told them, "I've worked hard getting through high school in three years. I'm going to take a year off before college."

I may have cheated myself out of one of the most formative years of my life by skipping over my junior year. It would've been much more fun to graduate alongside the kids I went through grade school, junior high, and my first two years of high school with.

We earned our sense of values by always trying to make our parents proud of us in all we did. I always looked up to Joe, my big bro, as a role model.

I needed to try to live up to my big brother's school achievements, too. Joe always won a place on the honor roll with straight A's. I never learned how to study for tests, struggling with them but excelling daily in class discussions. I studied a lot longer than Joe ever did, but never read well and found it hard to memorize facts. I may have even been a little jealous of my big bro. My report cards in high school showed lots of B's and C's with a smattering of A's, and even an occasional D in foreign languages.

I stuttered as a kid, but overcame it by the time I entered the seventh grade. I still stutter sometimes when excited, but I overcome it.

About The Author

Bill Collins was formerly a full time weddings-only photographer serving the Indy, Cincy and Dayton, Ohio regional wedding market for forty-five years. He was born and raised in Connersville, Indiana. Bill and his wife Sue live in Greens Fork, Indiana with their two pet cats.

Note From Bill: If you enjoyed reading Vegas Fever, please take a couple of minutes to rate it on Amazon.com and write a book review for me there. It really helps the book become established and more discoverable by others who might enjoy reading it. Amazon's rating system considers any rating less than five stars as a negative review, as such ratings lower the book's overall rating. Detailed reviews are especially appreciated, telling what you like about the book, what sets it apart from other books, and what pleasures others will get out of reading it. Early detailed reviews set an example for later reviewers to follow. Later reviewers will be more likely to also post detailed reviews if they see the earlier reviews are detailed.

Please type the url below into your browser right now to put your rating/book review on Vegas Fever's Amazon product page:
http://www.amazon.com/dp/B018ODEE60

Thanks so much,
Bill

Vegas Fever's Facebook page:
https//www.facebook.com/1498502047123770
Give it a Like while you're there. Thanks.

Bill Collins' Amazon Authors page:
http://www.amazon.com/-/e/B00LLQ715Y
Give it a like while you are there. Thanks

Acknowledgments

I'd like to especially thank Victorine Lieske, New York Times Best-Selling author of *Not What She Seems*, a mystery novel that sold more than 100,000 copies, for all her help. She critiqued several chapters of Vegas Fever for me, offering suggestions for improvement and even rewriting a few paragraphs for me. She taught me quite a bit about writing in the process. She also designed Vegas Fever's front cover and provided it for me to use free of charge. In addition, she also had me contact her current book editor, Cherise Kelley, who did the line edit for Vegas Fever.

Victorine is a prime example of everything an author should be. I thank her for all her help and the time she graciously provided in making Vegas Fever a better, more entertaining read.

www.ingramcontent.com/pod-product-compliance
Lightning Source LLC
Chambersburg PA
CBHW060421130626
46555CB00005B/2160